CUMBOTO

The Texas Pan American Series

Cumboto

By RAMÓN DÍAZ SÁNCHEZ

Translated by JOHN UPTON

Illustrated by Kermit Oliver

UNIVERSITY OF TEXAS PRESS  AUSTIN & LONDON

The Texas Pan American Series is published with the assistance of a revolving publication fund established by the Pan American Sulphur Company and other friends of Latin America in Texas. Also contributing to the cost of translating and publishing this book was the William Faulkner Foundation.

For Isabel

"... neither was there any such spice as
the Queen of Sheba gave King Solomon."

II CHRONICLES

PUBLISHER'S NOTE

Cumboto was chosen by the Ibero-American Novel Project of the William Faulkner Foundation as the most notable novel published in Ibero-America between 1945 and 1962. The first edition was published in Caracas, Venezuela, in 1950; this translation into English was made from the fourth edition, which was published in Caracas in the Colección Popular Venezolana in 1960. The novel has also appeared in French and Italian translations.

Ramón Díaz Sánchez was born in Puerto Cabello, Venezuela, in 1903; he died in Caracas in November, 1968. During a varied career he had been a factory worker, a proofreader, a newspaperman, a municipal judge; co-director of the newspaper *El Tiempo* of Caracas; and director of Culture and Fine Arts of the Ministry of Education. In addition to *Cumboto* he published several novels and collections of short stories, as well as biographies, essays, and works for the theater.

The Glossary was prepared by the translator with the assistance of the author.

CONTENTS

xii

PART ONE: *An Enchanted World*

Meeting at Dusk

From the large window of the house all you can see is the towering coconut grove that lies on the other side of the highway. The window faces north and is very wide, as though it had been designed to take in the entire landscape, with its thousands of waving palms and its pale sky, dotted with lazily soaring vultures.

There stands Don Federico, as he does every evening, with his El Greco profile and his silvery beard, his pale fingers drumming softly on the glass.

Don Federico is gazing off into the distance, dreaming of other days, turning over the past. Perhaps inventing it. A large diamond on the ring finger of his right hand shoots little pointed arrows of light around the room. I stand in the half-light of the library, regarding once again his aristocratic features, sharpened and drawn by the turmoil within: the straight Roman nose, the deep-set blue eyes darkened now by the shadows, the thin, pale lips. No one knows as well as he the history of these people, this country, and this plantation. For me, Natividad, who have lived with him all my life, it is an unforgettable story. If I had children I would want them to know it, too. It is a long and exciting tale, beautiful and sad, one that is well worth hearing.

At this time of day there are no longer any birds to be seen in the sky or in the trees. What remains of the sun is like a torn lip against the cup of the horizon. A greenish mist is rising from the sea, beyond the forest, enveloping the evening. For a few moments a yellow splendor glistens on the spiny crests of the cactus, on the acacias, and over the tops of the tall palm trees; then it passes rapidly through every shade of green before turning blue, indigo, and finally black.

As I stand here watching Don Federico, I'm not sure what role I'm playing. I don't know whether I'm simply spying on him, or displaying the age-old concern servants have always felt for their masters. In any event, the fact is that I have done the same thing every evening for more than twenty years. In a few moments Don Federico will pick up his cherry-wood cane, put on his Panama hat, and set out for his daily walk in the woods. Then his tall, slender figure, dressed all in white, will wander among the shadows as though he were trying to drown himself in them. And once again I shall follow him through the huge, empty night that is filled with somber blue shadows and the salty smell of the coast. I shall keep behind him, trying not to let him see or hear me. The darkness will wrap itself around us like a soft membrane, and the world will seem wider and emptier. The muffled roar of the sea in the distance will grow louder, and the two of us will go on, guided by the stars; we will never join each other even for a moment, each pretending to be unaware of the other's presence, but always knowing that we are there to protect each other.

If Don Federico reacts as I do when night falls, he must be feeling at this moment as if an icy drill were boring into his bones. It isn't fear, exactly—not that vague but irresistible terror that comes over Negroes in the dark. It is a kind of conscious and even defiant uneasiness that drives us to explore the night, sometimes along the path that leads to the beach, sometimes in the shadowy depths of the coconut grove.

Don Federico has been intimate with night ever since he was a child; he knows its deepest folds. He can identify every beat of its heart, every sigh. He knows the brief laughter of the owl, the chilling croak of the *chupa-huesos,* the wind's hand stroking the limbs of the trees, the *mapanare's* rippling caress, and the irritable sizzle of the rattlesnake. Always dressed in white, with his black necktie and snow-white hair, he stands out against the darkness as though he were surrounded by a kind of nimbus. This is the way we all see him: I, who follow behind in silence, and the other Negroes who peer out at him through the cracks in their doors and the chinks in the mud walls of their houses.

"There goes Don Federico," they say. "*Ave Maria!*"

And they cross themselves.

In their evening gatherings, amid the tobacco smoke, I have often heard them asking each other, as though hoping to find the clue to some mystery: "Bless my soul! Why in the world didn't Don Federico ever get married?"

I can well understand why this subject fascinates them. Don Federico's predecessors took wives and had children. He, on the contrary, is still a bachelor and lives alone on the seven leagues of his plantation. There are still some old men alive who can remember his grandfather, Don Lorenzo Lamarca. I knew his father and mother, Don Guillermo Zeus and Doña Beatriz.

"Why in the name of Heaven didn't Don Federico ever get married?"

It is a troubling question, that melts into the shadows like the night itself. Perhaps I am the only one who can answer it satisfactorily.

Don Federico sets out for his walk. Along the path a slender young man is approaching from the opposite direction. He seems to be in a hurry. As he passes the old gentleman he stops and stares at him. Why does he look at him like that? What does he see in him that so arouses his curiosity?

As Don Federico wanders off into the dusk, the other stands there, looking after him. When I come up to the visitor I see that he is trembling, like a man awakening from a dream.

"Is that the owner of Cumboto?"

His question is directed to me, his eyes fixed on mine. Something about him makes me very uneasy. Where have I seen that lean face before, those greenish, luminous eyes? Where have I heard that voice that touches you like the blade of a knife? He is a young man. A boy, almost.

"Yes," I answer. "That's Don Federico."

"And you?" he goes on. "Are you from Cumboto, too?"

"Yes, I am . . ."

"I must speak with Don Federico."

Before replying I examine his face more carefully, trying to find there the answers to the questions I've been asking myself. I don't really know whether I like this boy or not. His delicate profile, his slender hands, his cat-like movements awaken distant and painful memories. A suspicion has crossed my mind, and I hope I am wrong.

"Do you think I could see him?"

"Maybe you can if you come back to the White House tomorrow."

Later that night, as I reconstruct the scene on the path, I can hear the boy's voice so clearly that I find myself obsessed by it. It brings back a flood of memories that threatens to engulf me like a cataract. Our whole extraordinary, chaotic past passes before my eyes as my weary body lies motionless in the bed.

The light from the full moon in its cloudless sky filters through the leaves of the trees about the house. I stare at it through the open window, thinking that it must have shone like this when we were children, and even long before that: in the time when the first black settlers leaped from their canoes onto the shores of Cumboto. Those tormented beings who were hunted down like wild animals must have gazed at many moons like this one, thinking of their distant homes, while time brought about its slow transformation.

Seeing this boy has been enough to stir up in me the muddy bottom of the past.

A Primitive and Passionate World

The plantation still bears the region's original name—Cumboto—and stretches from the seacoast on the north to the foot of the mountain range on the south. Within its original boundaries villages sprang up, with their little squares and churches. It is crisscrossed by roads and rivers. The railroad line runs east and west, parallel to the main highway, and every day the piercing whistle of the locomotive makes us turn our heads and blink.

Along the coast the vegetation is coarse and twisted, like a Negro's hair. It is made up mostly of cactus, acacia, and other hostile plants. But farther inland, where the rivers moisten and soften the earth, the soil is black and the trees grow luxuriantly, with immense, spreading foliage at the top. Almost the entire estate was planted with coconut trees by some ancestor of Don Federico's, and a battery of vats for boiling the coconut oil was installed not far from the main house.

Once, when Don Federico's parents were still alive and the house was filled with laughter and he and I were children, I heard his father tell a story I have never forgotten. It was a Sunday morning and some visitors from the city were there. I was drilling holes in green coconuts to get the sweet, white milk to make a refreshing drink for the guests that hot summer day, and Doña Beatriz was playing the piano—some piece of music that was as slow and dark as the river. All at once Don Guillermo flung his enormous arms above his head and called out in his trumpet-like voice: "Listen, everybody!" he said. "I'm going to tell you about the settling of this country and the founding of this plantation."

Don Guillermo had been drinking a great deal of beer that morning, and he was as red as a crab.

"Before Puerto Cabello was built, the nearest town was Borburata, on the coast between the savanna of Santa Lucía and the beach called Gañango. Although it was a prosperous village, it was destined to survive only a short time. When Lope de Aguirre invaded the country the townspeople moved out, and the whole area was almost completely deserted. Some time later the Guipuzcoana Company was formed; this was a Spanish investment firm interested in exploiting the agricultural riches of Venezuela. That was the beginning of Puerto Cabello; the company, to protect its interests, built warehouses, walls and forts, a church, and a shipyard there. As for the Indians, we know hardly anything about them. It is generally believed that the people of Borburata and the employees of the Guipuzcoana Company were the first settlers, but that is not true: the Negroes had arrived before them."

The Negroes! These words caught my attention. Ever since I was a child

I've always had a curious mind, eager for information. Besides, I am a Negro myself, and Don Guillermo's remark could not have failed to interest me. Where had they come from—those ancestors of mine who occupied this land before the white people? How did they reach this coast? What did they do when they arrived? Don Guillermo, in his Sunday exuberance, was going to tell us about that, too. They were African slaves, he said, who had escaped from the depots maintained by European slave traders in the Antilles; they preferred to face the fury of the sea rather than suffer any longer under the mistreatment of their civilized masters. When the Spaniards took them captive and questioned them, they babbled amid a whirlwind of anguished gestures: "*Cum-boto! Cum-boto! Cum-boto!*"

That explained everything: *con botes,* with boats, in fragile little vessels and rafts made from the trunks of trees, they had ridden the waves for days before falling exhausted on the rocks where the sea licks the roots of the acacias. For months and even years they had toiled to hollow out the trunks, keeping them hidden in the underbrush. For them the sea was a leap beyond death, an interminable and heroic agony that was to reshape the history of the world. These persecuted people, too, made their conquest, armed only with fear. They were a gobbet of God's spittle on the white man's Christian enterprises—a black, fermenting spittle, rich in seeds for the creation of life.

Many of them were able to escape into the interior. The new land took them to its bosom, hid them in its green depths, and digested them like a gigantic stomach. Naked, barefoot, sweating, scratched and cut, they ran through the woods away from the coast, opening future roads for white civilization with their bleeding feet. Each one's physical endurance was measuring off the distances for a new geography. Their dark voices, hoarse with anger or fear and as cosmic as the night wind, shook the forests. Their weeping watered the roots of hope, and in their smiles there dawned each morning a promise of love. They went on carving out their destiny, turning each death into a sunrise. During the brief, trembling parentheses when they stopped to rest in their flight they sowed the seeds of new villages: in the south, Goaiguaza; in the east, Quisandal, the new Borburata, far-off Patanemo; in the west, Morón, Sanchón, Alpargatón, San Felipe . . . As a child, and later as a grown man, I was often tempted to set out through the woods and follow the rivers until I disappeared in the darkest part of the jungle, trying to find the old refuges of these first Negroes—dark dens where nature pulses with the heart of the great drums, and paths where the sharp odor of runaway slaves still lingers.

Those who were too exhausted or discouraged to go on were captured and remained on the coast, where their palm-thatched mud huts sprang up among the acacias like tumors on the irritated skin of the earth. From time to time manhunts were organized to bring back runaways, and then the woods rang with the cries of mastiffs. The plantation came into being in this way, and throve like a monstrous appendix of the seaport citadel. Puerto Cabello, so called because it was said that a ship could be moored with a single hair in its quiet harbor, represented the hard, driving ambition of the white man. It was no more than a spit of land surrounded by noisome waters, along whose banks Negroes peered out with dread in their hearts. The stubborn austerity and perseverance with which the Basque founders defied death in that fever-ridden valley was a definitive weapon in the history of European domination. Gradually, the fear of death would be overcome by greed, the town would grow within its walls and fortifications, and a little wooden bridge suspended over a canal would serve to unite and at the same time separate the two original worlds of the town: "Inside," where the masters lived, and "Outside," which was slave town.

I didn't get all this information, of course, from Don Federico's father. I learned some of these things in other ways, with the slow passing of the years, in the same gradual way that the obscure seaport town cut down its mangroves and abandoned the segregation of its little bridge. I have discovered, for example, that the development of Cumboto does not date from the early days of the Guipuzcoana Company, but came much later.

Cumboto's lands were divided up, fenced, crossed with canals, and given different names by the various colonizers who settled on them. With the passing of time, the original name was taken over and used by Don Lorenzo Lamarca, Don Federico's maternal grandfather.

People considered Don Lorenzo to be a strong and honest man, and he became known throughout the area as a just administrator. His elder son became a seaman, and was lost in a shipwreck. The other joined the priesthood, went off to heathen lands, and was never heard from again. The unhappy Doña Beatriz, his only daughter, became the wife of Don Guillermo Zeus, a foreigner whose nickname was *El Musiú*.

The Negroes who had reached a ripe old age—of which there are hundreds in Cumboto—used to tell how Don Lorenzo administered justice in his domain without ever once appealing to the established local authorities. His word was law, and anyone who had a problem ran meekly to him. Actually, he himself had not created this position of authority; he had acquired it along with the property. But he used it wisely, like the old feudal lords. He admonished and actually punished wrongdoers, even imposing certain forms of corporal punishment that had been forbidden as excessively cruel by the laws of the Republic, such as flogging and the stocks. Still, the people of Cumboto respected Don Lorenzo, and obeyed his orders as they would have those of a good father. And when all is said and done they were right, for it was he who provided them with land and seed so that they could plant their crops, with timbers and palm branches to build their houses, with water and the salt for their food, and, in short, with the air they breathed. He baptized their children and buried their dead; and, as he knew a little medicine, when the occasion arose he gave them pills for their stomach cramps and salve for their sores. No one ever rebelled against the authority of this severe man, whose mere presence was enough to abash a crowd of troublemakers carried away by anger or the fumes of rum.

This last is no laughing matter. Negroes and mulattoes are given to drunken sprees, and their parties often end in knifings, clubbings, and broken heads. They are quarrelsome and outspoken, and even though their disputes are soon forgotten, they like to underline them with blood. In Cumboto there are skillful instructors in the arts of fighting with the club and the machete; and the men, if they have no weapons, would rather attack with their heads, which are as hard as coconuts, than with their fists.

But with all this, the Negro is as gay and artless as a child. His life is a never-ending party, filled with laughter, singing, and constant chatter. He loves to play. His natural activity is horsing around. He behaves like the creatures of the forest—especially the birds, which are his favorites. There is no Negro who does not firmly believe that animals can talk and that there are people who know the secret of their language.

I have often wondered, while strolling through the countryside or watching the men cut coconuts on the plantation, which one of these beings with battle-scarred faces could have fathered me in the glow of some bonfire or on some river bank.

My first glimpse of the world was in my masters' big white house, where I found myself seesawing in terror between Don Guillermo's guffaws and the fearful silence of the rest of the family. Beyond the door that opened onto the patio lay another country, filled with uncertainty. To which of these two worlds did I belong—the one where brilliant sunlight shone like gold on the mango trees and made the darkened coconut meat gush with oil, or the other where its soft glow slid across cold, polished floors?

In trying to answer this question, I used to watch the Negroes and mulattoes on the plantation—chattering men and women submerged in toil as though in a river—and as I did so a great sadness came over me. They knew nothing. Almost all of them had been born here in Cumboto, and they loved these coconut groves where they had no choice but to spend their lives, beget children, and welcome death.

The men's work consisted of climbing the palm trees, bringing down the ripe coconuts, and loading them into huge, heavy two-wheeled carts drawn by somnolent oxen. The creaking of the ox cart is a plaint from the slumbering earth; the driver must drive his goad deep into the animals' hide to keep the team from falling asleep on its feet. The sight of oxen has always filled me with a feeling of infinite tenderness. They remind me of old people who appear at the doors of farmhouses to ask for a little water to slake their thirst.

Not far from the main house there were enormous sheds where men and women of all ages spent their days splitting mountains of coconuts with short, sharp machetes. After the outer husk had been removed, one skillful stroke of the machete on the inner shell released a flood of sugary juice. Then a

swarm of expert hands loosened the white meat with small knives called *rabones*. As the work went on, the sheds and the surrounding area were piled high with great white pyramids; later the meat would be spread out to dry in the sun before being thrown into the boiling vats.

Cumboto's work sheds were like huge hives, where black bees had been engaged in their merry task for generations. I often used to visit there and watch the fascinating bustle of hands and machetes and the forest of naked feet bathed in the sweet cascade. Every time a machete came down on a coconut shell and split it open with a dry crunch, a shiver ran up my spine. The coconuts made me think of human heads—Negro heads, to be exact. The fibrous, spongy exterior was like hair, pulled out by agile hands, and the stroke of the machete seemed to be part of a ritual sacrifice to the gods of the forest. The complicity of that army, that included girls with glistening skin and teeth like stars, culminated in a deed of indescribable cruelty when the *rabones* scraped out pieces of white brain from the skulls.

One thing I loved to watch was the sport called "popping coconuts," in which the Negroes engaged with genuine passion. The contestants, each armed with a dry, stripped coconut, took turns striking one against the other until one of them split open. They invested this game with an air of solemn liturgy, bringing into play cabalistic formulas and softly intoning mysterious words whose object seemed to be to propitiate the forest spirits. Once, when I happened to be near enough, I was able to make out the words of a muttered incantation on the lips of a smiling Negro boy:

> *Coquín, coquito,*
> *coco, cocón . . .*
> *Viejo virulo de verde ropón;*
> *pónmelo bueno,*

pónmelo pon,
dame la agüita con este pelón;
Coquín, coquito,
coco, cocón . . .

Choosing and preparing a coconut for this sport is a real science. Perhaps even one of the occult sciences. The contestant examines the shell carefully, holds it up to the light, looks at its "eyes," taps it all over with his knuckles, holds it up to his ear and shakes it to hear how the milk swashes about inside; then, not content with all this, he commends his venture to his favorite saint. The smaller coconuts are usually the hardest and the toughest. When the expert is satisfied with the results of his examination, he announces in the tone of an oracle: "This one a champion."

Old Cervelión was a tall Negro, thin as a lance, with a small, shiny head tacked onto the end of his body, who enjoyed the reputation of being the best judge of coconuts in all Cumboto. Cervelión not only could pick out the "champions," but knew how to treat them with mysterious unguents and manipulations. He was very fond of me. Once he took me by the hand and said very seriously: "I show you how to handle a coconut, so you be a good fighter."

He picked one up and began my first lesson at once.

"Now listen: grab the nut like this and hold it tight in both hands, with your thumbs held straight out, not too close together, not too far apart. You leave a little bare place where the other man going to hit your coconut. Don't let him hit it on a soft spot, else he'll flatten it out like a pancake. You got to mark the little hitting-place like this, with some spit, and scratch it all over with your fingernail. Whatever you do, never give the other man a chance to look over your coconut, else he'll break it on you first thing. When it's your turn to hit, grab it like this and hit him once, straight on, hard, from the wrist. Understand?"

He looked at me in a peculiar way, showing his tobacco-stained teeth, and repeated his question.

"Understand?"

I stood there looking at him, and didn't answer. Then he shook his shiny little head, so far above me, and said dubiously: "Uh-huh. Looks like I'm going to have to teach you a lot of things, boy. Listen here: we Negroes got to know a thousand tricks if we going to get along in this world. Look at me: I can't read, but people write to me. You mix with the white people, but you're black all the way through. They not going to teach you anything *they* know; so you got to look sharp if you want to live like a man."

One place I didn't visit until some time later was the big room where they boiled the oil in vats. Don Guillermo, *El Musiú*, spent a great deal of time there, and I was terrified of him. I never knew Don Lorenzo, the feudal lord, but I think I would have preferred his stern glance to Don Guillermo's dreadful laughter. It was this flushed and hairy giant, who drank beer like water, who had installed the large tubs for extracting the oil. His orders were always punctuated by impatient gestures with hands that were like vermilion hams; and often, without interrupting his laughter, he would use the point of his boot to make the workers move faster.

Out of the mists of my early memories rise the pale, slender figure of Don Federico, who was about my own age, and the blond, rosy image of his sister Gertrudis, who was a little younger than we. At that time, of course, I did not call him "Don," but simply "Federico." Neither of the two children had inherited their father's expansive and brutal humor. They were amiable children who had been placed under the authority of a European governess. They always seemed so intimidated that I grew to feel sorry for them—which is saying quite a bit. Their mother was a tall, pale woman with chestnut hair and startled eyes, who people said was not in her right mind. A veil of delicate melancholy had fallen over her, which seemed to isolate her from the outside world and lend her—in my eyes, at least—the air of a goddess. Hers was a sweet and quiet madness. She was, however, taken by strange impulses at times, and then she was apt to do surprisingly foolish things.

She was the only woman who ever caressed me as a child. Her bluish hand, soft and nearly weightless, would rest on my head while her eyes wandered along the paths of her thoughts. Her pale presence was like a ray of sunlight on the Lamarca plantation.

The White House

The owners' house is surrounded by a Spanish porch whose tile roof rests on round masonry pillars as strong as trees. The morning sun comes in through the porch to visit the large living room. It squeezes in through the windows, too, and pokes about in the rooms like a convalescent child. From the center of the porch roof, exactly above the front door, there hangs an old wrought-iron lantern, which is lighted every evening.

The White House, as it is called in the neighborhood, is more than a hundred years old. It stands in a clearing in the forest, a rifle shot away from the highway. There is an orchard near the house, with orange trees, pomegranates, guavas, rose apples, and other fruit trees. There is also a garden filled with roses, magnolias, jasmine, and several kinds of palms. The White House has two stories and many rooms. The living room, the library, and the dining room are on the ground floor; the bedrooms are upstairs. I sleep in a little room built of wooden planks between the kitchen and the bathroom, outside the main building. When it rains I cannot reach my room without getting wet, but still and all I would not trade it for the best one in the house. On its blackened walls, which are covered with stains in every imaginable shape, my fancy has created a whole world of good friends without whom my life would be very dull.

Inside the house there is an odd perfume, faint but persistent, redolent of the fragrances of the countryside. It is a heavy, discreet odor that fills the spirit with reverence. The walls are always clean and the floors glisten like mirrors. When I was small I used to feel the urge to dive into them and swim about. Whenever I walked through the living room I thought of a colored print I had seen over the cook's bed, and pretended that I was Jesus walking on the water.

The ceilings are so high that by late afternoon you can no longer make out the details of the moldings. This used to fill me with a vague terror. Still, I liked to look up and watch the shadows gathering, swallowing up everything. I remember that one day a bat got in, and after flying once around the room in a wide circle, let out an unpleasant shriek and fastened himself like an arrow in the dark gulf above me. "He's drowned," I thought, trembling. Then I immediately corrected myself. "No, he hasn't drowned, he's got mixed up in the shadows, he's melted into them like a piece of soap in water. Because bats," I reflected seriously, "are diabolical creatures, made out of darkness itself."

For a long time after that, whenever evening came, I could not cross that room without being overcome by a terrible uneasiness. I would look suspiciously above me and say to myself, "If I weren't so afraid, I'd stay here and see how bats are made."

No doubt what made the living room seem so mysterious was, more than anything else, the shapes of the furniture and the way it was arranged. The grand piano in the center was like a phantom ship anchored in an immense ocean. There were three soft, black leather armchairs, a couch covered in the same material, and, against the back wall, a large chest—also black—on which two silver candelabra gleamed. To get to the dining room you passed through a wide arched doorway, and to go upstairs it was necessary to climb forty-six steps of varnished wood that creaked slightly, as though mocking the people who went up and down. The door that led to the library was of carved mahogany.

At that time the inside cleaning girl was an ashy Negro who was built like a flute; she had only to stretch out her arm to reach the tops of the doors and to dust the pictures on the walls. Her name was Eduvige, and she moved noiselessly, gliding through the house like a lie. When I looked at her expressionless eyes and her mute and bitter mouth I wondered if she were really alive. I let my imagination run wild, and made up the most fantastic stories about her. At any moment I expected Eduvige to shoot up toward the ceiling and disappear, leaving behind only her extremely white dusting cloth as evidence that she had existed.

I had always been intrigued by the library. Whenever Eduvige was working there I stationed myself strategically in the dining room doorway, where I could peer in at my leisure. The variety and confusion of objects accumulated in that place, the impressive look of the glazed cabinets filled with books, the tables, the lamps, the trunks, the yellowing busts standing here and there, the dark paintings on the walls, the terrestrial globe perched high on a shelf, the thousand and one things of different shapes and colors, all ran together in my mind, so that no matter how hard I tried to remember them I was never able to retain any coherent picture of that fascinating world.

I wanted to go inside and stand in the midst of those objects, examining them, touching them with my hands, until I knew every one intimately. I suspected that there were marvelous things in that room, things that told of an existence I knew nothing of and yet vaguely sensed. But it was to be a long time before I could realize this dream. Meanwhile, I lived with the impression that the library held some terrible, tragic secret.

The dining room faced east, and the forest breezes and the soft music of the palms came in through its open windows. There, at a large table covered with a spotless linen cloth, the master and the mistress, the children, and the governess took their meals. They ate in silence. Eduvige served and I helped her by pouring water and taking the empty plates to the kitchen. I was given my orders by signals—brief glances that I learned to interpret perfectly. When there were guests, however, Don Guillermo's behavior changed completely. Then he grew talkative and spoke politely to his wife. He would even ask her to play the piano.

I forgot to say that on the ground floor there were also bedrooms for the silent Eduvige and the pallid governess, a woman with fair skin, freckles, and straw-colored eyes, who bore the exotic name of Frau Berza. She, too, hardly ever spoke. She knew how to smile, though, and more than once I caught her gazing thoughtfully off into the distance. She taught the children their reading, writing, and arithmetic, made them sing songs I found incomprehensible, and forced them to pound the piano keys for hours at a time. I shall never forget the unexpected sweetness in this woman's voice as she repeated the notes of the scale to engrave them in her pupils' minds:

Do . . . do . . . do . . . do . . .
re . . . re . . . re . . . re . . .
mi . . . mi . . . mi . . . mi . . .

Federico learned quickly; Gertrudis, on the other hand, was dull and inattentive. When he was not at the piano or reciting his lessons for Frau Berza, Federico used to amuse himself by drawing animals and landscapes with his colored crayons. Then I was able to be with him. I would stand there wide-eyed, following the movements of his hand, watching the colored lines run along the paper, witnessing the creation of tiny worlds in which I would have liked to live. With each new touch he would smile with satisfaction and hold up his picture for me to admire. Sometimes my impatience would be too much for me; I would forget my manners and allow myself the liberty of criticizing his work.

"Why don't you make that palm tree greener?"

"Because it's just right the way it is."

"You think so?"

"Of course."

We even used to argue.

"Who ever told you medlar leaves are green?"

"What other color are they? Can't you see for yourself?"

"They look blue to me, not green."

One day he threw me into confusion by asking: "Do you want to draw a picture yourself?"

He handed me his drawing tablet and sat there looking at me. I sweated blood that afternoon. When I finished my picture and showed it to him, Federico burst out laughing.

"What in the world have you done? Are these things sticking out of the tree supposed to be leaves? Good God! They look more like donkeys. Blue donkeys!"

His laughter attracted Frau Berza's attention; she frowned and whispered something in his ear. My friend hung his head. Then she turned to me.

"This is not your place. Go and sweep the floor."

My consternation was indescribable. I was hurt, and filled with strange new emotions. At that moment I understood how a human being could die of shame. My small, childish world, that with all its problems was tinted with the most beautiful colors, suddenly turned black.

Frau Berza Has a Secret

It would be difficult for me now, after so many years, to explain the real nature—or, if you prefer, the true form—of the suffering I endured because of the governess' rebuke. For some time before that—I don't know how long—I had been aware that Federico and I were not equals. I had realized that he was my superior because of a very simple reason: it was he, and not I, who was Don Guillermo's son. I accepted this fact objectively and calmly, and I would have remained quite content if it had not unfortunately occurred to Frau Berza to whisper in Federico's ear before flinging those cutting words at me. That was a revelation for me. There was an aspect of Federico's superiority he had known nothing of until that moment when Frau

Berza came along to suggest it to him. I did not know what it was all about, but it was not long before I felt the effects.

I spent miserable hours on my old wooden cot, turning it over in my mind and trying to figure it all out. The next morning I could think of nothing else. However, the bustle of the day's activities, the thousands of outside stimuli that attract a child's attention, and the subconscious urge to believe that none of it had really happened gradually anesthetized me until I had completely forgotten the matter. But about four in the afternoon, while Frau Berza was dozing in the dining room, Gertrudis came up to me with a furtive air.

"What was it Frau Berza whispered to my brother when she scolded you? You don't know? What a shame. I asked Federico, but he wouldn't tell me."

This volley from Federico's little sister reopened the wound that had already begun to heal over. Fortunately, for children there is a Providence whose function it is to desensitize those nervous centers where great sorrows are felt. If we adults were less cowardly, if we could retain even half of the vigor and good will of infancy, humanity would be incalculably less miserable. There was a moment in the midst of my dark ruminations when a tiny light appeared, and I clutched at it with all the tenacity of a castaway grasping a frail piece of seaweed. There must be some way to get around Frau Berza's cruel injunction. It would need only a little cooperation on Federico's part for everything to return to its former happy state. I must point out that I was not thinking of myself alone. I was sure that Federico was suffering, too; I wanted to alleviate my friend's loneliness as well as my own.

It didn't require a great deal of scheming. After lunch Frau Berza would usually sit and read in the dining room, leaning comfortably back against one of the pillars. Gradually her eyes would close, and her freckled hand would fall languidly on the pages of her open book. She would remain like that for an hour, sometimes longer. At the end of that time her eyes would open again, she would lift her hand to arrange her straw-colored hair, and she would go on reading until dinner time. It was this opportunity that Federico, Gertrudis, and I seized to renew our association.

The moment we were all together again—two days after the catastrophe— was an occasion for celebration. The fact that it was a mute celebration, a rejoicing without words, made it even more exciting. We tacitly agreed to communicate with gestures, so as not to wake Frau Berza; but we spoke with our eyes. What made me happiest was Federico's pleasure at having me with him again. I must say, to our credit, that not one of us shed a tear. Children cry only over trivial things. We were happy. That afternoon I took my revenge by drawing whole herds of blue donkeys. Federico watched, smiling, and instructed me with gestures to paint them red—even the ears. Suddenly my friend grew serious, raised his eyebrows, and put his finger to his lips. He moved his hands through the air before my eager eyes, trying to convey by signs something that I was not able to understand, apparently having to do with Frau Berza. At last, seeing that it was hopeless, he decided to resort to words and whispered in my ear: "Frau Berza has a secret."

Several days went by. By taking advantage of the governess' afternoon nap we were able to exchange a few furtive words occasionally, and Federico let me take his sketches so that I might admire them at night in my room. Unfortunately for me, the cook was lacking in artistic feeling; she put out the light without consulting me just when I was most absorbed.

My moment of revenge came one splendid night in June. It was hot, and the moonlight was like satin. As long as there were sounds of people moving about in the house I lay in my bed quite contentedly, examining Federico's pictures by the light of the silvery glow that came in through the window. The marvelous oceans, rivers, and forests he had created filled my mind with dreams of voyages and adventures. Suddenly I realized that everyone was asleep and that the house was silent, and my happiness ended. The moon, which until that moment had been a cordial friend, suddenly made me feel very uneasy. The cook was snoring nearby, snorting with the regularity of a blacksmith's bellows. Forgotten things, scattered words, shifting figures, all magnified by the silence, crowded into my mind. "Frau Berza has a secret," Federico had told me. What was Frau Berza's secret, and why should it concern me? "Go and sweep the floor." And who ever saw a blue medlar? "Frau Berza has a secret." The hours moved slowly. The sounds of the forest whispered in my ears and walked up and down my spine like restless insects. The moonlight—clear, steady, metallic, ghostly—poured into our little room and made everything look larger than life and unfamiliar. I lay there with my eyes tightly closed, but sleep would not come. Every once in a while I lifted one eyelid, very slowly, to regard the phantasmagoria that lay about me; but I immediately closed it again, so tightly it hurt. Time seemed infinite. The silence was immeasurable. It was useless to think about blue donkeys and Federico's smile; the words kept coming back, as insistent as the moonlight: "Frau Berza has a secret." I don't know how long things went on this way. Suddenly I heard a little stream of voices, and I had to clamp my mouth shut in order not to cry out. I thought of souls in Purgatory, who, I had heard, came out at night and walked about through the deserted countryside. But that couldn't be it, because there were only two voices. In spite of my terror, I could hear them more clearly every moment. And anyway, this wasn't Friday, but Tuesday. Perhaps it was the Ghost Who Walks Alone . . . But it couldn't be that either, because, as I said, there were two people speaking— a man and a woman.

The simplest thing would have been to put both hands over my ears under the patchwork quilt, shutting out that terrifying sound; but I didn't, for the simple reason that I didn't dare move a muscle. Fortunately, just when I was expecting to see the ghosts come in through the window, I recognized the woman's voice. "Why, that's Frau Berza," I said to myself. And at that moment my fear ran away across the fields with little skips of joy. I took my head out from under the covers at once and listened.

"No, no, Cruz María," Frau Berza was saying, "Please don't insist. I can't go with you tonight, not with the moon as full as it is."

I jumped as if I had stepped on a hot coal. I knew the other voice, too. It was Cervelión's son, the one who tended the cows and brought the milk in the morning. There could be no doubt. There was only one Cruz María in all of Cumboto, nicknamed *El Matacán* because he moved like a deer. There was a pause, and then the governess said: "Let me go, Cruz! Please, let me go! That's an order. I won't go with you again . . . Besides, didn't I tell you to bathe before you came to see me? You smell like a cow, Cruz."

"But I did take a bath this afternoon in the river."

"Well, the cow smell is still there, and it doesn't go well with making love."

My fear replaced by curiosity, I slipped out of bed and went to the door without waking the cook. The two figures stood before me, grotesquely magnified by the moonlight. Their enormous shadows seemed to glow against the white wall of the house. The man and woman were struggling, holding their breath. I stood motionless at the door, watching the fantastic scene. How immense the world looked under that bluish light! Cruz María was naked to the waist, and his skin gleamed like the shell of a huge June bug. Frau Berza's wrapper was so filmy that she seemed almost transparent in the moonlight. With his strong arms around her waist, Cruz María might have been embracing a pillar of smoke. Her long hair floated in the air in an unreal way as she twisted and turned to avoid his hot lips.

I found that my attitude had changed completely. Now I felt that I must defend this woman from Cruz María's hands and eyes and lips; but I didn't dare cry out for fear of summoning up Don Guillermo's flushed countenance, the cook with her enormous nightgown, and Eduvige's rigid, ashy face. I had little time to debate the matter, however, because just at that moment the two struggling figures happened to turn in my direction and froze where they stood. After a few seconds Cruz María suddenly leaped like a deer and shot across the garden, and Frau Berza came toward me with her hands outstretched. I felt her fingers on my throat.

"Tell me: how much have you seen?"

"Nothing," I whimpered, hypnotized by her glistening eyes.

"Be quiet! Keep your voice down!"

I thought she was going to strangle me on the spot. She could have, I'm sure, for her hands were strong and wiry. But suddenly, to my surprise, her behavior changed. She smiled.

"All right," she said gently, arranging her wrapper and smoothing her hair. "You're not going to say a word to anybody about this, are you? And I'll do something for you. I'll give you a pretty present."

She pulled me gently toward the door that led to the dining room and put her finger to her lips.

"Not a word to anybody, do you understand? Not to the grownups, or the children, either. Promise?"

I nodded my head.

"Do you swear?"

I nodded again.

"Speak! Say yes!"

"Yes."

She gave me a piercing glance and then, without another word, turned and walked down the hall to her room.

The following afternoon I whispered to Federico: "You were right: Frau Berza does have a secret. Last night I saw her fighting with Cruz María."

Federico smiled.

"I saw them, too."

"And you're not scared?"

"No, I'm not scared."

His smile grew broader and more enigmatic.

"She's the one who'd better be scared now," he said.

The Path of the Blue Donkeys

All at once, without really meaning to, Federico and I altered the rhythm of our lives, and dragged little Gertrudis along with us. What happened was so unexpected and fascinating that we felt as though we were enveloped in an intoxicating haze. I was amazed at Frau Berza's new attitude toward us. Some change of heart had taken place to make her so meek and eager to please that she no longer treated me with suspicion and was less strict during piano lessons. Actually, I should have known better than anyone what had happened to the governess; and yet it would never have occurred to me to relate this change with the scene that night in the garden. Of that episode I recalled only two things that had made definite impressions on my mind. One was Cruz María's inexplicable behavior and the strange gleam in his eyes; the other was the nice present Frau Berza had promised me, which I had not yet received although several days had gone by.

It was Federico who took the initiative in changing the rules by which we lived. With his enigmatic smile constantly on his lips, he watched for every opportunity to flout the governess' discipline. No longer did I have to lie in wait until Frau Berza began to nod in her chair before coming into the dining room to talk to him and watch him drawing in his notebook; now I did so with impunity whenever I liked.

"What are you hiding for?" Federico would ask scornfully. "Don't be scared, silly. Come on in."

And he would lead me inside and make me stand beside him, with my elbows on the edge of the big table. Then he would wink and whisper: "Don't worry. She's not going to say anything."

And, in fact, from then on Frau Berza merely regarded me very seriously, without uttering a word. She walked past me stiffly, her head held high and her eyes half-closed, as though the glare of the sunlight irritated them. One afternoon Federico surprised me by asking: "Do you want to learn to read?"

Without hesitating for a moment I said that I did, because it would all be part of the same adventure. Learning to read at Federico's side, out of his own book, under his direction, would be just as exciting as using his crayons to draw the fantastic leaves that he said looked like blue donkeys. Each letter I learned, which he introduced as though it were a new friend, had for me all the vitality of a being suddenly come to life, rising out of a world of dreams to become a part of my own existence. With their different names and shapes, the letters were tiny Federicos and Gertrudises come to join our company.

In his big book, with its pages stiff as cardboard and its multicolored covers, there were many familiar figures and scenes: intensely green trees, little houses with red roofs, appetizing fruits in tempting colors, little dappled cows that grazed in neat meadows inlaid with tiny flowers, and white children who seemed to be dreaming on the river bank. Although we lived so near the rivers of Cumboto we had only vague and colorless notions about them. I, for example, could not remember ever having been near a river in my life. As though to repay Federico for all the questions he was constantly asking me, one day I asked one of my own.

"Wouldn't you like to go down and look at the river?"

"The river?" he repeated, puzzled.

I simply pointed to the picture in his book, that delightful spot where lazy little Enrique lay in his canary-colored trousers, and turned my eyes toward the woods where the trees were gravely swaying. Both of us fell to dreaming. We spoke no more of this, but from that moment on I often caught Federico with the book on his lap, idly regarding the green mystery of the coconut palms.

"There are a lot of people I don't know about, aren't there?" he asked me one day.

"Where?" I demanded.

"Out there," he said, looking toward the horizon.

"I don't know . . ."

But immediately I corrected myself: "There's a fellow called Cervelión."

"Cervelión! What a funny name! Who's Cervelión?"

"Cruz María's father."

"And who's Cruz María?"

"The one who brings the milk early in the morning."

"Oh! And who else do you know?"

I didn't know anybody else, really. Cervelión himself I had seen two or three times at the *coquera*, but I distinguished him from other people only because of his fascinating lecture on "popping coconuts." Federico and I had long discussions about this while we were reading or drawing. I was amazed to see how entranced he was with the things I told him. He drove me crazy with questions about that unfamiliar world that I, because of my special position in the household, had the privilege of frequenting. I described it as well as I could, even adding some broad touches of my own; still not satisfied, he insisted that I draw it for him. As evoked by my pencil, Cervelión looked like a leafless coconut tree. One afternoon I found Federico very excited.

"Tomorrow we're going to the river," he told me.

"To the river!"

"Yes. Tomorrow Papá's leaving for the port. I heard him telling Don Serafín."

Don Serafín was the majordomo of the plantation, a silver-haired old man who hardly ever showed up at the house.

"As soon as Papá leaves," he went on eagerly, "we'll go and find Cervelión."

Federico's father did, in fact, set off very early the next morning on horseback, followed on another mount by a Negro carrying a gleaming machete. The children and the governess had breakfast in the dining room, while Doña Beatriz took hers in her bedroom. I was trembling with impatience and fear as I watched all this. When breakfast was over, and while Frau Berza was still at the rear of the house, Federico ran up to me and took me feverishly by the hand.

"Come on! Let's go, quick, before they call us to lessons."

As we crossed the threshold and our feet sank in the grass that grew around the house we felt an electrifying sensation of freedom. At Federico's side, looking all around in terror, came his sister Gertrudis. We walked fast, faces up, nostrils trembling as we felt the fresh young breeze that came from the blue horizon. The green, damp garden, in the midst of which rose the white mass of the house, seemed like a quiet sea bathed in the light of the rising sun.

"Where are you taking me?" little Gertrudis demanded.

Neither Federico nor I thought it wise to answer her. Her brother was leading her by the hand, making her skip to keep up. It was I who led the caravan, doing my best to keep us hidden in the foliage. Soon we were panting and sweating. Every few minutes Federico asked, "Is it much farther?" and his little sister, her small voice shaking with fear, kept coming in with her refrain: "Where are you taking me?" It was not long before we saw, rising above the vegetation, the tile roofs of the work sheds and the tall brick chimney of the vats where they boiled the oil.

"Look! We're almost there," I said.

When Federico emerged from the palm grove and stood staring at the *coquera*, he was breathless with wonder. The sheds were teeming, like a cage full of starlings. Only the older Negroes worked in relative silence. The girls were singing and the young men were shouting at each other and laughing with wide-open mouths. But when they saw us they fell silent. It wasn't my presence—which meant nothing to them—but that of Federico and especially Gertrudis that struck them dumb. And then I saw Cervelión's out-sized figure coming toward us with his phlegmatic gait, and I nudged my friend. The old man bent over me with a comic air of solemnity.

"Hello, boy! What you kids doing around here?"

"We came to see you," I replied, bending my neck back to look up into his face.

"You come all by yourselves?"

Without answering I took him by the hand and drew him to one side. I made him bend down and whispered in his ear: "These are Don Guillermo's children."

"Yes, I know. But what you want here this time of day?"

"Why, we're on our way to the river."

"All by yourselves?"

"No, you're going with us."

Cervelión stood up again and scratched his head. He raised his eyebrows, looked all around, and then leaned down again. His voice buzzed like a bumblebee.

"This is kind of awkward, boy. I don't want to get in any trouble with *El Musiú*. Why don't you kids go on home?"

"Because we want to see what it's like down by the river."

"I see."

Federico had come up to us, followed by his sister.

"You're Cervelión, aren't you?"

He looked very seriously into the Negro's face. Without waiting for an answer he took his hand and shook it.

"I'm Federico, and this is my sister Gertrudis. We've made up our minds to get to the river, no matter what. If you won't come with us we'll go by ourselves. All we ask you to do is show us the way."

"*Caramba*! Well . . . all right."

I was overcome with admiration. Just when I was beginning to regret having undertaken our adventure, my friend was displaying great courage and determination. His little sister, unconcerned, was looking all about her.

Without another word, Cervelión led us a few yards from the sheds and pointed toward the woods.

"Now pay attention to what I tell you. See that path going into the woods? All right, follow it straight ahead, and don't turn off anywhere. After a while you come to a barb-wire fence. Climb through it—but be careful. Then keep straight on. Pretty soon you going to come to a house with a tile roof and a nice, neat front yard. That's Ana's place—old lady Ana, the one who makes little candies to sell. Knock on the door and ask which way you go to get to the river. If you do what I say you can't get lost."

We looked at each other, petrified. What should we do? If Federico had asked my advice at that moment I would have said with no hesitation, "Let's go back home." But he did nothing of the kind. Undaunted, he turned to Cervelión and said: "Straight ahead on this path?"

"And don't turn off anywhere."

I had heard my friend reading a story from one of his books about a boy who fell under the spell of a magician, was transported through the air, and suddenly found himself in a strange world where he had delightful adventures. As we set out on the path that led "straight ahead" to the river, I could have sworn that we were in that same enchanted universe, and throughout the events that followed I behaved accordingly. I looked up at the thick foliage that made a great roof over us, and was certain that the sun had disappeared from the sky. There is a great deal of light in the world of children's dreams, but never any sun or moon or lamps. The houses and streets are lit by starlight, by gold and silver stars that tinkle like little bells and glow and sing when the magician touches them with his wand.

Invisible birds were warbling in the tall branches of the trees. From time to time one would burst forth with a sudden whirring sound and take wing. Startling noises shook the dead leaves at our feet as huge *matos* shot out with their tails in the air. It was all new to us and we were overwhelmed, rocked in a cradle of delight and terror. Men and women were coming and going along the path. We passed with serious looks on our faces, tense with the fear of being kidnapped and dragged away to distant caves.

Soon we found ourselves in front of the house with the tile roof and the nicely-swept front yard. Almost all the peasant huts I had seen were painted either black or red, and were filthy, with walls that cracked and peeled under the pitiless heat of the sun. They were as unsociable as wild animals hiding in the forest. This one, on the contrary, smiled at us from its window, under the green arms that leaned down to caress it. A soft breeze was stirring the leaves, dropping a shower of flaming-red, pulpy blossoms on the roof. Federico and I stood looking through the half-open door. Gertrudis had picked a flower and was playing with it. Somewhere inside a chicken cackled.

"Shall we knock?" I asked.

"Yes. You do it."

His imperious tone surprised me, but I didn't say anything. I rapped on the door.

"Who is it?"

"*Gente de paz.*"

"Comiiiiing . . ."

In a moment there appeared a girl a little older than we, whose slender figure made me think of a pencil line. She was dark and barefoot, and was engaged in combing her kinky hair, that dripped rivulets of water down her forehead.

"What you want?"

"Is this where old Ana lives?"

I was the one who asked the question. The girl frowned and pointed her comb at me.

" 'Old Ana?' What you mean, 'Old Ana?' You're pretty rude, if you ask me. The lady who lives here is my grandmother Anita."

Federico intervened in a conciliatory tone: "Don't get mad. We just want to know how to get to the river."

The girl made a face, glanced at me with contempt, and turned to give my companion her most delicious smile.

"Well, that's better. All you have to do is talk right, and we can understand each other. I just came back from the river with my grandmother, but..."

"But what?"

All her charm was directed toward Federico. With a knowing wink she skipped back into the house and soon reappeared with her rope-soled sandals dangling from one finger.

"I'll go back with you. Come on, I'll show you..."

Our adventure suddenly took an unexpected turn in the company of that restless, changeable, odd creature who oozed words from every pore. We no longer saw the world about us except through the magic of her tongue. Everything around her was familiar, she knew everything by its name, and she related everything, directly or indirectly, with her grandmother and herself.

"I like to go in the river with my sandals on," she said. "It's easier to get around. That's why they're all wet now—see? My grandmother Anita's always scolding me about something, but I don't pay any attention to her. She's so old, poor thing. Here's the road you take to Paso Real—and Goai-guaza, too, if you want to. You come to Tres Cruces before you get to Goai-guaza. You're not from around here, are you? You must be strangers. I went to Tres Cruces once with my father and my brother Prudencio. After you pass Tres Cruces you come to Barrial del Machete."

Sometimes she walked along beside us in a normal way, and then sud-denly she would begin to jump about as if she were skipping rope. Her long, thin arms whirled about like windmills, as though they turned on pins set in her narrow shoulders. Her feet—also long and narrow—showed such an individual and surprising mobility that they made me think of two funny little animals.

On a sudden impulse she ran up to Gertrudis and took her by the hand.

"Why don't you skip like me, dummy? Come on, make believe you're playing hopscotch."

But Gertrudis didn't understand. The poor child had had an apprehen-sive look on her face ever since we first met that human whirlwind. "Where does this erratic person get such annoying vitality?" she seemed to be asking. In her large, blue, dreamy eyes there was a look of astonishment. She was not far from tears.

As we followed our new friend, the path grew more crooked and nar-row, until we had to push aside the underbrush to get through. I confess that I was beginning to be uneasy; and when I turned around to look at Federico I saw that he had turned pale. Gertrudis, who was clutching her brother's hand, kept tripping over the ruffles of her petticoat and falling down. All three of us had grown silent. Our illusions were foundering in that tempestuous green sea. We didn't turn tail and run only because of the fascinating person who held us there by the power of her will.

"My name is Ana, too, same as my grandmother," she was explaining now. "My whole name is Ana Agustina, but some people call me Pascua, because they say I'm as gay as Easter morning. I know everything around here like the palm of my hand. My father's Ernesto, and my brother's name is Prudencio. He's bigger than me, but he'd better look out if he gives me any trouble. The other day he started pulling me around by the hair to show off in front of a girl named Carmita who sells tortillas, and you can still see the mark where I bit him."

Always jumping about, never pausing for breath, she made her way through that vegetable ocean as nimbly as a dragonfly. And all the while she flitted from one subject to another like a hummingbird in a garden.

"I'm a great dancer, did you know that? Whenever they have a dance around here they send for me. But I don't dance with just anybody. Don't you like dancing?" she asked Federico. "Where do you kids live? Are you from Puerto Cabello? Or Goaiguaza? I never saw you around here before—this one's face looks kind of familiar, though." (She was referring to me.) "You have to meet my grandmother. On the way back you can stop at the house, if you want to."

Suddenly Federico stopped, his hand on his chest.

"I can't go any farther," he panted. We all came to a halt.

His sister regarded him with terrified eyes.

"Are you tired?" Pascua asked. "Poor little kid! You're not very strong, are you? Stick it out a little longer, we're almost there."

At that moment a burst of laughter came from somewhere nearby, and we looked at each other uneasily. We could see no one, for we were practically drowning in vegetation. Overhead, through a wide gap in the treetops, we could see the brilliantly blue sky, dotted with little white clouds. It was so far away that we felt no larger than the crickets chirping in the thicket. A few seconds later the laughter broke out again, hoarser this time and more menacing in its gaiety. Gertrudis put her hands over her ears and began to scream. The laughter ceased, and a voice called out. "Don't be scared, little white girl. Nobody going to hurt you."

Cervelión's round, shiny head rose from behind a bush, his face illuminated by his smile. In that mouthful of yellowish teeth not a single piece was missing.

"You think I let you come all by yourselves?"

He chuckled. Then he explained that he had taken another path that only he knew. He spoke gently, with all the fondness of a servant for his masters.

"Come on with me."

The river lay only a short distance ahead, at the foot of a slight slope that ended in a strip of golden sand. There was a large stand of bamboo whose long lances leaned down to pierce the surface of the flowing water. A few little red flowers, like vivid drops of blood, sprinkled the river bank. There were others as yellow as gold coins and as blue as Nordic eyes. Some women who were washing clothes and bathing where the water was deep under the canopy of the bamboo began to scream and giggle. Cervelión pacified them in his lazy voice.

"You don't have to carry on like that. I can't see that far any more, anyway."

He turned to us and said kindly:

"You kids want to take a swim?"

Federico shook his head. I didn't think I wanted to, either. Everything was so strange and splendid that we needed more time to make up our minds as to how we really felt about it.

Grandmother Anita

Outside of Frau Berza, Eduvige, and the cook, no one at the White House knew about our adventure. But for the governess the affair took on the proportions of a tragedy. No sooner had we arrived home than she threw herself upon Federico and began to chatter at him excitedly in that guttural tongue I couldn't understand. Then she busied herself with Gertrudis' hair—which was in a deplorable state—with a violence that betrayed her repressed anger.

While Frau Berza was attending to his sister, Federico remained standing in the middle of the living room, next to the piano. As he regarded the governess' sloping shoulders the blood began to drain from his face. Then he said something in that unintelligible tongue that made her wheel about as though he had bitten her in the back of the neck. Her lips trembled, but she was unable to speak. It was as if something had collapsed within her. What had Federico said? I wasn't long in finding out. That same afternoon she stopped me in the hall near her bedroom and dragged me inside.

"You told him, didn't you? You told him, after you promised you wouldn't say a word to anybody!"

I was dumbfounded. There were tears in Frau Berza's gray eyes, and her face seemed sunken, as if a hundred years had left their mark on it. When I saw how her mouth was shaking I felt very sorry for her. Suddenly, I was no longer afraid.

"It wasn't me, Frau Berza," I cried. "I swear it wasn't."

"How did he find out, then?"

"I don't know. He told *me* about it."

The scene I witnessed the following afternoon was even more pitiful. Frau Berza, seated at the table with her hands clenched on her open book, was weeping softly before Federico. I couldn't help understanding some of what she was saying, for this time she was speaking Spanish.

"Be a good boy. Don't take the little girl with you. Please!"

When she saw me come in she took out her little lace handkerchief and held it to her eyes. Federico's face was pale, but he was smiling. I was afraid again.

From that day on—or, more precisely, from the moment I saw that smile of Federico's—my admiration for him was tempered by a vague impression that in some way he was not quite like other people. I found that I could no longer move or speak or even think except in the way he wanted me to. I even began having absurd dreams about him. In these dreams I invariably saw him as a smiling white cat with cruel blue eyes.

That episode was followed by a veritable orgy of freedom. Don Guillermo was often away, always in the company of a Negro on horseback, and we would leave the house as soon as he was gone. We got our fill of the woods, the river, everything that voluptuous world had to offer our newly-awakened senses. There were no lessons then, nor any drawing or piano scales to practice. No one stopped us or even asked where we were going, and even Eduvige hardly cast her sphinx's glance in our direction when we came home. Federico made only one concession to the governess: he no longer took Gertrudis along.

Our acquaintance with old Ana, Pascua's grandmother, dates from that time. We called on her for the first time one morning after a long swim near the bamboo grove. From that day on we never failed to visit her whenever we went to the woods. The prospect of seeing her in the midst of her neat household held an irresistible attraction for us. Her granddaughter's garrulity always rounded out this delightful experience. Like Pascua, the old lady loved to talk about herself; she was always bragging about how old and how strong she was.

"Us Negroes are tough," Grandmother Anita used to say. "How old you think I am? Look at me; I been eating bread for almost ninety years. Look at these teeth: not one cavity. When I was a girl, and proud of my looks, I used to clean them with twigs from the hot-pepper bush and pieces of licorice root. After I had my first baby, when I learned to smoke to calm down the pain, I used to scrub them with cigar butts. But let's not get off the track. I was talking about getting old. I always laugh at people who make out to be younger than they are, like they think it's the years that make them older. My grandfather lived more than a hundred years, and if a mule hadn't kicked him in the chest while he was shoeing it he'd still be around telling everybody what to do. He was a very funny man. No matter what happen, it remind him of a story or maybe even a poem. My boy Ernesto take after him, a chip off the old block. But the other one, Fernando . . . Better not talk about him . . . My boy Fernando," she added confidentially, with a malicious look, "married a white girl—to 'improve the race,' he said."

When she was in the mood, Grandmother Anita was a delight. Then she was gay and garrulous, and gathered everybody about her and was so entertaining that time flew by without our noticing it. Unhappily, this did not happen as often as we would have liked; the old lady spent most of her time wrapped in sullen silence or rocking back and forth, softly singing to herself.

Grandmother Anita was absolutely and totally black. Even so, when she was young she must have had a kind of special charm that appealed to men. She was undoubtedly tall and graceful, and must have displayed the piquant wit that still colored her conversation. By the time I met her, years and troubles had bent her figure and withered her flesh. In her appearance there was something of the African fetish figure. No one had ever been able to change her habit of wearing an enormous bandanna tied around her head, and on top of that a battered felt hat with a broad, shiny brim. Over her flat nose a pair of ancient steel-rimmed spectacles hung precariously—a superfluous ornament over which her little, watery eyes scrutinized everything about her. When she was absorbed in her sewing her lower lip hung down loosely and revealed her small, even teeth.

She lived with her younger son, Ernesto, and his offspring, Prudencio and Pascua. The elder son, the fabulous Fernando who had married a white girl, lived in the city and never came to visit her. Our gatherings almost always took place at the rear of the little house, around the kitchen fireplace. Her audience consisted of Federico, Pascua, and myself; Prudencio was at that time off working in the stables. Pascua was, as she herself said, "her grandmother's idol." In fact, this dark, wiry girl was the only person who could loosen the old lady's tongue. And what was even more interesting, she was the only one who could, on very special occasions, make her open the old mahogany trunk where she kept her heterogeneous store of keepsakes.

When her grandmother consented to unlock the trunk, it was like a party. We gathered in a ring about her, quivering with the same emotions Edmond Dantès must have felt as he stood for the first time in the cave of Monte Cristo. The clanking of the big bell that hung from the lock spilled out over the countryside like a hallelujah; we received it in our hearts, we opened our eyes to it, we breathed it in through our widened nostrils as though it were a perfume rather than a sound. Then we would stand in awed silence, hanging on her every word as her black, trembling fingers, with ritual deliberation, turned over the pieces of many-colored clothing, the jewels of gold and silver, the huge Madras shawls impregnated with ancient perfumes, the tiny cups of Holland china, and the strange musical instruments that aroused our curiosity more than all the rest.

Grandmother Anita's trunk was a fairy tale, not only because of the objects it held but because of the stories they illustrated. From what marvelous lands were those brightly-colored silk prints? Who were the people who had worn the yellowing batistes that only the old lady's fingers could handle without damaging them? Whose lips had rested against the gold rims of those fragile cups, and whose bosom had been adorned by those twisted chains, those pale ivory lockets with their delicate cameos, those *custodias*? The old lady told us how all these things had come into her possession at the death of her grandfather Mamerto, who in turn had been given them by his owner, a white gentleman.

"His owner?" Federico repeated, most intrigued.

"Yes. That's what my grandfather called him, you know."

When she gave this explanation that none of us really understood, Anita laughed sardonically.

"He called all the people in the big house that. He was the slave of a rich family who owned big coffee and cacao plantations. When the last of the masters went off to war, my grandfather was left in charge of the house."

"And that man never came back, Granny?" Federico asked.

"No, he never came back. If he had, this stuff wouldn't be here now."

"What would you do if he came back?"

"I'd give it back to him. That's what my grandfather told me to do before he died."

As I inspected the jumbled objects in the trunk, I was most fascinated by the musical instruments; by some silver amulets in the shape of tiny human limbs, ships, birds, and animals; and by an ancient chromolithograph of a general with a long, black beard and a row of medals across his chest. As for Federico, he would have given ten years of his life to read those letters written on blue paper and tied with a faded ribbon. Pascua was interested only in the skirts, the camisoles, and the vivid shawls.

Among the few keepsakes Anita allowed us to profane with our curious fingers were some small daguerreotype portraits, blackened and dim. We could hardly make out the faces of two women with straight black hair and two very stiff men, one of whom boasted enormous muttonchop whiskers. The effect these photographs produced in my mind was most peculiar. I saw them as the images of four ghosts, souls in Purgatory who were held captive in the tiny prisons of their portraits by some diabolic art.

"Who are they, Granny?" I asked.

"Four white people, relatives of my grandfather's master."

"But what are their names?" I insisted as I gazed at the blackened metal rectangles.

If the old lady had ever known, she had forgotten. Those fantastic people with their unreal faces had lived many years ago, when life and customs were very different. I gathered this from Anita's evasive replies, and, judging from the vague terror these grave faces occasioned in my mind, it must have been true. If the mere sight of their portraits, as dry and faded as leaves pressed in a book, could affect me so, what would happen if I were to meet them in the flesh? Anita's grandfather had called them his "owners," and perhaps she herself used the same term in her mind. Was I expected to think of them in the same way, to regard them with the same servile reverence and affection?

The problem arose every time I saw the four daguerreotypes, and for a long time was the source of one of my most acute childhood conflicts. Once I resolutely asked the old lady, "Granny, were these people *your* masters, too?"

She looked at me for a moment and said, "Yes, they were. And if they were still alive they'd be yours."

When I heard this astounding statement, in which there was a certain malice, I felt an indefinable uneasiness. My masters! The first thing that came to my mind was a cur called Corazmín, who showed up one fine day at the main house only to be kicked out the door by Don Guillermo. Corazmín was a white retriever with chocolate spots, gentle and affectionate but always hungry, given to poking his muzzle into every corner. He never came around the house again, but whenever he caught sight of one of us he followed him like a shadow.

"That dog!" Pascua used to protest furiously. "Why doesn't he follow his own masters?"

That exclamation was a kind of key to my preoccupation. Now that these people were all dead, whom should I regard as *my* masters?

For a long time after that I felt a secret distrust of Federico, which fortunately he never suspected.

Aside from the marvelous trunk, what attracted us to Anita were the delicacies she prepared from time to time and the stories she would tell when she was in a good mood.

I shall always remember with delight those dishes that even after so many years are still enveloped in the fragrance of coconut butter, anise, and Ceylon cloves. She made them with the hands of a goddess. She often spoke of the little-known riches of Curaçao cooking, of the delights of *banana-stobat, calás, sopita,* and *buñuelos,* but I can't say where she got these recipes because I never thought to ask. I can only claim to have wolfed down the products of her laboratory with insatiable gluttony.

On mornings when we found the old lady singing to herself, her lower lip drooping, we looked forward to spending a couple of happy hours in her company. That was the unmistakable sign that we were going to have *ventas,* or hair-raising stories, or even both at once. (I forgot to say that Anita's delicacies were known as *ventas* throughout the neighborhood, and that she herself took great pains to point out that the word specified that they were "for sale," so that there might be no mistake.)

In fact, whoever did not have at least a centavo to spend could be sure that he would not taste a *calá* or a *buñuelo*. It was only when the old lady's good humor bordered on madness that she let us have one of her confections on credit, to be paid for on the following Saturday. There was, of course, one exception in our group: Pascua, her beloved granddaughter.

I have referred to the laboratory where Grandmother Anita prepared her specialties, and the subject really merits a little elaboration. When it was *calás* she was making, she provided herself with a huge gourd bowl and an old tin pot. When the beans had been soaked in water in the pot and were softened and wrinkled like the skin of a drowned man, the old woman's fingers began removing the dark skins so slowly and carefully that it set our nerves on edge. When each bean was completely skinned and gleamed like a pearl, it was transferred to the gourd bowl. When the bowl was full she went on unhurriedly to the second step in the maddening process, which consisted of mashing up the beans together with a strange oily compound that contained the real secret of her magnificent art. The mixture was then beaten with a whisk of twisted twigs, examined frequently for the proper consistency, and tested by Anita's sibylline tongue. It was then carried to the blackened cooking-hearth, where an ancient iron griddle, carefully greased, was heating over a cheery bed of coals.

Watching Grandmother Anita test the frothy bean paste always filled us with excitement and ineffable wonder and respect. Our eyes followed the motions of the whisk and our hearts pounded with anxiety during the few seconds it took for the thick drop to fall upon the palm of that knowing hand. Our mouths watered as we watched the old woman's tongue, wet, broad, and as flexible as a serpent, emerge over her lower lip and lick up the sample. As she stood there, motionless, the suspense was more than we could bear. The question burst forth from our lips with gastric urgency: "Is it all right, Granny? Does it taste good?"

Depending on her mood and the direction of her thoughts were taking at the moment, the time for peeling and beating the beans might also be the time for telling ghost stories. I say according to her mood, because it was not unusual for her to prefer to hum softly as she worked, even when she was in the best of spirits. The sound of her voice was like the monotonous, soothing purring of a cat.

Now that the passing of the years has blurred the picture in my mind, I believe I can interpret that happy purring. Grandmother Anita loved to turn over her memories in her mind, to relive the past, and these tasks left her mind free for daydreaming. The patient painstaking preparation of her *ventas* opened a door within her that led to a hidden paradise. The old lady lived in her reminiscences. Her mind must have been a great deal like her trunk: full of jewels, vivid colors, guitars and mandolins, jungle perfumes, and barbarous superstitions.

It was these superstitions that came to the surface when she was in a communicative mood. They took the form of anecdotes, or, as she called them, "histories of devils and visions." Grandmother Anita was unaware of that civilized world of fairy tales where princes married shepherdesses after releasing them from the spells of wicked witches, let alone that literature wherein moved such refined personages as Little Red Riding Hood, Snow White, and Robinson Crusoe. Hers were *true* stories, dealing with events she could swear to, manifestations of a world that was no less real than the everyday one even though it lay outside the realm of human perception.

She always introduced her stories with one of two sacred formulas. She would begin, "You don't have to believe this if you don't want to . . ." or,

"No matter what people say . . ." The events she related had usually happened to her or to some close relative, such as her father, her mother, or her grandfather Mamerto.

"You don't have to believe this if you don't want to, but once I saw the ugliest, the scariest, the wildest thing you can imagine. When I was living in Borburata with my grandfather Mamerto, I saw a man walking around with his head in his hand."

This, naturally, was enough to make our hair stand up. But our curiosity was greater than our fear; huddling together as closely as we could, we cried out in chorus: "With his head in his hand, Granny! How could that be?"

And she told us about it at great length, accumulating details, gratified to see us so interested and frightened. According to her, the man was the founder of the plantation called El Quisandal, near Borburata, where she, her mother, and her grandfather had gone to live. He was a Spaniard who had refused to surrender to the patriotic forces; when he was taken prisoner he was decapitated with an axe in the presence of his servants. They buried his body in his own patio, with his head between his hands; and ever after that, his miserable soul, unable to rest, walked about the neighborhood. Sometimes he came out of a little wood and went into the house, while at other times he seemed to emerge from the coffee grove and stand in the center of the patio, gesturing as though he wanted to say something. But what could the poor wretch possibly say with his head no longer in its proper place?

She had also seen a terrifying spectacle which she called the "Shall I Come Down or Not?" This happened to her when she was a child; she could not remember exactly where, since she had moved about a great deal with her grandfather Mamerto.

"One night when I was a little girl I went outside into a big patio where there were lots of trees, and I saw a black thing hanging from a tall *samán* tree. *Samanes* attract unhappy spirits. Soon as I laid my eyes on that thing hanging there I was paralyzed with fear. Then I heard a hoarse, horrible voice say, 'Shall I come down, or not?' And another voice answered, 'Come down!' Then I saw an arm fall, all glowing with light. 'Shall I come down, or not?' the voice asked again. 'Come down!' the other one said, and another burning arm hit the ground. 'Shall I come down, or not?' 'Come down!' And I saw the head fall, like a ball of fire. And then somehow I got the strength to run away from there. I ran into the house as fast as I could and jumped into bed and pulled the covers over my head. Next day I told my grandfather about it, and he says to me, 'Girl, that's the ugliest vision I ever heard of. But what you ought to do, instead of running away, is say, "Come down, brother, and find rest in the name of God and the Holy Trinity." ' If you didn't say that, the evil spirit would make you lose your mind. The only reason I escaped without going crazy was that I wasn't a real woman yet."

It would be an endless task to enumerate all Anita's specters and those that had been described to her by her grandfather Mamerto, her mother, and her many relatives. She was acquainted with all the phantasmagorial personages that infest the Negro's world, finding their way into bedrooms, taking over houses, swarming in city suburbs, turning churches and graveyards into places of terror: the Hobbled Mule, the Little Cart, the Lady Hangman, the Souls in Purgatory, the tormented dead who drag their chains beyond the tomb, and the wretched misers who, having buried their money while they were alive, suffer after death until some pious soul digs it up again and pays for a few masses to take them out of their misery.

"No matter what people say, the spirits of the dead are always here with us. They come back to live their lives over again and do penance for their sins."

The old lady had a complete theory about the supernatural; it was a primitive and highly simplified one, but clearly defined. Her grandfather Mamerto had been an authority in this field—a *faculto,* as she called him. He had known how to drive out evil spirits and ward off all kinds of mischief by the use of charms and prayers. For her, the phenomena of "the other world" were divided into two distinct classes: souls in torment and demons.

"A lot of people think they're the same thing," she used to explain, "but that's a big mistake. Devils don't have anything in common with dead people —in fact, they torment them. Devils never do anything but evil; they scare people and try to damn their souls. They're the ones who whisper in a man's ear to make him commit horrible crimes, and heat up a woman's blood so she sins; they make a son turn against his father. They cause everything bad, make rivers flood, bring on earthquakes, and spoil the crops."

"About how many devils are there, Granny?"

It was always Pascua who asked this question, for women are more interested than men in the business of hell. Old Anita answered with the learned vagueness she always employed when she had to extricate herself from a tight corner.

"Lots and lots, so many you can't count them. But they're not all alike, and they don't all have the same power. Some can control whole towns, cities, and countries; other ones can only get a single house in their power; and some can hardly handle one human being."

There were minor demons in the orders and ranks of the infernal legions whose mission was merely to play mischievous pranks and startle people.

These were the goblins—tiny, mocking creatures who threw stones on roofs, dragged furniture across the floor, and broke dishes in the kitchen. Anita knew of more than one house that was inhabited by goblins. One poor woman, who made her living cooking *arepas*, was tormented by a goblin who overturned her pot of boiled corn every night, turned her water faucet on, and jiggled her bed when she was asleep. Another woman was always being slapped.

"Is there a boss devil, Granny?"

"Yes. He's Mandinga, the most powerful one of all."

Whenever she mentioned this name the old lady crossed herself with the utmost reverence and muttered, *"Ave Maria Purissima."* Mandinga, who was also known as Beelzebub, the Evil One, and the Enemy, made his presence felt only at times of great upheavels in the world, of national and world-wide catastrophes. Especially during wars. He was the angel of evil, the monarch of shadows whom the Lord cast out of Heaven as punishment for his over-weening pride. He reigned with absolute power over human beings and made them suffer.

Grandmother Anita's voice darkened when she spoke of these things.

"When Mandinga is running around loose, you better be afraid. Ruin, pestilence, bloodshed, and death go with him wherever he is. His goat's hoof burns the earth where he steps, dries up the grass, and withers the flowers. There are people who carry the devil inside them; they're never happy unless they're doing bad things. They're easy to recognize. When somebody does some evil to you, children, look at his face, his hands, and his feet; on one of these parts of his body he's got the mark of Satan."

PART TWO: *The Mark of Satan*

The Silver Spade

One day, to everyone's surprise, Doña Beatriz appeared at the dining room table dressed as though she were going to a party. In her sky-blue crinoline and her filmy shawl she looked like a large bellflower that had been blown in across the polished tile floor by the north wind. Her straight, shining hair was held in place by a bandeau, and in it she wore a handful of little blue flowers. Her eyes were moist and bright. I was helping to serve lunch at the time, and heard her say in a languid tone:

"I dressed early so as not to keep the General waiting."

Her children stared at her, open-mouthed. Frau Berza kept her eyes on her plate and busied herself with rolling her bread into little balls. Don Guillermo scowled and struck the table with his fist.

"The General? What in the devil are you talking about?"

"Didn't you know?" she said sweetly. "The General's coming today to inaugurate the railroad, and will join us for lunch afterward. I thought Papá had told you."

Don Guillermo's face was like a river in flood. His blue eyes turned pale and shot fire. I was fascinated by the white spots that came and went on his scarlet cheeks. Suddenly his loud laughter filled the dining room, like the fluttering of a flock of maddened birds. Doña Beatriz stood there, rigid and motionless, resting her hands on the edge of the table, which began to tremble. At any moment I expected her to let out a little cry and fall in a faint. But nothing of the kind happened. After a few seconds she put one hand to her bosom and slowly walked out of the room.

"The General!" Don Guillermo muttered. "That old fool!"

After this no one said a word. The only sound was the tinkling of the knives and forks on the porcelain plates and the noises of the tropical forest. But when the children were about to leave the table, Señor Zeus stopped them with a gesture.

"Do you know how long it's been since that famous lunch your mother got herself all decked out for today? No less than thirty years. That surprises you, doesn't it? She was only a girl then, and I hadn't even thought of coming to this country. I want you to know the truth, so listen carefully. Her father—your grandfather—told me the story. One of those bits of confusion known in this country as 'revolutions' had just succeeded, and the word 'federation' was being used to justify every idiocy these crazy people are capable of. The General your mother refers to was President at the time. He was the perfect nonentity, a typical product of the tropics, with all the qualities necessary to make certain kinds of women fall madly in love with him. Some day I'll show you his portrait, with his black beard and his chest covered with medals."

Don Guillermo explained that this "nonentity" was a fanatic about railroads; he could talk about nothing else. Actually , Federico's father said, the plans for a railroad between the port and the principal inland towns had been made by a group of local investors, among them Doña Beatriz's father. The construction was nearly finished when that absurd war broke out. The General was coming to inaugurate the small section that had been completed after his rise to power. This took place on the 21st of December, 1864. Old Don Lorenzo Lamarca, who was also half mad, had had made in London, especially for this ridiculous ceremony, a mahogany wheelbarrow trimmed in silver and a small spade of the same metal.

A silver spade and wheelbarrow! I was fascinated by the story, and waited for someone to make a comment or ask a question that would bring out more details. But Federico, his sister, and Frau Berza were as silent as statues. My imagination was running wild. Were these things among the extraordinary objects I had glimpsed in the library when Eduvige left the door open? But why had Federico's grandfather ordered a silver spade and wheelbarrow?

"The ceremony was held in Paso Real," Don Guillermo went on. "Your mother arrived in an open calèche drawn by two gray mares."

He stopped to look at his children; then suddenly, as if he had said something very funny, he burst out laughing.

"Two gray mares! Can't you see how ridiculous that must have looked?"

On the contrary, I thought it must have been very pretty. If Doña Beatriz had appeared in the same blue dress she had worn that morning, she must have looked like an angel. She must have floated along on the seat of the calèche like the blossoms that drop into the river and drift with the current. Perhaps she carried a silk parasol, too. Somewhere I had seen a woman like that, in a calèche drawn by gray mares, with a blue parasol in her hand.

Don Guillermo's voice snatched me out of the arms of my dream.

"The General made a speech, naturally, after which everybody applauded furiously. You can imagine what it must have been like. The Negroes probably saw him as an archangel come down to earth to set them free so they could lead the easy life enjoyed by the white people."

His sarcasm cut me like a sword. I have never forgotten it. It must have hurt Federico, too, for he turned pale and hung his head.

"He took the shovel," Don Guillermo said, "and dug up a little dirt from one place, put it in the wheelbarrow, carried it to another place, and dumped it. Immediately the first locomotive began to move."

"How beautiful!" I heard Federico say under his breath.

"Do you think so? Then I'd better tell you that your illustrious grandfather lost two hundred thousand pesos in that beautiful venture. But the funniest thing was what happened while the General was digging: the silver spade hit a skull . . ."

"A human skull?" Federico asked anxiously.

"No, it was the skull of a Negro."

I don't know why I think Federico's father said these things just to humiliate me. Years have passed, and I have learned a great deal from life and something from books; but this still puzzles me. If Señor Zeus didn't like me, why did he tolerate me in his house? I can think of only one answer: Federico. Federico was the only person in the White House who was allowed to comment on anything his father said, and even at times to contradict him. More than once that ruddy giant, before whom everybody in Cumboto trembled, had appeared to be disconcerted by something his son had said. I must have felt Federico's protection without realizing it.

As soon as Don Guillermo left the house that afternoon, Federico came to the kitchen looking for me.

"Come on, let's go look at those things in the library."

"In the library! How're we going to get in?"

Triumphantly, he showed me the key.

"How did you get it?"

"Frau Berza," was his laconic reply.

When we unlocked the door and went in, my whole body was shaking with a strange apprehension. As I stood in the half darkness, breathing that rarified air that smelled of naphthalene, I felt as though I had entered a tomb. Federico found his way across the room and pulled back the curtains. The light tumbled in, illuminating even the darkest corners. For a long time I stood gazing at that grotto where so many unfamiliar things lay jumbled together; in spite of the light it still seemed like a tomb. The shelves of dark wood, jammed with books, reminded me of the coffins I had seen the Negroes carrying to the city cemetery. A large table with carved sides, surrounded by four chairs with black leather seats, took up most of the center of the room. The table bore only one object: an ancient, intricate clock under a glass bell. In one corner, on a stand, stood a ponderous album bound in morocco with gold corners. A tinkle of glass made me look up. It was a huge crystal chandelier that hung from the ceiling, whose multicolored pendants were moving in the breeze from the window. There were so many fascinating things I didn't know where to look first. Above the book shelves, which were not very high, the wall was papered with large, faded roses and hung with some dark paintings. There were also some yellowing busts of personages with long locks and grave faces, lamps with colored glass globes, chests as big as sarcophagi, the terrestrial globe I had already glimpsed from afar, and a thousand other useless and discarded things I can't pretend to remember. Federico's voice awakened me from my trance.

"Look! The wheelbarrow!"

There it was, all right, hidden under the table. Federico pulled it out, and in it we saw the silver spade. When I saw how boldly he was moving things about, I was frightened. Surely we would be punished in some way for violating the last rest of so many dead things. The metal parts of the spade and wheelbarrow were dim, like the moon seen through clouds. Was this silver? Yes, it was; Federico set to work shining it with his handkerchief. Someone— I couldn't remember who—had once told me that if you looked at silver you exposed yourself to the Evil Eye; recalling this, I could not bring myself to look at my reflection in the surface of the spade as Federico was doing.

We searched everywhere, but we couldn't find the skull. It was actually Federico who looked for it, for I hardly dared even breathe in that terrifying world, standing on that thick carpet that muffled our footsteps. Only my pride and my determination to feel and behave exactly as my friend did kept me there, surrounded by a thousand imaginary perils. Then we heard someone playing the piano, and we froze in our tracks. No one had played it for so long that we were not only surprised, but frightened. The notes ascended gaily in a delicate spiral, sharp and clear, then suddenly became grave and slow, like a liturgical response.

"It's Mother," Federico said, frowning. "How long it's been since she's played!"

He went down the hall, and I followed him. There, with her hands on the keyboard, was Doña Beatriz.

"It's the Beethoven *Appassionata*," her son told me. He stood erect and reverent, as though he were listening to a hymn.

Doña Beatriz's arms were bare, and her white skin gleamed. We never moved during the whole time she was playing. Federico would have cut my throat without a moment's hesitation if I had made the slightest sound, the least interruption. An ecstatic expression had come over his face. As for me, I felt an inexplicable uneasiness, a mixture of anxiety and sorrow, so that I was in no condition to form any kind of opinion about the music itself. If anyone had asked me just then if I liked it, I would have said firmly that I did not; and yet I wouldn't have been telling the truth. Its tangled harmony, its capricious cadenzas, its surprising leaps from joy to lamentation, awoke such violent emotions in me that I was almost giddy. But when the music stopped I was floating in a delightful lethargy, like someone who has just emerged from a warm bath.

I was not able to talk to Federico any more that afternoon, for after his mother had finished playing he went to the window and stood gazing out for a long time. He was looking over the tops of the palm trees toward the sea. I didn't dare interrupt his meditation, but it seemed so strange that I began thinking about it. Neither he nor I had ever turned our thoughts toward the sea, but always toward the river. Through the palm grove that people called "the other side" ran the railroad, with its rumbling cars, its piercing whistle, and the thick trunk of smoke that shaped horses and black ships in the sky. Why had we never been curious about that part of the plantation? Why was Federico staring out there now? They were aspects of the same question—a question that preoccupied me for some time. As I wondered about this, my thoughts returned to the scene in the dining room and Don Guillermo's story about the cocky, bearded general who dug up a Negro's skull with his silver spade. A whole avalanche of questions came down upon my mind. Whose skull was it, and how had it gotten there? Did that general have any connection with the one whose picture I had seen in Grandmother Anita's trunk? Why was it necessary to dig up dirt with a silver spade and carry it somewhere in a silver wheelbarrow when a railroad was being inaugurated? Why had Don Guillermo spoken of these events with such contempt? I thought of what Anita had said about the mark of Satan, and I wondered why all white people behaved as though they bore this sinister sign.

After working all day in the sheds, Cervelión spent his evenings weaving palm leaves. Some of the other Negroes did the same. Others went down to the river to fish for crayfish, or set traps for birds, or chopped wood to make charcoal. Immediately next door to Cervelión lived old Venancio, a bald, fat mulatto who made his living selling birds to the foreign ships that put into the port.

When I arrived the two of them were working in a clearing in front of their houses by the light of the setting sun. Venancio was seated on a stool, putting the final touches on a cage made of palm ribs and leaflets. Cervelión, sitting with legs wide apart, was weaving long strips of palm into a wide mat which he rolled up at his feet. Venancio's hut was an aviary. The front wall and the interior were covered with clusters of cages of all shapes and sizes, in which hundreds of restless, nervous birds were hopping about and twittering. Suddenly from inside the house a *paraulata ajicera* shot out, perched on the old man's shoulder, and began to sing. Cervelión looked at me with a smile.

"How you like Coronela? She's playing reveille."

I was entranced. I would never have believed that a little bird could imitate the sound of a bugle like that, reproducing the martial notes with such perfection. Of course I had no idea what reveille was; but the notes themselves, the harsh, strident music, filled me with delight. My spirit was still heavy with the heart-rending sonata I had heard Doña Beatriz playing that afternoon, and the bird's brassy outburst was truly like an awakening.

"Her name is Coronela?" I asked excitedly.

"Yes. Coronel ought to be around here some place."

Venancio watched me out of the corner of his eye, smiling. He pursed his lips and let out a stream of short, melodious chirps. In a few seconds another winged arrow flew across in front of me and fastened itself on his other shoulder. It was a mockingbird. His yellow breast and black wings glistened in the last rays of the sun.

Coronel's voice was different. It was like a bell, or the lowest string of a guitar.

"Does he play reveille, too?"

"No, he strikes the hours and imitates animals. He barks like a dog, meows like a cat, brays like a burro, bleats like a goat, and laughs like a person."

I watched ecstatically as the birds hopped about on Venancio's shoulders and pecked at his ears and his bald head. What heaven I would have been in if Coronel and Coronela had been mine! One gray, the other black and yellow, they seemed like two enchanted beings—a prince and princess changed into birds, like those in the stories I had heard the workers tell in the sheds. Venancio and Cervelión went on smiling as they worked. Theirs was a happy world, simple and without neuroses. If these two, with their birds and their palm leaves, also bore the mark of Satan, it was well hidden that evening.

"What you doing around here this time of day?" the bird man asked me.

To which Cervelión answered, "He came looking for me. He got something on his mind."

He turned to me.

"Come on, spit it out."

I told them what I had seen at lunch and what we had found in the library. As I went on with the story the two old men looked more and more serious. When I had finished they regarded each other in silence; then Cervelión said solemnly: "You right not to touch that spade. It got a curse on it."

He said no more, and I didn't ask any questions. When I returned to the White House, it was getting dark and Eduvige was lighting the lamps.

The Devil's Business—In Black and White

I doubt that any boy has ever felt as I did that morning in July when Federico told me that they were going to send him and his sister to school in Europe. I didn't know what that meant exactly; but immediately I felt empty, and there was a bitter taste in my mouth.

"When are you going?" I asked.

"I don't know yet, but Father told us to get ready."

I asked no more questions. I went and sat on a rustic bamboo bench in the shade of a luxuriant mango tree beyond the work sheds, and thought about it for a long time. The word "Europe" had no precise meaning for me. It was an abstract, fantastic concept, like Heaven or Hell. Going there meant leaving this world, defying the laws of gravity, becoming different from ordinary mortals, turning into a god. The idea so overwhelmed me that when I looked ahead to the day of Federico's departure I could find nothing to compare it with but death—not his, but mine.

I won't say that the prospect of this separation grieved me, because I don't think that is the right word. It terrified me. It unhinged my life. Suddenly I found myself staring into an abyss. What was I going to do alone in that house without my friend's protection, at the mercy of his despotic father and the embittered Frau Berza? Many of the things I loved were going to disappear from my life, little things that were as important to my existence as air and food. In fact, many of them had already disappeared, by a kind of erosion of the spirit; but it had been such a slow, imperceptible process that I had not noticed. Perhaps they would all vanish in the same way. However, it was the suddenness of this announcement that turned it into a cataclysm.

One reflection led to another. If we had changed, it was no doubt because we were no longer the same persons. As I looked back on our delightful pranks and our wonderful, childish dreams, I was amazed to find an unexpected verification of this notion: four years had gone by since that day we set out like three small explorers to discover the river. Everything seemed the same, but everything was different. I reviewed in my mind the people about us. Don Guillermo was still the same big, square, florid man who was always guzzling beer; but the lines in his face were deeper, and his blue eyes no longer flashed as they used to. Doña Beatriz hardly ever came down to the dining room these days, and she never touched the piano. Frau Berza had forgotten that she used to smile occasionally. The cook had grown a little fatter, while Eduvige on the other hand had lost weight to an alarming degree. The only ones who seemed not to have changed were Grandmother Anita, Cervelión, and Venancio. Federico and Gertrudis themselves were far from the same. He had shot up like a reed, tall and thin. With his blond hair hanging over his eyes and his face covered with scarlet pimples, he looked like an ear of corn. His sister was now a conceited young lady with gold-rimmed glasses, and very chummy with the governess. And I? Good Lord! I was different, too; I could see that just looking at my arms and legs. I was stronger, and yet at the same time more timid. My voice kept changing pitch in an unexpected, involuntary way that embarrassed me. One afternoon when they were making fun of me in the *coquera,* Cervelión said with his comical gravity, "He changing his song like a chicken."

One day when I was bathing in the river I had noticed some tiny, coal-black, kinky hairs around my penis, and I found myself laughing nervously. The changes I had seen in Pascua filled me with surprise and wonder. She had grown, of course, but it was more than that; she had rounded out, and glowed like a fruit that is beginning to ripen. She was just as noisy and impudent as ever, though. What disturbed me most about her were the dark mounds that lifted the cloth of her blouse. Her glance was different, and she gave off a disturbing scent.

I think that I had not really paid much attention to these things before because of the emotional distractions I had found in my visits with Grandmother Anita and Cervelión and in my afternoons in the library. My curiosity had finally overcome the superstitious fear I had felt when I first stepped into that room. I began to spend many hours there, at first with Federico and later by myself, when the White House had fallen into its noonday lethargy, during the peace and quiet of the siesta. The only things I never touched were the wheelbarrow and the silver spade. But I leafed through all the books, even those I could not read, because I loved to look at the pictures. There were only a few in Spanish; the others, almost all printed in black letter type, were of no use to me. There were many adventure stories and other fascinating things; but after a leisurely sampling my favorite reading was reduced to two enormous volumes which I could open only by placing them on the table: a book called *The Races of Man* and a translation of *Paradise Lost,* both marvelously illustrated.

My racing imagination was plowing through new seas. From scenes of distant lands and bloody battles I leaped to the life of Satan in the shadowy regions where he was cast by the wrath of the Lord. For a time I was so spellbound by these pictures that I could not distinguish fact from fiction. I had heard people say, for example, that Satan and Mandinga were the same person, and that he was black; and I even found in the book on human races a tribe of African Negroes called Mandinga. And yet in *Paradise Lost* Satan did not look like a great, black bat; he appeared as a white-skinned, handsome young man with a magnificent head of hair and the wings of a great bird, like those of the Holy Ghost.

I discussed some of these observations with one or two of the people I knew outside the White House, and it seemed to give them something to think about. Neither Cervelión nor Venancio had any clear idea as to whether or not there were such things as white devils. Grandmother Anita, though, was sure of it. Of course there were white devils—maybe even more than black ones! What she couldn't tell me about these creatures! I was in the habit of going to her house nearly every evening (I was no longer afraid to go home after dark), and knew her household intimately. She and Pascua slept in the bedroom, while Ernesto and his son Prudencio bedded down in the little living room. When the two children were small they had had the measles, and had been confined to the bedroom; Ernesto had papered it with old newspapers to keep out the draughts. They were there still, the printed pages yellow and torn, and on one of them was a picture of a little black horse. I fell in love with it the moment I laid eyes on it. The simple silhouette, eyeless and featureless, galloped along with its mane and tail streaming out behind. I made up a little poem I used to say to myself:

> *Glad to see you, of course,*
> *Little black horse.*

There were some colored pictures I liked, too. Leo XIII, a fine, intelligent pope, looked out at us with a smile from an almanac that was pinned to the wall. There was an advertisement with flowers and perfume flasks and six exotic names, as intriguing as the open sesame to some hidden treasure:

> *Camia,*
> > *Des Roses,*
> > > *Lidilia,*
> *Sonia,*
> > *Le Muguet,*
> > > *Liseris*

Pascua's attitude toward me had never changed since the day we first met. There was a strange reserve between us, like a wall of ice, and my shyness was no help in breaching it. We hardly ever exchanged a word. I was not very expansive with her brother, either; Prudencio was as unpredictable as a young animal, and I didn't trust him. I spent my time with the old people. One afternoon, however, Prudencio showed me something that really interested me. He began with a disconcerting question.

"Hey, Natividad, you ever see a naked girl?"

I confessed that I hadn't.

"You want to see one?"

He took me aside and told me about somebody named Pastora, a "half-cracked" Indian girl who wandered about and gave herself to country boys like ourselves in exchange for a little fruit or a piece of bread. No one knew where Pastora had come from. She had simply appeared in Cumboto. She was not a Negro, nor a mulatto, nor a white woman. She was an Indian. She went barefoot and slept wherever nightfall found her.

"She knows some tricks, too. She makes little animals out of mud and spit."

Naturally, I wanted to meet Pastora. Prudencio took me to her that same afternoon in a secluded place in the woods, under a gigantic *jabillo* near the river. There she was, sitting on a sloping bank, absorbed in rolling a little ball of mud about with a twig. In her inky and tangled hair she wore every kind of forest trash. Her only clothing was an old dressing gown the color of blood, ripped and tattered, and the caked mud she had collected along the roads was flaking off her legs.

"Say something to her," Prudencio prodded me, showing his teeth like a small demon. "Go on, lift up her dress."

He raised it himself to encourage me. The girl paid no attention, as though she hadn't noticed we were there. She offered not the slightest resistance when Prudencio pushed her legs apart. There was a smile on her pale, full lips. He pushed her gently over on her back, and Pastora remained lying there with her head on the ground, her serene eyes fixed on the deep foliage of the *jabillo*.

"You see it?"

I stood there without moving, as tense as a bowstring, hypnotized by the

Indian girl's bronze body. I stared at her almost hairless genitals, her tiny navel, and her open thighs; I felt the blood pounding slowly and unrelentingly in my head. Prudencio knelt beside her and put one hand on her breast. He smiled up at me like a salesman displaying his merchandise.

"Go ahead, climb on! Us kids do it all the time."

But at that moment we heard someone coming, and had to run off leaving Pastora lying there in the leaves.

Later I was to come across her again and take advantage of her passive nature. I found in her semivegetable flesh the revelation my eager senses were looking for. She was not totally imbecile. She could talk, but only about the one subject that fascinated her: the little creatures born of her saliva. In her mind there was no doubt that birds sprang from ripe fruit, worms from filth, and lice from the accumulated dirt in the hair. She would sit under the trees for hours, staring sometimes at the branches, sometimes at the roots. She would spit on the ground and stir the little puddle with a stick; when she saw some minute insect emerge from the mud, her eyes would light up. Of all the men who had touched her insensible and indifferent body, she recalled only one face and one name: a certain Zacarías, who was old, one-eyed, and toothless. It was he who taught her to make her little creatures. He was really a great man; he could make not only worms and *piqui-juyes*, but rats, monkeys, and even horses. When Pastora spoke of Zacarías, she was transfigured.

"You know what? He has the sun in a bottle. I saw it. He showed it to me. At night it shines like a lamp. With that bottle he can make any animal, any size he wants. But he doesn't like to make horses, or cows, or burros, or goats, because then people come and take them away from him. They don't let him keep anything, not even a poor, mangy dog."

More than once it occurred to me to share all this with Federico, to reveal this sinful discovery Pascua's brother had led me to; but I refrained because I was convinced that Federico was not the same person he used to be. I could have sworn that he was avoiding me. One afternoon, however, I came across him unexpectedly in the library, thumbing through the big morocco and gold album. I felt uncomfortable at finding him there. Without turning his head, he said: "I've been waiting for you. Come and look at these pictures."

The first one was a dim photograph of a young woman in a net dress, with a cluster of dark curls falling over her shoulders.

"Do you know who that is?" he asked.

I looked at him and hesitated; I had guessed, but I didn't dare say what I thought.

"That's Mother when she was a girl." He gazed at the portrait for a moment, his head on one side and a gentle smile on his lips.

Then he turned the stiff pages to another photograph, this time of an arrogant-looking officer with folded arms and a very full and commanding black beard.

"And do you know who this is?"

"The General!"

Federico's smile grew broader. He turned back to his mother's picture and said, as though to himself: "That's how she looked in those days."

Then he closed the album and walked out of the library.

Naturally, I had to discuss this with Grandmother Anita. There was no longer any doubt in my mind that Doña Beatriz's general and the one in the magic trunk were the same man. I asked the old lady to let me see it again.

The only difference was that the picture in the album was in black and white and this one had been colored. This gave me an excuse to ask more questions. There was much gaiety in Cumboto in those days. The General had taken a liking to the place, and came to visit whenever he could. Grandmother Anita and her family watched from afar when he went out walking with Doña Beatriz in the garden. She was like a vision in a mist.

"Don Lorenzo—may God forgive him—was very happy to see them together. The General was still single. He came at Mardi gras to dedicate the new station at El Palito. He brought her a great big white mare as a present, and everybody wore masks. But after that things began to go wrong, and he had to leave the country. The *godos* came back into power. I used to see *godos* around here a lot; Don Lorenzo was too smart not to get along with everybody. Seems like there was one fat old fool—one of those people they called 'oligarchists'—who courted the girl, but she gave him the cold shoulder. When the General came back—that was in '70—what a party there was! Nobody around here had ever seen the like. But the White House was closed up tight, dark as a tomb."

"What happened, Granny?"

"The General had gone and married somebody else in Caracas."

"Poor Doña Beatriz!" I said to myself.

After a moment I asked, "Did she play the piano in those days?"

"She was learning to, I think. When the General came the first time, there was a music teacher living here. They said she was in love with him, but that's not true. The poor man didn't belong to her class. He disappeared one day, and people began saying Don Lorenzo had him murdered and buried in the coconut grove."

"They said her *father* had him murdered?"

"Uh-huh."

"What do you think, Granny?"

"I don't think anything, boy. I mind my own business and let the devil mind his."

The Death of El Matacan

The gunshot ripped the veil of night and echoed through the immense silence of the woods. I sat up in my cot with a start and waited, tense and expectant. I heard nothing more. As the last echoes died away my nerves relaxed and my imagination set to work. I went to the window. There was no moon, but the brilliant stars gave off a faint, dusty light that outlined everything in a blue haze. Then I saw a white shape moving toward the house.

If it hadn't been for the sound of the shot, I would have sworn that it was a ghost. But it wasn't. It was a living person, a person I knew. It was Frau Berza. Then I was afraid again, even more than if it had been a ghost. At that moment thousands of people for seven leagues in all directions must have been feeling just as I was—their hearts in their mouths, sure that death had once more crossed the boundaries of Cumboto. Death! How the Negroes' hearts must have been pounding from Paso Real to Goaiguaza, as they envisioned that fleshless figure who roams the countryside at night with his scythe, his empty eye sockets, and his terrible smile! Who was the damnable creature's victim tonight? There must have been many others besides myself who had guessed the answer to that question. Many of them had probably been waiting for this, night after night, for the past five years.

Still, I must confess I was not expecting it. That scene in the moonlight had taken place so long ago that I had forgotten it. Now that I was old enough to understand what was happening, I was amazed that this strangely-matched pair—Frau Berza and *El Matacán*—had continued meeting by night. Death, more constant than they, had lain in wait in the darkness with his infinite patience and his sinister smile. Every Negro in Cumboto must have been thinking the same thing. I could almost hear the muffled sound of their terror-stricken voices: "Lord, have mercy on his soul, and forgive us who have done no evil."

As I waited to see what would happen next, my imagination ran wild. I recalled the episode of the skull and the bearded general's spade. That nameless cranium was like a symbol of all the Negroes who lay buried in the widespread land of Cumboto, with coconut palms, mango trees, and *jabillos* for their crosses. Their juices had nourished these roots, sweetening the flesh of the fruit and the milk of the nuts, ever since those early days when those who had escaped the Antillean slave prisons first stepped on this firm shore. Cruz María, the ingenuous *Matacán* who had been dazzled by Frau Berza's white flesh, was going to add his tiny bit of humanity to the contribution his ancestors had made to the white man's civilization.

Cruz María was not all Negro. He had tawny eyes and skin the color of

ripening fruit. I could see him in my mind, with his sharp, mobile face, his full lips, and his curly hair. I said a requiem in my heart for his simple, deluded soul. It was not his sin he was paying for, but that of his mixed blood. Who had fathered him? Cervelión? That was what people said; and they themselves said so. But Cervelión was a Negro, and Cruz María was not entirely a Negro.

I hardly knew Cruz María. I had seen him only occasionally when I happened to get up early and meet him as he was leaving the milk can at the back door of the White House. I knew that he was very good-natured; he was always joking and whistling. Physically, he was nothing at all like Cervelión. How did he and Frau Berza ever get together? Which of them arranged their nocturnal rendezvous? When I first saw them together in the garden five years before, none of these questions had occurred to me because I was still a child. Now they were the wellspring of a growing fury—a fury that I must admit was mixed in my heart with a bittersweet feeling of envy.

Suddenly my room was flooded with light. Don Guillermo stood before me with a large lantern in one hand and a rifle in the other. He was wearing a red dressing gown and red leather slippers. I trembled in silence as he searched the room, shining the light in every corner and under the bed. His search was soon finished, for the room was small and almost bare of furniture. Then he stood facing me, tall as a lighthouse.

"Where have you been?" he demanded.

"Right here."

"You haven't left the house?"

"No, sir. The shot woke me up and I got up to look out the window."

"What shot?"

It was an astonishing question. In his enormous hand the rifle looked like a toy. If the silence had lasted a minute longer I would have fainted with fright. But he saved me by asking, "Did you see anything unusual when you looked out the window?"

I thought fast. Without a moment's hesitation I replied, "No, sir."

Without taking his small, piercing blue eyes from my face, Don Guillermo moved to the door.

"Get dressed and come with me."

Terrified and bewildered, and still in my bare feet, I threw on my jacket and followed that terrible man as he crossed the garden with great strides, armed with his rifle and lantern. Where was he taking me? What did he intend to do to me? Was he going to kill me so I couldn't tell anyone else about the shot?

As I hurried along over the damp ground I repeated every prayer I knew. I invoked the name of God and mentioned his Divine Mother and the court of Celestial Saints. If I had had an amulet of some kind I would have been less frightened; but I had none. I didn't own so much as a little palm-leaf cross that had been blessed, or a holy medal, or even a simple *zamuro* seed.

Don Guillermo was walking fast, and I was beginning to get tired. Maybe he was taking me down to the river. It would be easier to dispose of my body there. How would he do it? Would he shoot me, or would he give me a blow on the head with the rifle butt? Perhaps he had a knife hidden under his robe. Afterward he would throw my body into the river and the current would carry it out to sea. How horrible it would be to die in the ocean, torn to pieces by sharks! Still, it might be less terrible than melting into the earth as all those thousands of Negroes whose bones nourished the roots of Cumboto had done.

Don Guillermo suddenly came to a halt in the middle of a clearing, and I shut my eyes. His voice was muffled by the night air.

"Look carefully at the ground. Do you see drops of blood?"

I wanted to see something that resembled a drop of blood with all my heart, so that I could give him the answer he so wanted to hear. But God did not grant me that small happiness. It was he who found the first traces: large drops that glistened black in the lantern-light.

"He's somewhere around here," Don Guillermo cried triumphantly. "I've got him now!"

The bloody trail led toward the work sheds at the *coquera*, and became easier to follow every moment. As we entered the woods it left the ground and continued along the tops of the bushes.

"He couldn't have got very far," Don Guillermo declared. "That bullet was well placed."

The laborers' huts began to appear, like dark ships anchored in the motionless ocean of the jungle. It was pitch-black, and cold. Soft whispers, muffled sighs, and faint laughter seemed to come from somewhere deep in the earth, and I was filled with dread again. Everybody knew that the tormented souls and evil spirits that Grandmother Anita had told us about walked these paths in the dead of night. We would soon come across the hanging corpse that let fall its flaming head and limbs as it called out, "Shall I come down, or not?" In the midst of these terrors something else occurred to me: I knew very well where the trail of blood was leading us. But did Don Guillermo know? In a few minutes we would come to Cervelión's hut. God only knew what would happen then.

Luckily, Federico's father seemed to know less than I. I watched him as he stopped and stood there uncertainly, holding the lantern high to cast its light on the surrounding underbrush.

"It's no use," he said. "We've lost him. Tomorrow the vultures will tell us where he is."

I don't know if he spoke ironically; but the fact is that the group who called at the White House the following morning did look a little like those black birds. I watched from my window, not knowing exactly how I was expected to behave under the circumstances. There were Cervelión, Venancio the bird man, Pascua's father, Ernesto, and two other Negroes who worked in the sheds.

When I had got back to the house the night before, I had cried for a while and then fallen asleep. I had disturbing dreams, and awoke with a start as though someone had stuck me with a pin. My eyes were burning.

I never thought I would see an expression on any man's face like that on Cervelión's. His bloodshot eyes shifted from place to place, not seeing anything. His lower lip hung down inertly, wet with saliva. His long arms dangled loosely at his sides. His body was bent, and his flesh seemed to have wasted away beneath the drab clothing that flapped about his limbs. The others looked solemn and hung their heads.

Eduvige went out to speak to them.

"We came to tell Don Guillermo that Cruz María died early this morning."

Nobody said a word. Eduvige, as solemn as the tomb, went to deliver the message. In a few moments Federico's father came out. There was genuine surprise on his flushed face.

"So that's who it was!"

There was a gloomy silence. In the kitchen the cook wiped her eyes with the corner of her apron. After a few seconds Don Guillermo said, with some difficulty, "Believe me, Cervelión, I'm very sorry, but your son dishonored my house..."

What more could he say? We all knew, however, that there was something else he wanted to add. After another pause: "I shall pay for the funeral."

Then Pascua's father spoke up.

"We bury him ourselves, Don Guillermo. All we came to ask is you let us have the wake at Cervelión's house."

The pale, sunken face with its sharp nose and half-closed eyes hardly recalled the gay *Matacán* I had known. Framed in a white bandage made from a handkerchief, his features displayed a gentle serenity and at the same time a look of surprise. A man like this, who had believed that life was all fun and laughter, could never have expected love to end so suddenly in death.

By the time I arrived that afternoon, they had already put him into the black coffin. He was dressed in his white drill Sunday clothes. Around the coffin, which rested on two chairs, four candles burned in ancient copper holders. At the head there was a table with a white cloth, bearing a crucifix and a yellowed print of the Virgin Mary. Cervelión's hut was jammed with people from everywhere in the neighborhood. Every chair, stool, and chest in Cumboto had been requisitioned to seat the guests. The women gathered inside the house, sweating copiously; the men remained outside, talking and smoking and drinking, in the front yard where Cervelión wove his palm leaves. There was the odor of an animal's lair, of lilies, and of *camaza*. A smiling young Negro woman, who seemed to regard the occasion as a kind of party, offered me soda crackers, black coffee, and a small piece of white cheese. In the hut next door Venancio's birds were fluttering about.

Soon the women began keening. Or, rather, they began again, for they must have been weeping since the very hour of Cruz María's death. The first to begin was a fleshy mulatto woman with lascivious eyes, whom the men devoured with their glances. Then came a thin, glistening girl who bawled like a calf. Soon they were all weeping and deploring their terrible tragedy. But it was only a passing fit, soon silenced by the oppressive heat in the room. The screams and sobs quieted down like birds at nightfall in the nests of those weary throats.

No matter how unobservant I might have been, I could not have failed to observe the coolness, the hostility, even, with which I was received. Sidelong glances were cast in my direction as though these people were examining me for the best spot to sink their teeth. Pascua didn't return my greeting. I felt the rancor of a hundred hearts; there was an underground current of wrath, like a river searching for an outlet in the darkness. I understood at once: every one of these men, women, and children—Negroes, mulattoes, and *zambos*—had seen me with Don Guillermo, *El Musiú,* the night before, trotting along at his side in the darkness like a retriever leading his master to the wounded game. I was Don Guillermo's hunting dog; they were the forest creatures who had watched from their hiding places. I could picture them peering out through the chinks in their doors after they had heard the shot, then slipping soundlessly from hut to hut to discuss it. Perhaps Cruz María had fallen before reaching Cervelión's house; perhaps they had taken him up in their dusky, loving arms.

In the midst of that turbulent sea of sweating bodies in the small room I saw Cervelión's face, outlined by the yellow light of a candle that stood near the head of the coffin. He seemed to be asleep. His emaciated figure was huddled in a chair, and Venancio stood beside him. Again, I was afraid.

I could really have expected no other treatment. If it hadn't been for Cervelión, I wouldn't have gone through all this; my affection for him was stronger than any fear. It was unthinkable that he should be my enemy. Besides, Cruz María's death had horrified me. I had suffered his death throes with him. I would make Cervelión, Venancio, and the rest of them understand this.

The hours slipped slowly by, licking the open wound in my heart. I cowered uneasily in a corner, like a persecuted dog, and listened to the conversation around me. I learned that Don Guillermo had made some objections to the wake, on the grounds that the body would begin to decompose if it remained unburied so long, and that Ernesto, Pascua's father, had told him not to worry because they had ways of preventing that. They spoke with awe and respect of Cervelión's unbroken silence, and of Cruz María's tremendous endurance in running and leaping like a veritable deer for nearly half a league with a bullet in his chest.

"They didn't call him *El Matacán* for nothing," said a belligerent-looking young mulatto.

"He was a real deer, all right," an old Negro observed thoughtfully.

These comments were interrupted by a broken sob, and a woman loudly broke out the banner of her lament.

"Ah, my darling *Matacán*, they called you *El Matacán* because you could run so fast and because of the color of your skin . . ."

Like a litany, another voice went on: "Because he was so gay and had such soft eyes . . ."

And a third: "Because he never hurt anybody . . ."

And a fourth: "Because he fed in the woods at night . . ."

And a fifth: "Because he wouldn't eat anything but the tenderest grass . . ."

And the first voice again: "That's why they killed you so cruelly, little *Matacán.*"

After a pause the litany went on again, more softly now as the voices of the mourners were muted by fatigue. One woman recalled the day she met him on the way to the river, and he told her he was on his way to take a bath, and she told him to be careful because there was a bad fever going around, and he said he wasn't afraid of fevers or anything else, and she told him not to be so cocky, and he said he wasn't worried because he was protected against any kind of evil . . .

"I ran into him once on the road to Puerto Cabello," another woman went on in a reminiscent tone, "and he was wearing a brand-new blue suit. I asked for my *medio del estreno,* and he said he didn't have any change, and I said he owed it to me, then, and he said to remind him about it some other day, and I said *he* was the one who better not forget. Ah, Cruz María, my child!"

. . . "He was so good! And he had such a big heart! One day when he was a boy he was eating a papaya and I asked him for a piece and he gave me the whole thing. I said why did he give me all of it, all I wanted was a slice, but he said to take it because he didn't want any more. Ah, Cruz María, my child!"

. . . "Lord, what made *El Matacán* look at that foreign woman? What curse was on him that he couldn't see how dangerous it was? And is nobody going to punish that white she-devil? Surely he hadn't gone to her room and dragged her out every night against her will for nearly five years! She was old enough to be his mother. It was perfectly clear that the boy was a victim of the lust of her dazzling white flesh. Ah, darling *Matacán*!"

A fat Negro woman, her brow glistening with sweat, was keeping off the flies with a small green branch.

The Bird Man's Stories

Federico left for Europe without even saying good-by. I watched from behind the library curtains as they climbed into a carriage and drove off in the morning mist. There were four of them: Federico, his father, Gertrudis, and Frau Berza. The governess was wrapped in a veil that hid her face, and sat as stiff as a mummy. It was the first time I had seen her since Cruz María's death. I believe that by Don Guillermo's express orders she had remained shut up in her room for more than a month.

I was preoccupied all day, filled with foreboding. The White House was still and melancholy. At noon I saw Eduvige taking lunch up to Doña Beatriz, and in the late afternoon Federico's mother came downstairs and sat at the piano. She played something I had never heard before. It sounded like a lament. "Is it possible," I thought, "that that red barbarian wouldn't let her say good-by to her children?" My heart was heavy.

The carriage returned at nightfall, through the bluish mists that envelop the coast at that hour of the day. Don Guillermo had his supper alone in the dining room, and that evening he paced back and forth for a long time in the garden near the back door. I slept almost as badly as I had the night *El Matacán* died. I thought about Federico, on his way to some unknown land, and I kept wondering what my life would be like from then on. The following morning I awoke with a start; I had the feeling that someone had been watching me as I slept.

It was not long before my strange apprehension was justified. It happened while I was serving Señor Zeus his breakfast. As I was clearing the table, he regarded me steadily for a moment and then said, so sweetly and gently that it made me shudder: "Now get your things together and go to Cervelión's house. Do you understand? You're not needed here any longer. He has just lost a son, and you'll be company for him."

I stood in the center of the dining room with my mouth open, frozen to the spot. Don Guillermo stood up, smiling.

"What do you think about that, eh? Amusing, isn't it? You've been shut up here too long. You need to live out in the open air, with your friends."

Suddenly his face grew stern and terrifying, and he stamped his enormous foot, shaking the whole house.

"At once! Do you understand?"

So it was that my life changed overnight. It was a radical change, with nothing to soften the blow—a vertical and catastrophic fall. In Cervelión's hut, where there had been hardly room for the poor old man and his rolls of

palm matting, I had to learn to move like an insect. Fortunately, the mats made a soft, cool bed; but I was humiliated by my new status. I spent the first night silently weeping. Cervelión's attitude, his mute indifference, hurt me. I hardly had to explain to him what had happened. He made not the slightest objection to my sharing his lodgings; he took me in as he would have a small, homeless dog—and then never looked at me again.

I soon decided, however, that Cervelión's silence was not a sign of any hostility. It was merely a symptom of his mental state, of the dull pain that was drilling into his small head like a persistent louse. I think he was living a kind of double inner life, for I often heard him conversing with some invisible person. It was Venancio who drew him out of this introversion by making him talk and insisting that he go on with his weaving.

As for me, there was more to come. On the morning after my departure from the White House a stout Negro named Juan Segundo called at the cottage and took me to the stables.

"You going to work here," he told me. "You going to do the job *El Matacán* used to do."

This Juan Segundo was an evil-looking fellow; it made people shudder just to look at him. He was unpleasant and irritable, and made the most of his reputation as a bully. He always carried a club or a machete, and regarded everyone suspiciously with his little red eyes, like those of a wild boar. His mouth was huge, and when he spoke its interior showed blood-red, like a gaping wound. His thick tongue leaped about inside like a scarlet toad in its cave. His nickname was *Luango*.

At first I was sent to tend the oxen that pulled the coconut carts. Later I was put in charge of the cow barn. I learned to milk and take the animals out to pasture, and to sing them rustic songs, which they seemed to understand.

I was also taught to brand the half-grown calves. Soon I was unrecognizable, stinking of hay and manure, and covered with ticks. At night, too demoralized even to clean myself up a little, I would go to listen to the laborers who gathered in the sheds to discuss their problems.

It was a stupid, empty life, to which these timid souls tried to give some meaning with dark, superstitious beliefs. They were like so many animals, dirty and cunning, without morals, with no concept of beauty. As I sat and listened to them dragging out their anecdotes, a heavy despair filled my mind like a mist. When I had lived in the White House I had acquired habits that were to remain with me always; at least, I thought so at the time. These inclinations now fluttered about inside me like little, frightened birds. I would never get used to living this way, nor would I ever feel at home among these sly, mindless creatures who could talk of nothing but their misery. Where, I asked myself, had Cruz María found the courage to bathe in the river every evening and then walk half a league through the darkness from his hut to the White House? I wouldn't have been able to do it. I wouldn't even have tried. I wanted nothing more than to rot away and be eaten up by the green flies that swarmed over the manure heaps.

Gradually, however, I began to see things in a new perspective. Life took on a new dimension that I would never have suspected if I had not had the opportunity to live this way. There were certain charms about this obscure, creeping existence that I would never have known in any other way, even if I had lived for centuries. When these people perched on tree trunks or sat in their doorways or lay on the cool grass in the twilight, their voices were warm and slow, like a stream of honey or like wax dripping from black candles. Inside, they were veritable bonfires of repressed desires and passionate fantasies. The ends of their cigars glowed in the dark like animals' eyes, flashing the coded messages of their unrealized dreams from one end of the plantation to the other. Of their faces only the flashing of teeth and the porcelain glitter of eyes could be seen in the night.

It was there I learned that all Negroes are not the same, nor even similar. Even among those who can be called pure-blooded, there are differences ranging from physical characteristics—the shape of the head, the contours of the nose and mouth—to the most subtle variations in intelligence. There are some who are genuinely ugly, brutish, frightful-looking; but others are delicate and beautiful. Juan Segundo, *Luango*, was a member of the first group; Grandmother Anita must have been, in her youth, one of the second. Among the women, some displayed admirable physical traits and graceful bodies. Nor was their hair the same. There were marked differences in texture, from the tight, kinky mat which is called *pegón* to the silky curls the women tried to straighten with coconut oil.

Their stories revealed various degrees of intelligence and wit. Some were extremely simple, elementary; others were complex and full of humor. Some narrators specialized in hair-raising tales of gruesome and supernatural matters, with ghosts and witches; others told gay, inventive stories in which bubbled man's respect for the courage and cleverness of the forest animals. The exploits of Uncle Rabbit and Uncle Jaguar were endless, and Venancio the bird man knew them all. With his bald pate, the color of ripe tobacco, and his bishop's smile, Venancio was an expert at holding his audience's interest and relieving the heavy atmosphere that hung over the group after a procession of phantoms and demons. He was credited with inventing all the nicknames for Cumboto's inhabitants. He had christened Cruz María *Matacán,* Prudencio *Pitirrí,* and Pascua *Culebrita.* From the first he called me *Bachaco.*

Venancio was very versatile; he knew every kind of story and told them all equally well. People with morbid tastes would ask him for tales about dead men, and he would comply by relating events that had taken place in Cumboto itself. There were paths, for example, that no one used after six o'clock in the afternoon because they were haunted by "spooks" who appeared sometimes as human beings and sometimes as animals.

"They're the ghosts of the Spaniards who lived here a long time ago, see? I've seen them lots of times. You can always tell a spook because he doesn't walk on the ground; he slides along through the air . . ."

But other people preferred the entertaining fables about animals or princes and princesses, and he accomodated them all with the same good humor. And then there were his stories about Pedro Grimales (whom he sometimes chose to call Rimal or Rimales).

"Pedro Rimal went to visit Heaven one day. But when he got there St. Peter was just shutting the gate, and told him, 'You can't come in, Pedro.' 'Please, *Tocayito*,' Grimal begged him, 'don't leave me outside, because night's coming on and I'm afraid to go all the way back to Cumboto in the dark.' While he was talking, this Grimal—who was very good at getting into places—got his head and part of his body through the gate. This made St. Peter pretty mad, and he jammed the gate shut and left Rimales there with his rear end hanging outside. Just then some wasps came by, and they saw Rimales' rear end they thought it was a *campate* and crawled in. It felt so good that Rimal began laughing. This made St. Peter madder yet, and he said, 'What you laughing about?' 'I'm laughing because I'm getting such a good feeling on my other end. I don't want to come in now; I want to stay right here and enjoy it.' 'What kind of a good feeling?' St. Peter asked. 'Here, let me try it.' And he opened the gate and let Rimales come in so he could take his place. But St. Peter was awfully old, and all wrinkled, and the wasps didn't like the way he tasted, and instead of tickling him they stung him. Poor old St. Peter ran all around Heaven howling and scratching and looking for some coconut oil to put on himself. When the other saints saw him in such a fix they all began laughing. Then Our Father himself came in person to see what all the fuss was about, and when St. Mark told him what was going on in Heaven, He started laughing, too, and wanted to know who it was that played such a trick. 'It was Pedro Grimales, Lord,' said St. Anthony. 'A little man from Cumboto who just arrived.' 'Well, bring Pedro Grimales to me! I want to meet him.' St. Joseph brought him, and Our Father couldn't stop laughing. 'Look here, Pedro Grimales,' He said. 'I haven't had such a good laugh for a long time. If you want to stay, I'll make you patron saint of the wasps.' And so Pedro Grimales stayed in Heaven."

Stories like this, along with those in which Uncle Rabbit tricks Uncle Jaguar into crushing his own testicles or losing his skin, were hilarious to the Negroes. The other kind made them thoughtful and uneasy, and they silently clutched their amulets. There is a fantastic variety of these amulets: some are simple, natural objects, while others are complex artifacts made of surprising materials. Venancio the bird man, for example, owned a beautiful black ball. This curious formation found in the stomachs of ruminants is known as a "bull ball," and the Negroes believe it has the magical virtue of driving away evil spirits. He also had a little bottle filled with mercury, which he regarded as a miraculous living being. When he held the heavy, silvery vial between his fingers it was like the eye of some diabolical animal. He fed it by dropping in small *medio real* coins, which the quicksilver greedily devoured. Pascua's father's amulet was a handsome ring made from a horseshoe nail. Both Prudencio and his sister dreamed of inheriting this object one day. Others had rabbit tails, tusks of wild beasts, little scraps of snakeskin, rattlesnake rattles, and pieces of wood that had been carved by the light of the waning moon. I finally came into possession of a modest amulet of my own, like the one I had wished for one night not long before. One evening when I returned to Cervelión's house, feeling terribly depressed, Prudencio gave me a *zamuro* seed. The *zamuro* is a plant that grows in the woods, and is rather hard to find. Its seed is lens-shaped, as hard as stone, and looks like a bird's eye. Alas for the Negro who does not own one! All kinds of misfortune will befall him, and nothing he undertakes will turn out right. Negroes provide themselves with many amulets, but each one possesses special powers. To get money there is nothing like a bit of hangman's rope. To combat the Evil Eye many remedies are recommended— the purple *cariaquito*; the stone found in the stomachs of certain fish; the "sign," made by extending the index and little fingers; clutching one's left testicle, and so on—but none of these works as well as the *zamuro* seed. It is the universal amulet against small tragedies, and in spite of everything my reason has told me about ignorant superstitions, I cannot live without it.

My friendship with Prudencio was rather odd and intermittent. At times he was indifferent to the point of not even nodding when we passed each other; at other times he would treat me with an almost exaggerated kindness. He was that kind of person: as changeable and restless as a bird. Venancio had nicknamed him *Pitirrí* because he moved quickly and was always whistling like the little songsters the old man used as "pipers" or decoys to attract mockingbirds, bluejays, and blackbirds.

The day I joined the community and was put to work in the stables Prudencio planted himself before me and broke into insolent laughter.

"So they kicked you out, eh, *Bachaco*? And I bet you thought they were going to take you to Europe with them!"

I was tempted to throw myself on him and flatten his grin against those fleshy lips; but I was too depressed to say a word.

After that he often came to the cow barn to invite me to Grandmother Anita's house; but I always refused, for I was filled with a stubborn resentment toward the whole world. I wouldn't even have gone to see Cervelión if I had not had to sleep under his roof. The old man was gradually coming back to life, forgetting his bitterness. One evening he looked me over carefully and asked, "Why you so dirty? Why don't you go down to the river and take a bath?"

It was as if someone had opened a faucet within him. He went on in a melancholy tone: "He used to take a bath every evening . . . poor kid. Remember once I told you we Negroes got to watch ourselves? He didn't pay any mind; he got himself mixed up with the white woman. How many times I talked to him! 'Look, Cruz María, get away from that woman. White people are nothing but trouble.' But he wouldn't listen. He thought he was pretty smart. He thought *La Musiúa* really loved him. Loved him! Sure, she loved him to climb into her saddle, and that's all. And where's my boy now? Where's his poor, wandering soul? I light candles for him and pray for him, and I sit waiting for him in the night. But I never see him."

He wasn't crying. His eyes had always been red and moist. But his voice was heavier and sadder than before. I think my presence did his heart good; he was at last beginning to find some solace in my company. More than once I caught him watching me, his mouth half-open and his lips trembling. Now his neighbors were beginning to come and chat in his doorway, and before we knew it a new circle had formed in the front yard where he wove his palm leaves.

One evening when I came back from the cow barn I was surprised to find three tall, thin Negroes who looked very much like Cervelión. They were his brother Roso and Roso's two sons, who had just arrived from Morón. The physical resemblance between the two brothers was amazing: the same small head covered with ashy wool; the identical bloodshot, watery eyes; the same pendulous lip; the same slow, gentle voice. Nevertheless, there was something about Roso that made him decidedly different, something that showed in his every movement. Perhaps it was his cold, oblique way of looking at you, or perhaps it was the way he used gestures to emphasize his words. Besides, unlike the Cervelión of the old days, he spoke very little.

It was Venancio the bird man, more than anyone, who was delighted to see the visitors. He had known Roso since childhood; they had grown up together and shared many adventures. In the presence of his old friend there was a radical change in his stories. They no longer dealt with souls in torment or Pedro Grimales or Uncle Rabbit; now they told of a long, cruel war in which the two friends had fought. As though a withered garden in his heart had burst into bloom again, Venancio was filled with gaiety; he fluttered and chirped like one of his thrushes. Memories of the past came over him in waves, pouring from his lips in a uncontrollable flood. He did all the talking. He would shake Roso by the arm and say, "You remember, Roso? I guess you haven't forgotten the time . . ."

What a clever black devil this Roso was! He got to be a sergeant in General Zamora's personal guard, no less. The black rascal! When Zamora, who was a blond mulatto, attacked and defeated the fierce Colonel Pinto at El Palito, almost all his men were Negroes from this coast: from Morón, and Sanchón, and Alpargatón. That was where Roso and Venancio joined him, together with a man named Jeremías who was later killed by the *godos* and left on the savanna to be eaten by the vultures. Venancio saw them finishing him off, and was able to get his belt buckle as a souvenir. Venancio explained that vultures scream and dance about as they fight over the entrails. He drove them off and approached the body, which had turned white after death.

When he stood up with the buckle in his hand, he froze with fear; Zamora himself was standing behind him, watching the operation.

"And you know what the towhead said to me? He said, 'Look here, black boy, don't hang behind robbing corpses on me, or I'll decorate *you* with a vulture.' "

By the Holy Virgin, what a man! And how he loved setting fires! Venancio did, too, apparently; for when he told how the general ordered the fields of wild grass set ablaze, he drew deeply on his cigar and sat there gazing at the glowing rosebud of fire as though he were hypnotized.

"This was a man who never carried any prisoners around with him. Once I saw him order ten *godos* shot because they wouldn't tell him where they had hidden some guns. He called *El Adivino* and said: 'Look here, *Adivino,* say the *de profundis* for these boys, because pretty soon they're going to take a long, cold trip, unless they tell me where they've got the rifles buried.' And you know who *El Adivino* was? He was a Negro and Indian half-breed who was worse than Zamora himself; that's all I need to tell you. He traveled with the troops led by a man named Espinoza, where he was sort of a doctor and priest. Killing people, looting, raping women. He claimed he was a witch, and said mass in the village churches. When we were getting ready for a battle, the general would call him and have him talk to us; the bastard always said the same thing. He tried to look like a priest and wore the robes, but I think his contract was with Mandinga, not with God. I say this because he had so many people killed and used to think up ways to torture them. Once I saw him throw an old man down on the ground, tie his wrists and ankles, and rip open his belly with a rake. Right in front of the old man's son. He took the white and Indian girls to Espinoza and stripped them in front of their families for the officers to enjoy, one after another. They did this in every town they went through, so that the people were terrified and ran off into the woods. Espinoza had eyes like a snake, and he gave all his officers names of wild animals: one was *El Tigre,* another one *El León,* another *El Caimán,* and so on. But one morning when Zamora got out of the wrong side of bed he had his men tie Espinoza up in a little town square and put four bullets in him."

These new stories of Venancio's had a sensational effect; his audience shuddered, fascinated. Their eyes sparkled as they listened to Zamora's exploits. The ends of their cigars telegraphed their excitement through the darkness. The atmosphere vibrated with fear awakened by those long-past events, and grew heavy with lust. Here were death and mystery and sexuality. A phrase that remained in my mind was the one Venancio used when he spoke of *El Adivino*: his contract was with Mandinga, not with God. I had heard someone use these very words before, but I couldn't recall the person or the circumstances. It must have been a common expression. I decided to ask Venancio about it later.

I, too, was fascinated by the bird man's new stories, which seemed to be endless and went on night after night. Roso was content to listen, occasionally nodding his head in approval. He seldom made a correction. As the saga went on, he himself was beginning to take shape as a magnificent hero. He had been a member of the firing squad that executed Martín Espinoza. And what had Venancio been doing all this time? Ah, he was having his little adventures, too.

"I wasn't a very good soldier. Why should I deny it? But I had to keep moving like everybody else. When I had some of that brandy mixed with gunpowder they used to give us before a battle, I turned into a devil. And I'm not going to deny I made the most of it. We were all waiting to hear our officers say, 'Help yourselves, boys!' That meant we could break into the rich people's houses—or anybody else's—and take anything we wanted. That meant *petateo* . . ."

At the sound of this word, Venancio rolled his eyes upward, savoring the memory. *Petateo* meant chasing the women, pulling them out from under beds and out of wardrobes, dragging them away from altars where they were praying, tearing them shaking with terror from their mothers' arms. Then the men would take turns raping them as they lay there naked, covered with welts, tied hand and foot on the palm mats that covered the floors. Venancio could never hope to relate everything that had happened in those glorious days, those days he would never live again! His descriptions were so vivid that I could see the mob of drunken Negroes, their trousers unfastened, hands waving in the air, eyes flashing, as they fought over the white flesh that was nearly lost to view in the midst of that slavering horde. How many children had been born of these couplings? How many mulattoes with variegated eyes, with vengeful and angry blood? As I listened, I thought of Cruz María and

Grandmother Anita. She had said, "When there's a war, it's because the devil's loose." In the war Venancio was describing, it was the black devils against the white devils.

"How many did you lay on the mat, old Venancio?" Prudencio wanted to know, his mouth watering.

"Whew, boy! I lost count . . ."

"White ones?"

"Every last one. You think I was going to bother with black girls? Man, what bodies! What legs and breasts and waists! How that white skin gleamed next to this charcoal! The charcoal was burning pretty good, too . . ."

"If only those days could come back again, Venancio!"

"How they going to come back? Nothing was ever any good after they killed Zamora. Falcón took over and everything went to pieces. If Zamora hadn't died things would be different. *We'*d be the masters now."

At one of these evening gatherings Prudencio came up to me and said in a low voice that Grandmother Anita wanted to see me. I wondered about it all the next day. In the evening, after leaving the cow barn, I went down to the river and took a bath in the swimming hole under the bamboo, where one marvelous morning with Federico I had opened the windows of my world. As I lay there with the moving water caressing my skin, a thought suddenly cut into me like an arrow: I remembered the day we heard Cervelión's loud laugh in the bushes, and how terrified we had been. And then, how gently and sweetly the old man had reassured the frightened Gertrudis! "Don't be scared, little white girl. Nobody's going to hurt you!" Nobody had hurt us, in fact; he had come to make sure of that. And yet, on the other hand . . .

On my way home I stopped at Anita's house. She made me sit down beside her and touched my face with her black, withered hand.

"Prudencio tells me Cervelión's brother Roso is here in Cumboto . . ."

She looked at me for a moment and went on: "They tell me Venancio's been telling stories about the five-years' war, and I hear you're enjoying them."

There was a pause while she looked at me again.

"Is that true?"

I shrugged my shoulders. I didn't feel like talking.

"Now, look here, boy," the old lady said. "Watch yourself. You don't know what life is. Some people in this world worship the flesh, and some people worship the spirit. That Roso and that Venancio don't care much about the spirit."

The Flesh and the Spirit

"The devil's so wise because he's so old." This is one of our popular aphorisms, and I saw how true it was the next time I visited Grandmother Anita. The experience gained in more than ninety years of living had provided the old lady with an infinite fund of wisdom. She must have sensed my state of mind at once, and realized that unless she resorted to some dramatic device she would not be able to hold my attention. She did so at once.

"You think Cruz María was Cervelión's son?"

I looked up at her. She smiled with satisfaction.

"Well, if you do, you're wrong. He wasn't. Somebody left him in a basket one night on his doorstep. He had just been born."

I hardly needed to open my mouth, for the questions were tumbling out of every pore.

"And you know another thing? Roso's here in Cumboto because he's up to no good."

In Anita's opinion, Cervelión's brother, who so resembled him physically, was his exact opposite morally. She, too, had known him since he was a child, and knew all about the life he had led. He had always been a rebel, a malcontent. When he was a boy he ran away from his masters' house in Goaiguaza and went up into the Yaracuy mountains. He and some other runaways traveled in a pack. They committed all sorts of outrages—robbing travelers and even raping white women. She could think of nothing more abominable. Leaving his masters was bad enough, but for a black man to lay his hand on a white body was unthinkable. She had been a slave, and so had her grandfather, her mother, and her whole family. Their happiness depended on that of their masters, and they shared their sorrows with them. She was still a child at the outbreak of that terrible war that was to go on for so many years with so many changes of fortune: the war between the Creoles and the Spaniards. Her masters at the time were the Arguíndegui family, who later disappeared and were replaced by the Lamarcas. The gentlemen and the young ladies in the daguerreotypes she kept in her marvelous trunk were Arguíndeguis. When Anita was between twelve and fourteen, the so-called patriotic army under the command of Simón Bolívar (who was a colonel at the time) took possession of the entire coast and the area around the city. Cumboto, Goaiguaza, and all the other neighboring villages had to provide food for these ravenous troops. There was a massacre; the fort was abandoned and the old people and children were taken to San Esteban. Many of the women were left pregnant, and later gave birth to soldiers' children. It was a time of great suffering.

Bolívar was driven out of the port, and the Spaniards held the field; but there was still much unrest, for the demon of politics had sunk his claws in everyone's heart. Even among the Arguíndegui family—not only the men, but the women, too—there were two factions: the patriots and the pro-Spaniards. Anita heard them arguing, using words she did not understand, and asked her grandfather Mamerto what it all meant. The old man merely said, "It means the devil's loose, my child." In 1814 General Ribas took the coast. Then came General Mariño. But the fort still held out. Things went on like this for more than ten years, until one day General Páez appeared and everything changed. General Páez was inspired by the god of war.

"We never walked so much as we did then," Grandmother Anita recalled, struggling up the slope of time with her herculean memory. "My grandfather went all the way to Valencia on foot, over San Esteban Hill, which was where the road went then. He carried messages from old Don Carlos Arguíndegui to the families who lived there. Once he even went to Caracas . . ."

"On foot?"

"On foot . . . and he was over seventy then. We were living in San Esteban at the time, on the cacao plantation. One day little Miss María Belén sent me to the port, on foot, to take a message to Julián, a Negro slave belonging to the Iztueta family, who lived on the Street of the Mangrove. In those days the streets in the seaport had other names. As you went in from this side you went along Soledad, or Jesús, or Tamborete (the *tamborete* was the water tank on Alcantarilla); then you followed Negocio, which was later changed to Valencia; you turned off on Ballajá or Paso Real; you went down Cocos a little way and got onto Alante, which later was known as Iglesia and then as Colombia. The Iztueta house was in the part of town called "Inside," and so you had to pass through the military stockade to get to it; but the Spanish guards never gave us Arguíndeguis any trouble because we were royalists. But this time I was going to be a traitor..."

"You, a traitor? I don't believe it."

"Well, you got to believe it. It's always made me worry about the salvation of my poor soul. I don't know if I'm damned or not. All I was doing, really, was obeying María Belén's orders. The poor thing was only trying to save her father's life. But still, it was a treacherous thing to do, and from that day on the family had nothing but bad luck."

Grandmother Anita thought for a moment, her weary head nodding under the brim of her big hat. Through that gray, kinky poll the past was marching, with its joys and sorrows, its lace and elegant coiffures, its blue and red uniforms, and its snowy plumes. But then came the shadow of the bloody wing of war, and the glow of oil lamps and the glitter of gilded pussy-willows disappeared; in their place glistened the black skin of fleeing slaves, and the white, frightened faces of the masters as they looked behind them and saw death clutching the tails of their horses.

"Old black Julián Iztueta used to come to Cumboto two or three times a week. Sometimes he traveled as far as El Trapiche or San Esteban. He came looking for provisions for his masters, because the town was surrounded by the patriots and nobody could get food. One day General Páez showed up in person at the White House and put Don Carlos under arrest. He locked him up in one of the rooms with two guards to watch him. He was furious, and said terrible things. He was like a lion in a cage. 'If you don't tell me right now how that Negro gets here from "Inside" and back again, I'm going to shoot everybody.' My boy, that was a terrible time! I was there when the General ordered the firing squad to line up and they brought out Don Carlos with his hands tied behind his back. Then little María Belén couldn't stand it any longer, and she poured out the whole story. She said Julián jumped into the water and went through the mangroves in a place hardly anybody knew about. With just his head sticking out, he got to the coast near a point called Poza Azul on the road to Borburata, and then walked more than three leagues to reach Cumboto. That's how Negroes used to help their masters in those days."

The old lady was so moved by her reminiscences that tears had come to her eyes. I could see Julián's figure, submerged in the murky waters of the mangrove swamp, with his tiny head floating like a fallen blossom. General Páez had him followed and taken prisoner. They gave him his choice: collaboration or death. It was María Belén who finally persuaded him to betray his masters. Grandmother Anita wept as she repeated her words. " 'What can we gain by all this, Julián? They'll have to give up someday, when they're all starving to death. Besides, we're not Spanish; we're Venezuelans. The king is a thousand leagues away, and he doesn't know anything about what we're going through. All he cares about is our cacao. This is your country, Julián, our country, The General wants our country to be free. Do you understand?' " Julián seemed to understand. The word *patria,* homeland, was new to him, but it made his spine tingle. A few nights later, the Iztuetas' Negro slave led the liberating troops through the mangrove swamp, and the Spanish forces were taken by surprise and defeated. Many of them fled down Morián Street, followed by Páez's men. The street has been called Lanceros ever since.

At this point in her story the old lady's anguish became unbearable. She doubled over in pain, and her head rocked back and forth like a pendulum, as if refusing to accept the past. She hardly had the strength to murmur: "When Don Carlos found out what his daughter had done, he hanged himself from a roof beam in his room. And from then on the family had nothing but bad luck."

She paused. Then she gathered her strength and went on: "The whole country was jinxed. There were wars and more wars, miseries and more miseries. All the devils in Hell were loose on the land, and blood ran like a river that had burst its banks. My grandfather Mamerto never got any rest; he was always carrying orders, or shoeing horses, or making bullets. We were always on the move: from here to the port, from the port to San Esteban, from San Esteban to Quisandal, from Quisandal to Borburata, from Borburata to Patanemo. We went, we came back, and we went again. The young Arguíndeguis joined Páez's party. The General used to come to the house sometimes. They gave parties for him. Antonio, the older of the two brothers, played the violin; Francisco played the flute; María Belén the piano; and little Matilde the mandolin. The General was a jolly man, strong as an oak, with a big head covered with a tangle of chestnut hair. He had a very nice singing voice. I think—may God forgive me—that María Belén was in love with him."

According to the old lady's account, Cumboto was like the mouth of Hell, and the nearest city—Puerto Cabello—was like Hell itself. There must have been continual fighting. One day an ugly mulatto appeared and began to harangue the Negroes. He told them to forget about Páez, because he had been defeated, captured, and deported. He no longer existed. Why pay any attention to a corpse? Besides, the General was a fraud; he talked a lot about liberty, but the Negroes were still enslaved, They would have to wait for some other generals—like the Mongas brothers—for liberty to be a fact. "You're free now, don't you know that? What world are you living in? You're as free as the air, as the birds, free to do anything you want, to go any place, to dress the way you want to, to go into the church and kneel on the prie-dieux or the embroidered carpets. There are no masters any more. White people are just the same as black people." Grandmother Anita heard him. Her first reaction was one of fear, and then she found that she hated this intruder. But that exalted mulatto was not to be the only one who spoke this way. There were others, who cried out so eloquently that many Negroes went off with them. Those who stayed behind were confused. But not she. She had never had any doubts about her destiny. White was white and black was black; and the black man was destined to be the slave of the white man. Some time after that, a man in Goaiguaza put one of his slaves in the stocks. "Aren't we free now?" growled the others. "Why are they still putting us in the stocks?" "Kill him!" someone urged the man who had been punished. So the Negro climbed a tree, slid down a branch, and got into his master's house through a window. He crushed his skull with a piece of firewood as he lay sleeping. Then he ran away. There were others who followed his example. They roamed about the countryside, robbing and killing, until war broke out again. What were they fighting for? For equality, for liberty, because the Negroes who were no longer slaves now wanted to be masters. It was all terribly disconcerting, and Anita did not understand it.

She looked up suddenly and threw a question at me.

"You know who the Negro who split his master's head open was? It was Cervelión's brother Roso."

No one could persuade Grandmother Anita that Roso's life was any better than hers, either before the advent of freedom or after it. She had always been free, just like her grandfather Mamerto. She went wherever she liked. And what better place to go than her masters' houses? They had many relatives, and they owned plantations in every settlement along the coast. Old Mamerto's comings and goings were an object of wonder for the white landowners. "Good Lord," they said, "this man is made of iron!" And they would write to their relatives: "Mamerto is off again. We don't know where he's going this time, but if he shows up at your place take good care of him, because he's getting very old." When he died, after being kicked by a mule, his granddaughter inherited his privileges. Her body was free, but in her heart she was still a slave. White people persecuted and hated and killed each other for reasons she did not comprehend. Liberals against conservatives, and vice versa. Her masters were said to conservatives. Why? She didn't understand that, either. When and how had the change taken place? In the distant days of her youth, after Don Carlos Arguíndegui had hanged himself, she had heard General Páez say, "What a conservative the old man was!" And later, speaking to María Belén and her brothers and sisters, he had said, "You young people are doing the right thing. Youth should be liberal." And yet the liberals drove the Arguíndeguis off their lands, persecuted them, and called them conservatives, just as they had the general. She never saw them again, but the property, the houses, and the trees were still there. Nothing had changed; so why should she?

"They'll come back some day, and I'll be here waiting for them. Then I'll hand over the things in the trunk they left with my grandfather. I knew them when they were rich, when the little girls were pretty as princesses. And then I knew them when they were poor and old and scared, without a rag to wear because everything had been taken away from them. There was a time —I was just a girl then—when the young ladies never wore a dress twice. They would use it once and then give it to the servants. When the liberals took over the house, the girls had no clothes to run away in. I had to give back the dresses they had given me."

A new element of confusion and fear came into my life with that narrative of a bygone world I had never known about before. In a way, I was linked to that world, although I wouldn't have been able to say just where or how. The name of Arguíndegui seemed to be connected in some way with a terrible secret. In all this, which objectively belonged to the past, there was still much of the present and the future. Federico was not an Arguíndegui. Neither was his grandfather, nor his father. His mother was the daughter of that famous Lorenzo Lamarca about whom there were so many legends. I would have liked to clear all this up by asking Anita certain questions; but I didn't know how to put them in words or where to begin. Besides, there was a certain muddled quality about the whole thing that added to my bewilderment. It was as though Grandmother Anita, who struck me as a little incoherent, had related the story almost without meaning to, perhaps even in spite of herself. Where had she begun? With Roso's life. She wanted to warn me against this man about whom she knew so many terrible things. And then she had brought in Cruz María. And what had she told me? That he was not Cervelión's son. There were so many extraordinary things! The old lady's mind was wandering, probably. But in her ravings there was a certain consistency, as well as a moral drive that was almost frightening.

It wasn't until the following afternoon that I got everything straight enough in my mind to ask her a concrete question.

"Who were Cruz María's parents, Granny?"

But her mood had changed. She stared at me with dull, empty eyes and did not answer.

I stayed around the house for a time. I made some meaningless conversation with Prudencio, and stood for a while looking at the fascinating scraps of newspaper on the wall: the little black horse, the countenance of Pope Leo XIII, and the six exotic names of perfumes that seemed to be some kind of magic formula.

When I was leaving, the old woman beckoned me with her palsied hand.

"You living in Cervelión's house now, aren't you?"

"Yes, I am, Granny."

"I want you to look around the house and see if you can find an odd-shaped basket. If you do, look through it when he's not around and try to remember every single thing that's in it, so you can tell me. And if you find some embroidered baby clothes, I want you to bring them to me. Don't worry, God's not going to punish you for it."

She seemed to be getting older every minute. She laid her hand gently on my arm.

"When you do God's work, He's never going to be angry with you."

The Highest of All Powers

The restless odor of the sea. The sonorous evening breeze that hangs garlands on the cliffs and draws music from the abyss. Its immense hand tolls the bells of the coconut palms as the moon begins to come up over the black treetops. The world turns blue and sulphur, and millions of fireflies glow over the green water. A Negro and his girl are walking along the path. I see their sharp silhouettes and hear their muffled voices, tangled by the fingers of the wind. There in the phosphorus of the night are all the ingredients of the world.

I did not love the sea. I feared it. Only the memory of Federico could have made me cross the highway and enter that region of winding paths referred to by the people of Cumboto as "the other side." This happened one evening at the beginning of June, when the jungle was throbbing with the staccato lament of the drums. They had finished their hymns for the *Cruz de Mayo*, and were beginning the sonorous panting for St. John's Eve.

During the past few days I had been thinking fondly of Federico and his sister; their memory hung about me wherever I went, as though it were one of those perfumes advertised on Grandmother Anita's almanac: *Camia*, or *Liseris*. Some sorrow is so voluptuous and sweet that it cloys. This was like that. What had hurt me more than anything was not having been allowed to accompany Federico to the ship and see him off. He must have known about this traditional Negro celebration in June. Some time or other he must have heard the tense, sexual rhythm of the drums and the cries of the women invoking the saint. The sound must have been carried by the east wind through the mercurial silence of the night to the windows of the White House. Still, he probably never saw, as I did, those dark figures moving through the shadows with their chants and lamentations. At times I felt the urge to follow them into the darkness and saturate my spirit with their faintly sulphurous odor, but I was afraid. Besides, I wanted to be alone.

I climbed a small hill that rose above the palm trees to catch a glimpse of the sea. It is called the hill of *María la O*, and is surmounted by an abandoned hut built of palm branches. From there you can see the railroad below, silvery and endless, curving along on its ties like the tail of a gigantic comet. The line runs along an elevated roadbed at the foot of the mountain. Farther on, where the coconut palms end, the land is partly flooded, forming a dark, yellowish swamp. Then comes an expanse of porous rock that shines in the moonlight like dull enamel. I once heard Don Guillermo say that this rock

had been formed by millions of sea snails washed up by the waves over count-
less centuries.

In June, the moon along this coast has something monstrous and unhealthy
about it. At times it turns red, like a tumor that is about to burst; at others it
is as yellow as if it had been bitten by millions of malarial mosquitoes. The
Negroes read special meanings into the shades of color and the spots that
appear on the moon's face, and do or refrain from doing certain things
when it is waxing or waning. It had done me a great service a few days earlier
by curing me of a bad cold, with fever and aching bones, that I had con-
tracted in the damp, filthy cow barn. Actually, what really cured me was a
potion made from several kinds of bark (prepared by Pascua according to
Grandmother Anita's recipe); but if I hadn't taken it at the proper time of
the moon, it would have had no effect.

I was at that time so harassed by a combination of physical and spiritual
miseries that I was not sure I would be able to remain in Cumboto, or at least
on the Zeus property. More than once I thought of running away, to be free
to make a life of my own. But I didn't do it. It was the need to think these
things over that made me seek solitude. The sight of the distant sea was
painful to me, but it was perhaps less tormenting that my cot of palm mats
in Cervelión's house, where the silence seemed to make the shadows loom
larger, troubling my mind so that I couldn't sleep. Besides, Juan Segundo
gave me no rest. Life in the cow barn was becoming unbearable; but the idea
of leaving, with no plan or direction, no compass to guide my steps, terrified
me. I felt so weak and helpless!

This was the season when the Negroes are in the habit of making their
predictions of the future by the use of magic rituals. One of these rituals con-
sists of filling a clear bottle with water and pouring into it the white of an

egg. This is done on St. John's Eve at the stroke of midnight. The bottle is tightly corked and kept in a quiet, dark place for six months. On Christmas Eve, also at midnight, the bottle is taken from its hiding-place and the shape of the egg white is examined. Its appearance tells whether things will go well or badly for us during the coming year. One really has to use some imagination to find significance in these capricious outlines. Something that resembles a coffin, no matter how vaguely, means death; if there is some similarity to a ship, it means a voyage; if it looks like a house, it prophesies happiness; if a man, a long life; if it is round like a coin, it means wealth.

Shut up in Cervelión's hut, alone with my troubles, I prepared a bottle for myself. Then I wrapped it in a scrap of cloth and put it away in a box that I used for a trunk. I would wait six months, and the egg white would foretell my destiny. That night, like several before it, I had Cervelión's hut to myself; the old man had left earlier in the evening, as had all the Negroes in the neighborhood. The steamy air of Cumboto shuddered with the sound of the drums, burning in the night like scattered bonfires. Snatches of human voices that were like flickering flames reached my ears; the loudest were the women's, who were writhing and leaping convulsively. They were invoking the saint, merging with his savage essence: *San Juan! San Juan! . . . San Juan! . . .* And the drums hammered out: *Cumboto! . . . Cumboto! . . . Cumboto! . . .*

One of those voices must have been Pascua's. I thought I recognized it amid the throbbing confusion. It was a high, sharp voice that made me think of moonlight and of a serpent poised to strike. Neither she nor her brother would fail to be there in the flickering light of the bonfires, chanting their hymns to St. John. How lucky Prudencio was, to think only of childish things and spend his time whistling like the birds! How I envied him! Every afternoon I saw him stroll past the cow barn in his new cotton suit, slapping his starched trousers with the inevitable little black *chaparro* cane. On Sundays he went into Paso Real to show off his village elegance, with his kinky hair plastered down with coconut oil, and with his piercing, intricate warbling, like that of some visiting canary. It was his dream to become the best whistler in the world and conquer all the prettiest women with his *merengues* and waltzes. He had probably forgotten that vagrant Indian girl called Pastora who lay down in hidden places in the forest and let the boys relieve their tumescence in her, like adolescent fauns. I remembered her well, and it touched me still to think of her large chestnut eyes with their long, black lashes, placidly regarding the sky as we pounded her body. I thought of Frau Berza and *El Matacán,* too, and wondered how they had made love. There was something morbid in this memory, for I had been faintly envious of Cruz María; my envy still persisted, beyond the threshold of death. If I had been asked to choose a hero for Cumboto, there would have been no question in my mind: Cruz María embodied all the elements of a myth. How and where had he and Frau Berza made love? How had he looked, naked, as he moved against the governess' pearly flesh? She had probably not been indifferent, as Pastora had been. I thought of her room, where she dragged me the day of our first trip to the river. I remembered her odd perfume, that seemed to be a mixture of *resadá* and mint, her extreme cleanliness, her few pieces of handsome furniture. On a little bedside table I had seen the portrait of a man with a blond beard and a sailor's cap. I doubt that Cruz María had ever entered that room. No, probably he had never laid his reeking body down on that soft, fragrant bed. "You smell of cows, Cruz María!" she had said as she pushed him away. Still, she had wanted him again; but she had gone to him in the woods, as she would have to a handsome wild animal.

All these memories came back to me slowly and gently that hot St. John's Eve, and I caressed them like pets that had come to nuzzle against me in my solitude. But the figures who were most persistent were Fernando, Grandmother Anita's son, and Doña Beatriz; they whirled and fluttered about me like pigeons. Both seemed to be surrounded by a golden light; but while Fernando's form was dark and indistinct, Doña Beatriz's stood out sharp and white and proud. For me they were mysterious and unreal. They existed, but only as models or patterns for an ideal way of life. I saw Fernando as an ideal that was in the process of drawing nearer, as yet imprecise and indefinite; Federico's mother was moving away, still clear but about to begin the inevitable process of dissolution.

On evenings when I didn't take the path to "the other side" to look at the sea from the hill of *María la O*, I would go to the White House, taking care that no one saw me. I would look in from the garden and watch Eduvige serving Don Guillermo his supper. I would stare at the library window and picture myself there, leafing through the thick volume of *Paradise Lost*. At any moment I expected to see Federico come out of the house and invite me to go to Grandmother Anita's with him. One evening I saw Doña Beatriz. Darkness was falling fast. Suddenly a light came on in the living room, and her tall, slender figure was silhouetted against the curtains. I stood there for a long time without moving; then the light went out, and I walked away sadly. Another night while I was watching, someone began playing the piano. It was an unmistakable sign that Don Guillermo was not at home; perhaps he had gone, as he often did, to the city. Doña Beatriz was playing the same slow, fluvial music I had heard earlier; for a moment I was tempted to walk into the dining room and listen, as I had in the olden days. The music stopped abruptly, and it was a long time before I heard it again.

I was reliving these scenes in my mind, there in Cervelión's house, when I heard footsteps approaching. I crawled along the floor until I reached the back door, and waited to see what would happen.

Cervelión's hut was no different from the others in Cumboto; its walls were of reeds plastered with mud and it was roofed with dried palm branches. The interior was divided into an enclosed section that served as the living room, and an open area at the rear that looked out on the palm grove, which was the kitchen and the storeroom. Here I slept, on a bed of palm mats. The night wind caressed my body, the moonlight covered me at times like a sheet, and the rain, when it came from the north, washed my feet.

The moon was directly overhead, enormous and astoundingly brilliant. Its malevolent light cast a dull glow on the leaves and the trunks of the trees. Then I saw what looked like more tree trunks, moving in single file toward the hut. I waited, motionless. One by one they entered the living room. My problem was to watch and listen without making my presence known. Why? I don't know, exactly; but what happened later showed that my instinct had not misled me.

From my bed, where I had crawled, I heard a murmur of voices from the other room. Someone struck a light, and the closed door that led to the kitchen was slashed where the yellow glow came in through its cracks. I heard Roso's low voice, and a woman answering him. Whose was that strident voice? I found out later that she was a mulatto named Trina who lived on the outskirts of Tres Cruces.

Gradually a tide of curiosity rose within me. I could hear voices and footsteps, but I had to know what those people were doing. The yellow light between the planks of the door obsessed me. I couldn't stand it. I, too, was a Negro. Why shouldn't I slip to the door like a serpent and put my eye to one of those cracks? I would try it, and let it turn out as God willed. Slowly, straining every muscle, I inched across the polished surface of the palm leaves and rolled off onto the ground. Lying there, leaning on my elbows, I could see through the crack. There they were, looking slightly distorted because of the narrowness of the slit, those dark figures I had seen moving through the trees. There were seven of them, all kneeling in a circle in the center of the room. I couldn't see the source of the yellow light that lit their faces, but I judged that it was several candles, because of the flickering. I could make out Roso, who was facing me, and his two sons. The woman and Venancio were in profile; Cervelión had his back to me; and next to him was a Negro I didn't recognize.

Their shadows reached from the floor to the roof beam, in the shape of a huge cocked hat. The tiny heads of Roso and his sons were outlined against the wall, and seemed to have grown enormous ears. Then I saw the shadow of an arm stretched out along the ceiling, across the roof beam, apparently driving stakes into the other heads. It was Roso, putting cigars into their mouths and lighting them with a candle. When he had finished, he entoned solemnly:

"We come here to invoke the exalted powers and the soul of Cruz María, *El Matacán*. Let us concentrate our thoughts so no outside forces can disturb our labors."

Seven heads nodded in agreement, and the little room was filled with a hoarse unison response that seemed to come from the bottom of a well: "So be it."

"Brother," Roso said in the same liturgical tone, "present the objects that will help us in our purpose."

An enormous shadow arose, blocking out the light for an instant. Cervelión had stepped aside, and now I could see what his figure had hidden from me. On the floor in the center of the circle lay a doll made of white rags, and around it four burning candles.

"Sister," Roso went on, "bring out what you have provided."

The woman obeyed without rising. Her hands busied themselves with a dark bundle and drew out the body of a lifeless serpent—smooth, limp, long, and repulsive. It was a rattlesnake. She seized it in both hands and held it aloft like an offering.

"Seven years old, brother. Count the rattles."

"Your word is enough, sister."

It all happened very quickly. Cervelión soon returned with something large and square. I was suddenly overcome by a violent shudder. The basket! The odd-shaped basket Grandmother Anita had asked me to look for! Where had he been hiding it? I had looked everywhere. The ceremony that followed was so astounding and was over so soon that I was incapable of thinking. My whole life was concentrated in my eyes, and my heart was pounding in my chest. Cervelión had taken his place again, and Roso now held a piece of white cloth, yellow in the candlelight. From my lookout I could see its lace border, the sharp creases where it had been folded, and the black, red, and yellow stains that covered it. Roso's eyes were turned toward the ceiling in a kind of ecstacy, and from his lips issued a strange, tuneless chant. Then he spoke.

"He was naked when he came, and clothed when he went away . . . Tell the story, brother."

Cervelión responded: "He was left with me one night, and I warmed him and was a father to him. He was my son."

"Let the debtors pay their debts," Roso chanted.

"And let him who causes pain suffer pain," the woman answered.

"Oh, soul of Cruz María, *El Matacán,* come and help us in these labors. The man who killed you must die."

"And let the white kill the black no more."

The seven heads were bowed, and Roso and the woman were carefully and solemnly carrying out some maneuver I could not see. I could guess, however: it was some ritual with the dead snake, the swaddling clothes, and the doll that lay on the floor among the lighted candles. Then Roso and the woman returned to their places; they held out their arms before them, palms down, and Roso began a kind of litany:

> *Powers of the hidden world,*
> *Soul of Cruz María,* El Matacán:
> *Blow your breath of death*
> *Over what we have prepared,*
> *And bring Guillermo,* El Musiú,
> *On his own two feet . . .*
> *By the grace of this day*
> *And by the great powers,*
> *Let him suffer,*
> *Let the blood rot in his veins,*
> *Let his life drain away,*
> *Let his tongue fail him,*
> *Let his heart beat no more . . .*
> *Oh, highest of all powers,*
> *Oh, souls of all who died*
> *At another's hand,*

Blow now your cold breath.
Let the entrails of this rattlesnake
Begin their solitary journey,
Let this blood, colder than death,
Bathe the heart
Of the man who took your precious life,
Cruz María, El Matacán,
Son of Cervelión.

When Roso finished his eyes were turned back so that only the whites were visible. Then the woman spoke: "So be it."

"So be it," the others repeated in unison.

The woman's hands were red and wet with the rattlesnake's blood. I was dizzy and sick. I flattened my face against the dirt floor and breathed the acrid odor where so many Negro feet had walked.

Phantoms

The news was brought to the house by a terrified Negro, who told his story with exaggerated signs of grief.

"I found him down there, stone dead."

"Down there" meant on the river bank, where Don Guillermo lay face down near the water, as though Death had wanted to baptize him in the slow, muddy stream before he died.

There were no signs of violence beyond the two little marks on the back of his right hand, which was black and swollen like the rest of his body. His face and bull neck were puffy and ugly. Even the eyes that once were blue had turned black.

They brought him to the White House in a hammock and put him in his bed, and Eduvige and some other women took off his clothes to wash the body.

"Rattlesnake bite," Eduvige observed laconically.

"Must have come down like a ceiba tree struck by lightning," one of the women ventured.

The wake was silent and gloomy. The night wind rattled in the palms, and from the huts scattered over the plantation came the sound of prayers that went on until dawn.

"May God have mercy on him, may he rest in peace . . ."

But the throbbing of the drums and the wild chanting for St. John never stopped.

During most of the night there was a gentle, caressing breeze that barely disturbed the little burning lances of the candles. But about dawn the wind came from the sea and swelled the curtains like a ship's sail; the windows creaked, and the light danced mournfully on the walls and ceiling. Outside, the palm trees moaned.

Doña Beatriz presided at the wake; she came downstairs at midnight, dressed in black, and silently took her place at the head of the bed. No one had informed her of her husband's death. When Eduvige saw her she betrayed her surprise by barely lifting her almost invisible eyebrows. The women who had helped wash and dress the body kept repeating: "May God have mercy on him, may he rest in peace . . ."

Thus passed that unhappy night, with its accompaniment of wind from the sea, litanies, and distant drums. When dawn was breaking Doña Beatriz stood up, went to the bed, and lifted the white handkerchief that covered her husband's face. In her own there was no expression whatsoever. She silently and solemnly returned to her room, where she remained until several hours later when relatives and friends began to arrive from Puerto Cabello, from Goaiguaza, and from neighboring plantations.

He was buried with great ceremony, in an imposing coffin of mahogany and silver, like the wheelbarrow. The funeral coach, weighed down by the enormous corpse and a hundred wreaths of flowers, sank its wheels deep into the sand of the patio. Many people had gathered in the corridors, the living room, and the library, and sat solemnly staring into space with their black suits and white faces. Some of the men who worked on the plantation accompanied the procession to the city cemetery. I was dumfounded to see Cervelión, Venancio, and Roso and his sons walking along with the others. Only five days had passed since that unforgettable evening of witchcraft, and already Don Guillermo was dead; his blood had rotted in his veins, as Roso had demanded, and the powers of the hidden world had slaked Cervelión's thirst for vengeance. A horror as cold and clammy as the rattlesnake blood I had seen on Trina's hands went up my spine and into my heart as I remembered these things.

My perplexity increased every time these considerations returned to gnaw at my mind like some small, persistent rodent. There were many things to see in the city—streets, houses, and people—that under any other circumstances would have left me open-mouthed with wonder; but I couldn't rid myself of one disturbing thought. "After we've buried Don Guillermo, we'll have to go back to Cumboto and I'll have to face Cervelión. What am I going to say to him? What's he going to say to me? And what about Roso, and Venancio?" I might be able to avoid this situation by moving to Grandmother Anita's house; but could I do that without asking her first? Besides, the truth was that I wanted, deep down, to face Cervelión. I had to hear what he had to say. Perhaps he was innocent. Had all that fantastic business on St. John's Eve really happened? Perhaps it was all a wild creation of my feverish mind. I did not trust myself completely in such matters. It would not be the first time I had imagined things, absurd dreams that had seemed to take place before my deluded eyes. And finally, there was no way of being sure that what had happened was not pure coincidence. There was "something" in me that would not let me believe in Negro witchcraft. I told myself that it was all a ridiculous farce: the magic spells, the incantations, the "prepared" objects. But this "something" influenced only a small part of my mind; the rest of it believed, helplessly, with all the intensity that fear can lend to such ideas. I was a believer especially at night, when the moon was bright and the wind moaned.

I had been struggling consciously—and, in a way, desperately—against this duality in my own mind for some time. My intelligence, which had been partially awakened by contact with certain books and people, was striving to overcome the shapeless monster that lived in my heart. I pictured my soul as a miasmal swamp wherein floundered the small, white, feeble figure of my urge to improve myself. It is humiliating and odious to realize that one is held prisoner by such superstitions. These things—I told myself—cannot be, must not be; nature is logical and reasonable; every phenomenon has its explanation. And yet, as soon as the right circumstances came along the implacable beast returned to enslave me. And then I was a greater believer than anyone. Something of the kind must happen to drunkards who in lucid moments dream of liberating themselves from the tyranny of alcohol. The swamp is limitless.

The small, white figure in my mind looked like Federico. It was he who had begun that formidable task of redemption, which would perhaps never be completed. It was he who had introduced me to the world of beauty and logic.

But then he had left me to my own devices in the middle of the road, in the middle of the swamp, and I felt as if I were drowning. The way in which Don Guillermo had met his death was a decisive blow aimed at my mind. How would Federico have reacted if he had seen what I had? I wondered. Even so, I was glad he was no longer in Cumboto, that he was not here to see his father's black, distended body. Blacker than *El Matacán*'s, or mine, or Cervelión's.

The return trip from the cemetery was swift and silent. By the time we reached Cervelión's hut it was dark. He struck a match and lit a candle. When he raised it over his head we saw a woman sitting in a leather chair in one corner of the room.

"Eduvige!" I exclaimed.

We stood there, intimidated, without saying a word. Cervelión hung his head, but Roso was regarding Eduvige with a frown. The woman stood up and walked slowly toward us. Her sharp, ashen face was framed by the folds of a black kerchief. Her eyes were half closed, as if the light hurt them.

"This is your doing," she said, facing Cervelión. She paused to look into each of our faces, and went on: "Don't you deny it. I know all about these things, but I never thought you . . . If it had ever crossed my mind that you'd get such an idea in your head, I would've stopped you."

And then, with a sudden, violent movement, she buried her face in those damp, spidery hands, and her whole skinny body, flat as a reed, shook with her hoarse sobbing.

"What am I going to do now?"

"What about my son?" Cervelión said. "My son doesn't mean anything?"

But this question, instead of pacifying Eduvige, seemed to enrage her.

"Your son!" she screamed. "What son're you talking about?"

Her face had turned pale. White! Her eyes were as cold and hard as the stones in the river.

"Your son! Who do you think you can fool with that story? You think anybody in Cumboto doesn't know he wasn't your son?"

Then something happened that I never expected to see. Cervelión put out his huge arms and seized Eduvige by the throat.

"Shut up, damn you!"

It was Roso who kept him from strangling her on the spot. Cervelión stepped back, panting, and stood leaning against the mud wall. Eduvige straightened her kerchief and moved toward the door. She turned and said: "You're criminals, every one of you! But from now on he won't be able to fool people any more. *I* was the one who left that boy on this doorstep. You hear? It was me! Me! Now you know!"

As the woman's figure melted into the shadows Cervelión was overcome by a kind of frenzy. It was an incredible spectacle of fury. The words burst from his lips incoherently, with the violence of a whirlwind.

"It's a curse! Everything here's got a curse on it! They kill black people like animals. And white people, too. Mysterious things! Mysterious!" (He fastened his burning eyes on me, and I thought I would faint with fear.) "Remember what I told you about that silver spade? Go and pick it up, so you'll be cursed, too! I told you not to touch it, but if you want to, go ahead and take it in your hand. Yes, she left him at my door, but he was my son. Why should I care who his mother was? He came naked and he went away with clothes on. You remember, Roso? That's what you said."

His eyes were like wounds, raw and bleeding flesh; then suddenly they turned into cataracts. He wept like a child abandoned in the night, his face hidden in his shaking hands. The tears ran down between his fingers, and as I watched them I remembered the milk that oozed from the coconuts when the Negroes knocked them together in the sheds.

Coquín, coquito,
coco, cocón...
Viejo virulo de verde ropón;
pónmelo bueno,
pónmelo pon,
dame la agüita con este pelón;
coquín, coquito,
coco, cocón...

Why had these nonsensical verses come to my mind? It had been so long since I had heard them. In the presence of the old man's tragedy they were grotesque and inappropriate. They were like a sneeze of the soul. I tried not to think of them, to drive them out of my mind. But there they were, jumping about in my head as I watched Cervelión's little coconut head, racked with sobs. My God! How despicable I was! How stupid and hateful to have to strain every muscle to keep from laughing!

Cervelión's voice went on, and every word fell like a stone. When I heard Doña Beatriz's name I no longer felt like laughing.

"Don Lorenzo was going to kill Doña Beatriz's first baby, the one she had before she was married, with that spade. They don't think I know. He was going to bury him in the palm grove. There's gold buried there, too. And where there's gold buried there're Negroes buried, and there's a curse..."

When Negroes begin imagining things, their fantasy knows no bounds;

the borderline between the natural and the supernatural disappears, and the absurd becomes part of the very air they breathe. After the death of Don Guillermo, *El Musiú*, spirits and demons ran wild in Cumboto, and the inhabitants vied with each other in reporting all kinds of apparitions. Many of them had seen the ghost, some in one place, some in another. Prudencio assured me he had come across it on the path to the river when he was returning from his bath. He was not able to describe it in any detail because he had immediately taken to his heels in fear. Juan Segundo swore he had glimpsed it from a distance, near the bamboo bench under the mango tree by the *coquera*. He almost fainted with fright. He went home by another path and locked himself up in his house near the cow barn. But there was one odd thing in Juan Segundo's story that coincided with some of the other reports: the ghost by the mango tree looked more like a woman than a man. It floated along like a white mist in the evening shadows, rising and falling. They all said they had seen it at twilight, when the last light of the day was turning to shimmering blue shadows.

"I saw it from far away, too," declared one woman who worked in the sheds. "But I made the sign of the cross and it went away."

It had appeared to her near the gate that opened onto the highway. There was a rustic bench there, too, made of palm trunks, but she couldn't say whether the phantom had been sitting or standing. It had no face, she said.

"No face, and no feet."

"How did it move?"

"It floated through the air, like the little tufts of cotton that fall from the ceiba trees."

Nobody could understand why it hadn't shown up before this. Until now Cumboto had not been favored with this distinction that was enjoyed by the other estates in the neighborhood: it could not claim to have a private ghost. From time to time Negroes of both sexes had reported having seen shades and specters or hearing strange sounds—voices, or the clanking of chains—but these were possibly transient ghosts, or strays, and were never seen or heard again in the prescribed manner. A guest from the other world who is a constant and familiar visitor becomes with time inoffensive and even indispensable. One runs into him in the hall, the garden, or the kitchen, and steps around him as calmly as one would a broken board in the floor. Many of the neighboring houses had ghosts of this kind; the only exception was a mansion that belonged to the Ramírez family in Tres Cruces, where an apparition had taken up residence thirty years earlier. This ghost was so malevolent that it did not rest until it had driven the owners away. The Ramírez plantation was abandoned, and soon went to ruin.

This new specter that so upset all the Negroes did not really interest me very much. Any other time, perhaps, I, too, might have been fascinated; but now all my emotions were involved in events in which I thought of myself as playing an important role. The scene in Cervelión's hut the evening of Don Guillermo's funeral had opened up tempting, labyrinthine paths in my imagination. I strolled excitedly along these paths, and always came back with the same disconcerting answer: I would never find out anything unless someone who knew the facts was willing to tell me. I discarded Cervelión and Eduvige at once, and then, naturally, thought of Grandmother Anita. But perhaps she, too, would prefer not to speak of matters as grave as those that Cervelión had vomited up in his fit of rage.

As I tried to think of some clever way to arouse the old lady's interest and draw her out, more questions occurred to me, adding to my confusion. For

example: Who would be the head of the White House now? Its demented
mistress? I didn't think so. On the contrary, I was sure that it would not
be she. Eduvige, then? And who was Eduvige? Did Grandmother Anita
know? Did anyone in Cumboto know? It would have surprised me if anyone had known, for all the time I lived under the same roof with her I never
saw her speak to anyone or heard anyone mention her name. She was like
a shadow.

When I arrived at the shack I stopped at the gate, open-mouthed with
amazement. There, in the clean-swept front yard sprinkled with red blossoms from the bucare tree, a great pile of furniture rose like a rampart:
beds, chairs, tables, cupboards, chests. Pascua and Prudencio were going
and coming with boxes and bundles. *El Pitirrí* was whistling cheerfully, as
usual. His sister glanced at me, raised her eyebrows, and then went about
her business as though she had not seen me. It was Prudencio who broke
the news.

"We're leaving."

After a few moments I was able to ask: "But you didn't know about this
last night!"

"No. *He* decided early this morning."

He was his father. Ernesto had made up his mind suddenly. He was going
to Morón or Sanchón—Prudencio was not sure—to load sugar cane, which
paid better than working on the coconut plantation. And he was taking them
all with him, whether they liked it or not.

The brother and sister seemed to be delighted with the idea of leaving.
At last they were going to travel. They had been in Cumboto for a long
time, and were beginning to be bored. Ah! They would see new villages,

new people, new scenes! Since Don Guillermo's death, life in Cumboto had been very gloomy. And dangerous, Ernesto added in a mysterious tone. That one death would not be the end of it, as it would be if it had been a miserable Negro; there was trouble coming, and he wanted no part of it.

"There's that ghost walking around," Prudencio said, with the air of someone who was in the know. "What you got to say about that? Don't you think these things could mean the world's coming to an end?"

After that I talked with Anita. She didn't mind leaving, apparently.

"But you're not young any more," I shouted at her angrily. "Aren't you ever going to settle down anywhere?"

She kept on smiling; her head shook continually, a sign of old age that had grown more severe in the past few months. Turning her head in my direction was a great effort, and her eyes, always watering, were now useless. She resorted to her sense of touch. Her dry, trembling hand touched my leg, then my arm, and stopped when it reached my breast. Then she spoke for the first time.

"What can we do about it, my son?"

"This is inconsiderate," I protested. "You're in no condition to be jerked around like this."

"Sure I am. I'm used to it by now. And you know I always loved traveling. And anyway, poor Ernesto asked me if I thought I could make it."

"And you said yes."

"Of course I said yes . . . because I can."

"It's not true! You can't!"

I headed for the door, furious. But her voice stopped me.

"Listen to me."

I returned to her side peevishly. Her hand found mine and squeezed it.

"Come closer."

I put my face next to hers.

"Where are the children?"

"Out by the gate, getting things ready."

"Let me see your face."

Her fingers moved with exquisite gentleness over my skin and carefully followed the outline of my features. I have never since had the feeling of being so thoroughly examined. Her hand penetrated me, producing such a sensation of sweetness that tears sprang to my eyes. No one had ever touched me like that before.

"I had two sons," she said. "You know that, because I told you once. One left me when he was about your age. But God is very great. You can have sons without giving birth to them. Don't be sad, don't cry. We still have many things to see and a lot to talk about."

I watched the departure of the slow, creaking ox cart from my hiding place behind a nearby fence overgrown with carnations. The household goods were piled in a pyramid. Grandmother Anita and Pascua rode on a plank that had been fastened across the front of the cart for that purpose. Ernesto, with the long goad in his left hand, and Prudencio, still whistling, walked in front of the animals. My heart was breaking. It was such a deep, desolate, impotent sorrow that I almost enjoyed it. Now I was completely abandoned and alone, and there was a certain bitter, almost sensual pleasure in the thought. As I looked at the old lady's black, bent, shriveled figure and her face that was like a dried-up date, I reflected that her departure marked the end of an important period in my life. My youthful innocence was leaving with her.

I stayed there until the cart disappeared around a curve in the road and the sound of its creaking was lost in the distance. Then I went back to the hut, entered by the kitchen door, and walked through it in silence. In the living room I looked at the bare spots on the whitewashed mud walls where once had hung the portrait of Pope Leo XIII and the almanac with the names of those exotic perfumes: *Camia, Des Roses, Lidilia, Sonia, Le Muguet, Liseris.*

In the bedroom I could see the marks where Anita's and Pascua's cots had stood for so many years. The faded newspaper with the picture of the little black galloping horse was still hanging on the wall. "'He's black and free, like Grandmother Anita," I thought. The same figure appears on the coat of arms of our Republic; they say it symbolizes freedom. But it is white. Why is that? Have white people ever been slaves?

It was the hallway between the living room and the kitchen that saddened me most. Anita's rocking chair had occupied the same spot there for so many years that it had worn a hollow in the hard dirt floor. I leaned down and stroked the spot lovingly.

In the fireplace, which was a platform of timbers plastered over with red clay, nothing remained but three blackened stones and a little heap of ashes. It was here that the old lady had heated the iron griddle to cook the little flour tortillas and the *calás* of white beans.

I stood in those deserted rooms for a long time, alone with my dark thoughts. As I reviewed the events of my brief existence, once again there came to my mind the image of the swamp with its tiny white figure struggling to keep afloat.

PART THREE: *Let There Be Light*

Strange People

When I arrived with the milk can that morning, Eduvige met me at the kitchen door.

"Go this minute and take a bath," she ordered. "Then put on clean clothes and come right back."

I had seen this woman at the same hour every morning during the four years that had passed since that scene in Cervelión's house; and in all that time I had never heard her open her mouth before. Naturally, I was surprised. I looked at her questioningly, but she pulled herself up very straight and pointed down the path imperiously.

"Get moving!"

I obeyed. As I had foreseen, it was she who ruled in the White House now that Don Guillermo was dead. Everyone obeyed her.

When I returned, she gave me my instructions.

"Hitch up the little buggy, then drive to El Palito and pick up a lady who's coming on the ten-o'clock train. Here's her name on this piece of paper."

The thought of bringing a guest to the White House was exciting, for it would provide food for gossip in the *coquera*, in the sheds, and at the various evening gatherings. For four years the White House had been the focal point of certain intrigues about which we had made wild conjectures. I, too, had been caught in the net. At first I had put up a futile struggle against the influences of my environment; but finally I surrendered and became a gossip like all the others. As the horse plodded toward El Palito that morning I reviewed what had happened to me during those years.

Shortly after Don Guillermo's death a stranger had come to live at the house. He was an odd fellow, in whose personality there was a disconcerting mixture of madness and perspicacity. If he could have straightened out the hump on his back he would have been a fairly tall man. He had a lean, red face whose skin hung in folds; his beak-like nose and small blue eyes, hidden behind enormous spectacles, gave him a vaguely menacing look, like that of certain tamable birds such as the *guacharaca* or the bittern. He usually wore an absurd brown and green checked suit whose trousers ended a little below the knees, like knickers. From there to his ankles his legs were wrapped in canvas leggings, and he wore huge hobnailed boots. He was never without his heavy cane that ended in a metal spike, like an ox goad, a little green hat with a red feather, and a cloth bag that hung from his shoulder. When he first arrived someone in the *coquera* dubbed him *Guacharaca*, which was what everyone but myself called him. He reminded me more of one of those old, skinny sleepy horses that suddenly surprise us by fastening their teeth in our hand. When he told me his name—Herr Gunter—I immediately thought of Frau Berza. Why did they have such funny names?

Herr Gunter was said to be Don Guillermo's brother. He had come to Cumboto to look after the children's interests until they became of age. At least that's what he said, in his wretched Spanish. Don Serafín, the majordomo, had submitted to his authority without question, and turned in his accounts to him every Saturday. Eduvige seemed equally willing to accept him as master; so he did as he pleased in the White House. For the most part Herr Gunter gave the employees little trouble, since he spent his time in the jungle, looking for small creatures of all kinds. I accompanied him more than once on these excursions, and we visited every part of the plantation. I couldn't understand more than a quarter of what he said. At first this was maddening; but I soon realized that he was generally talking to himself, and so it didn't bother me any more. It was my opinion that there was a screw loose somewhere in that square head, with its short, red hair that stood up in spikes.

He seemed to be especially fascinated by the towering trees, hung with heavy ropes of vines and parasitic plants. He would go up to their trunks, sometimes standing up to his neck in the underbrush, and poke them with his cane.

It may seem strange, but the fact is that Herr Gunter's presence in Cumboto was partly responsible for my change of heart about leaving. After Grandmother Anita's departure, and then that of Cervelión and his brother Roso, I fell into a state of melancholy that approached despair. It was a time I don't like to remember. And then one day Eduvige ordered me to take the new *Musiú* out and show him the plantation; and my life, suddenly altered by contact with this odd being, returned to its normal course like a river that recedes after a flood. After that first excursion I found that this eccentric man attracted me fully as much as Federico's father had repelled and terrified me. At the time, I would not have been able to explain it. His gentleness, his gestures, his soliloquies, his mad dashes after a lizard or a butterfly, his sudden ecstasy at the sight of a plant, his way of plunging into the river without removing his shoes and leggings, his brusque questions and his total indifference to my replies—all these things disconcerted and at the same time amused me. Among the great variety of objects he carried in his shoulder bag was a book with a dark cover which he consulted frequently— I suppose to look up the scientific names for plants and reptiles. Whenever there was one he could not find there, he would stand for a moment, perplexed, scratching his head; then he would shrug his shoulders abruptly and continue on his way. All this amazed me. At his side I learned many useful things, although they were never to be of any actual service to me.

Herr Gunter and I made several trips deep into the forest. Sometimes he called me Natividad, and sometimes "boy." He learned the names of plants, animals, and people very quickly. One day I asked him why he didn't carry a gun. He fastened his little blue eyes on me through his almost cylindrical glasses and replied with inexplicable fervor: "Oh, no! I might think at you a bullet to shoot!"

Even today, as I remember those words, I shudder without knowing exactly why. I can't decide whether he meant to compare me with a wild animal or to imply that he was not to be trusted. Later he confessed that he was interested in nothing but plants, bugs, and animals. As though wishing to remove any possible doubt of this from my mind, he invited me to see his collection. This was how I came to enter the White House again, nearly two years after Federico had sailed away. My heart was pounding like a piston. As I followed Herr Gunter across the living room I ran my trembling fingers surreptitiously over the top of the piano. Everything was just the same: clean, severe, sweet-smelling. I looked up at the ceiling and remembered watching the bat. There was not the slightest sound to disturb the silence. Doña Beatriz was upstairs in her room, dead, perhaps, but as incorruptible as the ancient saints. It was only in the library that I found certain minor alterations. The large table, for example, was completely covered with wide, flat boxes shaped like trays, under whose glass lids lay the creatures *El Musiú* had brought home. This was the collection he had spoken of. In one tray were butterflies of every imaginable color and shape; in another, hairy black spiders, gigantic centipedes in a repulsive shade of purple, beetles with antlers like those of a stag, and scorpions as large as crayfish. As I forced myself to stand and stare at that bristly conglomeration, afraid to hurt Herr Gunter's feelings, I reflected that here had been brought together, in a kind of psychological synthesis, all the malignity of the smaller forms of life. My uneasiness reached its height when I found myself before the case filled with snakes. They were beyond my powers of description. There were so many of them, large and small, gray, green, ringed, and evil. Herr Gunter's eyes were glittering like two drops of prussic acid in the bottles of his spectacles, and his mouth had drawn itself into a reptilian slit. All these creatures were dead and preserved; but to me they were still alive, lying there quietly waiting for an opportunity to scatter throughout the house and spread death.

Herr Gunter was dissatisfied because his collection was far from complete. Specimens of some of the most interesting fauna of this latitude were missing, he said; among them was the rattlesnake. When I heard this I felt sick, as the memory of St. John's Eve crashed into my mind with all the violence of a stone thrown through a window. He must have noticed my reaction, for he bombarded me with questions.

"Are you afraid of her? Why? Has she bite someone? I can cure such, you comprehend. I possess the remedy."

That day he gave me a lecture on snakes, and scribbled some words on a scrap of paper which I learned by heart without understanding them, just as I had memorized the names of the perfumes on Grandmother Anita's almanac. The rattlesnake's scientific name is *Crotalus terrificus,* and its venom can be counteracted with anticrotaline serum; the bite of other serpents can be treated with an antibothropine. These words stuck in my memory, in various permutations. I repeated them mechanically, like someone shaking a bottle before using the contents: *Terrificus, bothropicus, crotalicus; crotalicus, bothropicus, terrificus.* And whenever I thought of the cold, dead, slippery rattlesnake in Trina's hands that night in Cervelión's hut, my stomach turned over.

I don't know how I managed to keep my secret from the shrewd Herr Gunter. One day he showed up at Cervelión's house, where I was still living, and began examining everything about him, making no attempt to hide his curiosity. I watched him, wondering if he had found out anything through some other channel. Suddenly the uproar of Venancio's birds attracted his attention, and he went out of the house like a shot, without a word. He stayed at Venancio's a long time. This made me nervous and suspicious. Venancio was not only in on that terrible secret—which, after all, involved me only indirectly—but knew others that concerned me alone. Among other things, the bird man had some knowledge of my future, for it was he who had interpreted the shape of the egg white in the bottle I had prepared. My vague, uncertain future! (The gummy white mass in the water had taken the shape of a plant at the bottom of the sea, with many long, trembling, transparent fingers reaching upward. Venancio studied it for some time, and then said in a thoughtful way: "They look like bars, but I can't be sure. You better be careful, anyway. The only bars I know about are in prisons." "Are they going to put me in jail?" I asked. "Could be. That's why I say be careful.")

Venancio had remained in Cumboto. For a time he had been wary of me; later, when our friendship was renewed, we never mentioned certain names that might have made both of us lower our eyes. But our relationship was never the same after that. There had been an irremediable loss of innocence. Although we were still friends, there was a certain caution and reticence between us. This is why I was concerned about his conversations with Herr Gunter.

With all these considerations, I was forming a rather confused and contradictory notion of this man. In the long run I couldn't decide whether I feared him, or hated him, or liked him. My most vivid memory of him stems from something that happened in the woods one day. We were walking along a path near the river when suddenly I heard a light, angry rattling. I stopped short and called out: "Don't move!"

It was all I could manage to say. I must have been as pale as death. I pointed with a trembling finger at a gray rattlesnake coiled in the dead leaves beside the path. Its rattles were quivering, and its triangular head, a foot above the ground, was aimed in our direction.

"Lovely!" Herr Gunter cried with delight, his little eyes dancing behind his spectacles. "Very lovely!"

It was all over in a few seconds. With the speed of thought he pulled a heavy hunting knife from his belt and cut a long, stout branch, the straightest he could find. He cleaned it of leaves and twigs, and with a length of steel wire from his shoulder bag made a running loop at one end. I watched him, shaking. He held the branch out toward the serpent, and coolly waited for the attack. I had never seen such a thing before. The reptile's head lunged forward like a hammer, and its curved fangs slipped off the green bark, staining it with a yellow fluid. I don't know whether it saw through the trick or if it felt that it had done enough, but it didn't strike again. The sun glistened on its body for a moment, and then the snake began to slither away toward the bushes. But Herr Gunter was too quick for it. The horrible head was now in the noose, which closed around its evil neck. What happened next was even more exciting: the powerful body thrashed about, making Herr Gunter's arms shake. Then it wrapped itself around the branch. At last it began to relax, grew limp, and finally fell to the ground and lay still. It was dead, strangled. Not until that moment did I notice that Herr Gunter had taken off his glasses.

After that I could go and look at the rattlesnake in the library. I often stood before the glass-topped case and examined it carefully. I wanted to know everything about it. It was like the one I had seen in Cervelión's living room.

The privilege of entering the library whenever I liked had been given to me by Herr Gunter, and I was filled with gratitude. Once again I could leaf through my favorite old books, and pick up the silver spade. This object no longer inspired me with the old superstitious terror. It is amazing how our perspective changes as time goes on and we meet new people.

Herr Gunter found me there one day and began asking questions.

"You lived once here, did you not? You know all the house? It has not underground tunnels or secret places? Tell me, have you seen plans? Maps? You know what are maps?"

He didn't wait for my answers. He knew, undoubtedly, that no matter what he asked I would say I didn't know. That same day, and for several days thereafter, I found him engaged in a curious task. He was searching every corner of the library, and looking through every book.

And now I was on my way to El Palito to meet another guest. The events of the past three years had provided me with a fund of memories that was to lend me strength during the trying times to come. I had no idea who the new visitor would be, but I had a premonition that with her would come new anxieties.

I looked at the piece of paper Eduvige had given me: *Laura Lamarca,* some unknown hand had written. Whose hand was it? Eduvige's? Herr Gunter's? Doña Beatriz's? I shivered as I remembered Doña Beatriz. Not long before I had thought of her as though she were dead, an incorruptible cadaver. Since she bore the same last name, Laura Lamarca must be a relative of hers. Then it must have been Doña Beatriz who wrote on this scrap of paper. It was her handwriting! The letters were large and round. She had written in violet ink, and had probably blotted it with sand.

Waiting! I had never done anything else all my life. In the station at El Palito I sat down on a bench of wooden slats, painted yellow. Its seat and back were curved to fit the body. It was comfortable and pleasant to sit there on that piece of furniture that invited meditation and sleep.

On one side rose the rust-colored mountain, covered with wild vegetation; on the other lay the green, sparkling sea. A few palm-thatched huts dotted the narrow valley where the railroad ran, and there were a great many cattle calmly grazing. Soon the train from Valencia arrived, and several people got off. Laura Lamarca had her daughter Teresa with her. I took them to the buggy that was waiting on the road.

More Strange People

I might almost say that it was that scrap of paper with Laura Lamarca's name on it that inspired me to write this story. Someday, I told myself, I shall have to tell Federico all this; and from that moment on I resolved to put down everything that took place in the White House, every act and word of its inhabitants. I must add that it was not Herr Gunter and Laura Lamarca who intrigued me most. It was Eduvige.

I had always held a high opinion of that silent, frigid woman, a deep respect for her character and intelligence. "She doesn't talk," I thought, "because she has so much to say." Good Lord! What would happen if she were to speak! Grandmother Anita, who had boasted that she knew the lives and secrets of every person in Cumboto, had never pried into Eduvige's life. She passed her by quickly, and kept out of her way. I hadn't remarked this before, but now that I was once again in the presence of this ashen sphynx I remembered it clearly. Neither Anita, nor Cervelión, nor Venancio wanted any trouble with her. That night when we came back from the cemetery and found her in the hut, Cervelión had turned pale; and in spite of his uncharacteristic fit of rage, I think his subsequent emotional outburst was owing to his fear of having her for an enemy. I often wondered if this had been the reason for his and even Grandmother Anita's sudden departure.

When we returned from the station at El Palito it was Eduvige, as usual, who came to open the door. Her face was expressionless as she stood to one side to allow Laura Lamarca and her daughter to enter the living room. Indicating with a gesture that the newcomers were to remain there, she went upstairs. I followed with the suitcases. When she knocked on Doña Beatriz's door, I heard a soft, meek voice say, "Come in."

I had gone upstairs automatically, without thinking, assuming that the Lamarcas would be given one of the bedrooms on that floor. I stood at Doña Beatriz's door, awaiting further orders; as Eduvige had left the door ajar, I looked in. I hadn't meant to, but the temptation was too great. I shall never forget what I saw; that scene is as indelible in my mind as the portrait Federico had once shown me in the morocco-covered album. Surrounded by the rosy glow of her bedroom, Doña Beatriz's face was framed in an enormous snowflake of exquisite lace.

I was dazzled. In a moment Eduvige came out and with a gesture ordered me to take the suitcases to a room at the end of the hall. Then the new guests came upstairs, and I heard Laura Lamarca announce that she was hungry.

In the days that followed I was to see these two women often, in the house and outside. I would come across them in the garden, on the paths, even at the *coquera*. One day I was surprised to find them at the stables. The mother stopped me to ask where the path led, and when I told her she said she would like to explore it.

"I'd like you to come with us. Will you?"

Mother and daughter were inseparable. The one, small but sturdy and domineering, with her large head sprinkled with gray hair, always led the way; the other followed, as tiny and fragile as a straw. Thus they came and went at all hours, looking at everything. They never exchanged a word. The girl followed her mother silently, as though drawn along by an invisible thread. Teresa was young, but she seemed ageless. Her eyes were dull and irresolute beneath those eyelids that never opened completely, and on her wan lips there was an expression of innate weariness.

As I had foreseen, these new personages created a great stir among the Negroes at the *coquera*. They were regarded with the same wonder that Herr Gunter had inspired earlier. I watched them peering from their doorways or hiding behind trees to follow the two women's movements, just as they had done before with Don Guillermo's brother. These wild, shy hypocrites almost hoped they would be caught and questioned by the women, if only to get a good look at them and hear their voices. This did happen to one little Negro boy from the *coquera* whom Laura caught by surprise. But he couldn't summon the courage to look her in the face; he wriggled like a fish and escaped into the woods while his friends watched from afar, laughing.

Laura Lamarca wanted to make the Negroes like her and trust her. She tracked them to their lairs and waved and called to them along the road. But they remained aloof. She asked me one day, "Why do they run away from me? Talk to them, tell them I'm not going to hurt them."

I did speak to a few of them, just to please her; but I put no enthusiasm into it. I, too, mistrusted these women, and wondered why they had come to Cumboto. Now I would have to divide my time between them and Herr Gunter. Luckily, he seldom needed me. Not even he was immune to the general curiosity.

"Who are these people?" he asked.

Since I didn't know myself, exactly, all I could say was, "They're members of the family."

"Of the family! Whose family?"

"Doña Beatriz's."

He said no more, but from that moment on there was undeclared war between them, a campaign of espionage in which I was to play an important role. I must confess that I enjoyed the situation and served both sides with pleasure, even going so far as making up things to upset them. In a word, I was acting as a spy for both factions. It was not long before there were three. One morning as I was leaving the milk can in the kitchen, I saw Eduvige motioning to me from the dining room. When I approached she said gravely, "I want you to tell me everything they do."

"The two women?"

"All of them."

My position as informer enabled me to enter the house again and loiter about. In addition, I became a friend of Eduvige's. I was more interested in keeping this powerful woman's good will than in anything Herr Gunter and the Lamarcas might have said or done. Every morning after breakfast the Lamarcas visited Doña Beatriz in her room, while Herr Gunter went to see Venancio. What fun it was to follow him through the woods as he talked to himself, gesturing all the while! I was not able to hear what he and the bird man said to each other, however, for I didn't dare try to sneak into Venancio's hut. If he had caught me, the very least I could have expected was a beating.

I delivered my information to *El Musiú* at my house—Cervelión's former home; I met the Lamarcas at the *coquera*; and my interviews with Eduvige took place at the White House.

One morning the crazy old man asked me, "What does a gourd tree look like?"

I described it as well as I could, but he was not satisfied.

"Show me one."

I took him to one of them. He examined it carefully, walked around it, stuck his steel-tipped cane into one of the large gourds that hung here and there along the trunk, and then pulled out his black book with the scientific names of plants and animals.

"*Crescentia cujete,*" he read aloud. " 'A member of the bignonia family.' "

"We use the gourds to make bowls and cups and spoons," I told him. "The leaves are good for toothaches. The wood is hard, but flexible. It bends, but it won't break . . ."

But he was not listening. He had begun drawing the tree in the notebook he carried in his sack. As I watched him, the past came winging back to my mind like a dove. Once again I was with Federico, my elbows on the dining-room table, looking on as he drew pictures with his crayons. I remembered how I felt the first time I took a crayon in my own hand and reproduced the forms and colors of nature. Medlars and blue donkeys! Desperately, I tried to remember Federico's exact words and the sound of his voice on that occasion, but I could not. Recalling visual images was relatively easy, but sounds had melted away like a sigh.

Herr Gunter was an expert draughtsman. In a few rapid strokes he copied the tree with admirable precision. There it stood like a person, alive on the white paper, stubby and knotted, with its arms pointing to the sky and its enormous fruit hanging almost to the ground. In Grandmother Anita's house there had been many cups made from these gourds, from which I had drunk coffee and corn soup more than once. Cervelión and most of the other Negroes had used them, too. When I told Eduvige about this excursion, she raised her eyebrows and looked very interested.

"A gourd tree? You sure?"

"Of course."

She said nothing more, but I got the impression that she knew why Herr Gunter was so curious about the *crescentia cujete*. Laura Lamarca's reaction was quite different.

"Why do you suppose that crazy man wants to know about a gourd tree?"

Surprisingly enough, she came looking for me two days later.

"Are you quite sure it was a gourd tree?"

"Yes, *señora*."

"He didn't ask anything else? He didn't mention any particular gourd tree? He didn't want to know whether there was one growing in any particular place in the palm grove?"

"No, he didn't say anything about that."

From that day on they dispensed with my services and did their own spying. I was surprised to see Herr Gunter give up his trips into the woods and spend his time in the coconut grove on "the other side"—that is, near the sea —and even more astounded when I saw Laura Lamarca following him with the tenacity of a bloodhound. From the hill of *María la O*, where I hid for that very purpose, I was able to watch the naturalist as he held a piece of paper in his hand and paced off the distances between a gourd tree and some points of reference nearby. I couldn't make out what these landmarks were, and, judging from his actions, I don't think he knew himself; but it was great fun to watch. Herr Gunter would plant his cane in the ground and walk from one place to another in long strides; then he would squat on his heels and look back and forth between the sea and the highway. He must have had some information written on the piece of paper, for he consulted it at every step and scratched his head. Laura Lamarca looked on from her hiding-place behind some palm trees.

And then I was nearly bowled over with surprise. Right there beside me, as though it had sprung from the earth, stood Eduvige's ghostly figure.

"What you doing?" she asked.

She could see for herself. Her glistening eyes were cold with hatred.

"Go back to the house and get an axe."

When I came back both Herr Gunter and the Lamarcas were gone. With her usual terseness, Eduvige commanded:

"Cut down that gourd tree. Cut down every one you can find around here."

For me that was to be a time of surprises and problems. My mind seemed to be floating along on a winding, misty river, and there was to come a moment when all these small enigmas would empty like little streams into a shining sea. The image of the shining sea came to me one afternoon when I had a vision. I was on my way from Cervelión's shack to the White House when I saw the ghostly figure sitting there on the bamboo bench at the foot of the mango tree. The phantom! I was confused, but my mind was working at full throttle. Other people had seen it in different places, white and vaporous, hovering above the ground like a beam of light, permeated by the pink and gold of twilight. But I knew who it was. I knew the moment I saw it. That's

why I wasn't afraid. My uneasiness turned to rapture and ecstasy. Her soft brown eyes were smiling at me, and her hair shimmered indistinctly in the last faint rays of the setting sun.

She raised her hand slowly and beckoned me. As I drew nearer her radiance seemed to envelop me. Then I heard her troubled voice.

"Come. Don't be afraid."

I stood before her, drinking in the marvelous whiteness of her skin. She wore a dress of filmy net, and from her shoulders hung in liquid folds a glittering blue cape with a collar that fell down her back.

"You're not afraid?"

"No, *señora*."

"You're luckier than I. Listen carefully. I need someone to protect me. I'm surrounded by people who hate me, who persecute me and spy on me. At night, when they think I'm asleep, they come in and search my room. They go through the drawers and cabinets and look under my bed. What do they want? I don't know. I've been thinking a great deal, and I remembered that you and Federico were like brothers. Just like brothers! That's why I came to find you. Watch out for me until he comes back."

"Is Federico coming back?" I was filled with joy.

"If he loves me even a little, if he hasn't forgotten I'm his mother, he'll have to when he reads my letter. You're going to mail it for me."

She took an envelope from her bodice and handed it to me. I took it mechanically. Then she added: "You will go this very night, so nobody will see you. No one must know. Will you promise me?"

If there were any words to answer her, I didn't know them. Then she said, simply: "Go."

And I went.

Are You Happy Now, Dear Ghost?

"Today I returned to the White House to live. I no longer have to enter like a spy or a thief. Federico said, 'You can come back.' " These were the first words I wrote as I recorded my latest experiences. Later I added, "What will Eduvige say?" And then: "And what about Herr Gunter and the two women?"

When I saw Federico disembarking from the great, black ship, I recognized him at once in the middle of the multitude of men and women who were coming down the swaying gangplank. I knew him in spite of the fact that he looked nothing at all like the boy who had left five years earlier. It was odd; I was disappointed that he had changed, but I realized spontaneously, automatically, and immediately that he could not and should not have looked any other way. The delicate lad who had seemed so weak but who was actually tenacious, rather sardonic, and even a little cruel at times, could only have turned out to be this pale, slender young man with the serious face who was coming to meet me so unhurriedly and calmly.

"You're from Cumboto, aren't you?"

"Yes, sir. I'm Natividad."

He showed no reaction at the sound of my name, as if it awoke no memory within him.

"Did you bring a carriage?"

"Yes, sir. I came in the gig."

He handed me the heavy woolen overcoat he was carrying on his arm, which I put in the gig, and ordered me to follow him to the customs to pick up his bags. The road that had once led from his heart to mine seemed no longer to exist. There had been a landslide at his end. As I walked behind him toward the customs shed I examined his back and made my inventory. His shoulders were broad and strong, and under the dark material of his suit I could see the movement of his muscles. On his recently shaved neck there was the faint line left by the razor, and a few red spots where it had irritated his skin. I saw Venancio among the swarm of people on the wharf, with two or three cages filled with parrots; I noticed that he never took his eyes off us. This made me uneasy—as if my thoughts weren't dark enough already—because I could not persuade myself that he was there merely to sell parrots. But I soon forgot about him and turned my attention back to Federico.

He wore a green Tyrolean hat, with its inevitable feather, like Herr Gunter's. There could be no doubt that there was a certain family resemblance; this was emphasized when Federico took off his hat for a moment and I saw the way my old friend now wore his hair. There was the same high, square outline, the same pitiless cropping that left his crown barely covered with a thin carpet of red bristles. His head was exactly like that of the half-mad snake hunter. Trying to find some small vestige of our mutual past, I did my best to remember how Federico used to look at me. It was useless. Nothing of that old expression remained. He had never looked at anyone in any other way but this. It was the same with his voice: he had never spoken in any other way. Carried away by a bittersweet current of sentimentality, I tried for a moment to imagine how certain phrases would sound now on his lips— things we used to say when we were children together—"blue donkeys," for example. But it was beyond my powers of imagination. They were phrases he had spoken, but they were no longer his; they were mine.

The Federico who was marching along before me now spoke firmly and distinctly, very sure of himself. There was a certain metallic, guttural accent that hardened his speech, although I'm sure that a grammarian would have found no errors in it. He walked erectly, almost stiffly, with his chest thrust forward and his head held high; and whenever he spoke to anyone he clicked his heels together. Perhaps all this had been there when we were children, and I had never noticed it before.

On the way home he hardly spoke. We were in two widely-separated worlds, he on the seat and I on the driver's box. By this time I had accepted the fact, and would not have dared turn around to see what he was doing behind me. He was probably looking me over as I had looked him over there on the wharf; or maybe he was regarding the landscape, or simply dozing. When we crossed Alcantarilla Street I thought about the day we came to bury his father. That was the first time I had ever been in the city, and now I was almost a grown man. Two shady lanes lay before us, either of which would take us to Cumboto. The one on the right, which went through Paso Real, was the shorter; the one on the left was the prettier, and was called the Well Road because it ran beside the aqueduct of heavy masonry that had been built in colonial times to supply the seaport with water. I would have liked to ask Federico which road he preferred, and I even pulled the horse to a halt in the vague hope that he would tell me. But he said nothing; so I decided to take the Well Road. Actually, Federico could have had no reason to prefer one to the other. He had been on only one of them—the road to Paso Real—when he had come to the port five years ago to set sail for Europe. I realized that my friend had no basis for comparison; they were both the same to him. And then I began thinking that a world he had forgotten was passing before his eyes, while his heart was filled with memories—who could say how intense they were?—of the world he had just left. I wondered what that world was like. I knew nothing about it, and didn't dare even try to imagine it. It must be splendid and awe-inspiring, I told myself; it must be worthy of free, strong men.

We passed by the inlet to the aqueduct, where in olden times the water had begun its journey to the town over those ancient stones set in place by the Spaniards. There the water came down from the mountain; along the stream was a path that led south to the plantation at Pitiguao. A little farther on, at El Paraíso, a group of burro drivers were loading their animals and calling to one another in loud voices. A woman standing in the doorway of one of the houses asked, "I wonder who that *Musiú* is?"

I began thinking about Doña Beatriz. I recalled our meeting at the bench under the mango tree, and her troubled voice: "I need someone to protect me. I'm surrounded by people who hate me. You and Federico were just like brothers . . ." I smiled. I had believed that, too, and my heart had swelled with pride. What a fool I had been! I thought I was going to be the champion of that fine lady who was so persecuted! I had taken the role so seriously that for six months I had slept out in the open, like an animal, just to be near her, where I could come running at the first sign of danger. I was proud of my loyalty and my physical endurance. Anyone else wouldn't have been able to stand it. When it rained, or when the wind from the sea was too cold, I would sneak onto the porch and huddle in a corner. I came to recognize all the sounds in the night. I was fearless. I became as hard as iron. Federico didn't know this, and possibly never would; but I wasn't going to tell him. Still, he had behaved like a good son. He had come back to Cumboto.

We got home in the middle of the afternoon. As Federico leaped from the carriage, the front door opened, and there was Eduvige, as skinny and flat as a broom straw. He didn't even notice her. He was looking about him, and I thought I saw his face grow softer. Yes, there could be no doubt of it: the past was coming back. As I stood there with his trunk on my back I felt a stab of joy.

One after another, the guests came out to greet him. First there was Herr Gunter, and then Laura Lamarca, followed by her daughter Teresa. All three regarded the new arrival with curiosity and uneasiness. He turned to them and waited. Laura was the first to introduce herself; her voice rang with false enthusiasm and affection, like the clucking of a chicken.

"I'm Laura—Laura Lamarca, your mother's cousin. This is my daughter Teresa, your cousin."

Then Herr Gunter came forward; he spoke in German. When they shook hands, all four heels clicked together, dry and precise. Federico turned to Eduvige.

"You're Eduvige. I remember you well. And this is Natividad." (He pointed to me.) "There's nothing you have to tell me. I suppose my mother still has the same room. Am I right? I'll take the one that used to belong to my father. Later I shall want to speak to Don Serafín. Draw my bath. I'll have dinner in the dining room with the members of the family."

These last words were spoken over his shoulder as he went upstairs to his mother's room. He stayed there for a while and then went to his father's bedroom, which had been locked since the day of the funeral. I didn't see him again until supper time, when I was about to return to my hut. He called me from the top of the stairs, and I waited until he came down.

"Natividad," he said, "my mother tells me that you haven't lived here for some time. You can come back here to stay as you used to."

My heart leaped, and I raised my eyes to his face; but his expression was so cold and indifferent that something within me went limp, like a flag when the wind dies. I didn't even say "Thank you." I merely nodded and left. That night, in the same little room with its walls of rough planks from where I had watched Frau Berza and *El Matacán* in the moonlight, I wrote on a scrap of paper: "Federico said, 'You can come back.' " And then I thought, as I sat staring out into the garden, "But was it Federico who said it?"

Everything in the White House was about the same as it had been when I lived there before. Except for Herr Gunter's specimen cases in the library, the outsiders had not dared to make any changes. I had no idea what they had done in their rooms; I wanted to find out, but there seemed to be no way. They were all very careful not to leave their doors open.

After Federico's arrival the battle shifted its center to revolve about him. It became a furious contest to gain his favor. In all fairness, I must say that Herr Gunter showed more dignity than Laura Lamarca. Her machinations bordered on the grotesque. She never stopped talking about her kinship with Doña Beatriz, and about how she loved the whole family. Her father had been Felipe Lamarca, Don Lorenzo's brother, who had died on the Apure plains after having built up great herds of livestock. The wars had decimated his cattle and fevers had ruined his health. When she was very young she had married a wicked man who "ate up" her inheritance and left her pregnant with Teresa—that marvelous creature. When she heard—she didn't say how—that her cousin had been widowed and was in poor health, she flew to her side. She did everything in her power to be of help and comfort.

As for Herr Gunter, he had come from central Europe when he received the news of his brother's death. He would have been here before, but it wasn't until then that he knew just where Guillermo was. Someone had said he was in Brazil, and others had thought it was Patagonia. The New World was huge and beautiful. Its greatest attraction was its variety of reptiles, even though it could not claim the cobra. He had lived in India, where he had done intense botanical and zoological research. At first, Federico listened with great interest and examined his collection. He, too, had studied these subjects a little, but not so much as to want to spend his time in long conversations about snakes and insects. He was more interested in books than in little creeping things, and above all else, in the piano.

Laura Lamarca reacted to Herr Gunter's unintelligible observations with eloquent grimaces of distaste and contempt, and Federico's indifference to them delighted her. She and her daughter were not scientists, nor did they have the slightest pretensions to any knowledge of artistic or literary matters. They were good Christians, as they had proved by watching over poor Doña Beatriz day and night while that insufferable ophiologist chose to turn the house upside down, tear the pages out of books, and dig up the plantation in search of God knew what mysterious treasures. This was the invariable subject of her table conversation, which became more and more vehement in the face of Federico's continued silence.

Why was he so indifferent? I couldn't understand it at the time. He behaved as though these people did not even exist. At no time did he betray the slightest curiosity as to how they spent their time when they weren't there making nuisances of themselves. He took his meals with them as though they were all travelers who had met casually at some inn. As for Eduvige and me, he paid no more attention to us than to the others.

It was I who cleaned his bedroom. I had to bathe and keep myself sweet-smelling. I spent hours there. Federico had many suits and a great supply of linen, as well as numerous bottles of perfume and jars of pomade. On his table were photographs of two women, one of whom wore glasses. He had also put up snapshots of himself, taken in the woods or in the snow, wearing a heavy overcoat. In one of these the two women appeared, too; in another he and one of the girls were sitting on a stone bench, the ground about them covered with a snowfall of feeding pigeons.

Federico spent most of his time in his room, when he was not in the library reading or leaning on the window sill and gazing out at the palm trees. Once I found him looking at the sea through a telescope. I never saw him enter his mother's bedroom again after that first day; but I did see him leafing through the morocco-covered album that held the photographs taken of her when she was a child. I often saw him strolling around the living room, regarding the family portraits that hung on the walls. I saw him go out on the terrace and stand there contemplating the sky filled with stars. I, too, stared at the stars, wonderingly. Peace had come to our world. The spasms of the early days were over—those days when the Negroes leaped from their boats onto the rocks and were hunted with mastiffs. The word *Cumboto* no longer throbbed with terror as it had on the lips of the captured fugitives. Everything was peaceful now. And yet there was an almost imperceptible trembling in this wildly fragrant air.

I knew that in the silence of night, when the lamps were lit, there were eyes watching us through cracks in doors and gaps in mud and wattle walls. In those eyes all the distilled fury of the past lay sleeping. The white master was dead, and his son was a new and unknown quantity. How would their world—the world of the subservient—be affected by the arrival of this pale, silent lad who looked out at the night from his solitude?

On the fifth day, however—how well I remember!—there was a remarkable change in Federico's routine. It was in the morning, when the sun knifed into the living room. I saw him come downstairs slowly and go to the piano. He raised the cover and began toying with the keys. His white hand ran lightly up and down, and at its touch the notes burst forth like a cloud of butterflies. I was watching from the dining room, sure that something extraordinary was going to occur any minute. He stood there for a few moments; then he sat down on the bench and began to play in earnest. I was bowled over. A cascade of notes and trills, like crystal tinkling in the breeze and water tumbling into an abyss, filled the living room and flooded out over the countryside. I was overcome, enveloped and swept along by that marvelous torrent. I soon recognized the composition—it was one I had often heard Doña Beatriz playing; but now, under Federico's flying fingers, it had a new elegance. It was as liquid and transparent as the morning rain.

At that moment Herr Gunter came running into the house and stood stock-still at my side.

"Ah!" he murmured. "The Beethoven *Pathétique*."

He took off his glasses and began beating time with them. His little blue eyes, grown pale, stared into space. Soon his head was bobbing up and down, too, and he was humming along with the music.

Then another person came upon the scene. Doña Beatriz came slowly down the stairs. She was dressed in white, as always, with a filmy shawl over her shoulders. A shaft of sunlight cast a nimbus over her figure as she stopped on the landing. I stared at her, enraptured. And in my mind I asked, "Are you happy now, dear ghost?"

Walk!

Federico's behavior couldn't have been stranger. He had been back in Cumboto for nearly two months and had never once stepped out of the house to look over his property. Not once had he shown any interest in the people at the *coquera* whom we had visited together when we were children. He had never asked about Grandmother Anita or Cervelión. All the scenes that he had found so fascinating at one time had been blotted from his memory; they had been supplanted, no doubt, by others that now occupied his thoughts. I would have given my right arm to know what it was all about. It did not take me long to think of one possibility: one of the girls whose portraits he had brought home was probably an important factor in his abstraction. And then I thought of something dreadful. Perhaps he was planning to go away again. That would explain his lack of interest in the plantation and its people. Don Serafín, the elderly majordomo who reported to him every Saturday, had more than once offered to take him on a tour of inspection of the coconut grove, the woods, the work sheds, and the boiling vats; and every time he had been left waiting with the horse he had saddled.

The only thing Federico seemed to enjoy was the piano. The selections he played must have been very evocative for him, judging from the passion he put into them. His favorite was the Beethoven *Pathétique*. He came back to it again and again, plunging into its mournful waters and abandoning himself to the current like a man trying to drown himself in a river. I knew nothing about music at the time—I don't know a great deal even today, though merely listening gives one, inevitably, a certain familiarity—but his fingers touched the keys with such precision and the strings gave out their cataract of notes with such brilliance that anyone would have been bewitched. Federico's mother, however, never again came downstairs to listen. It was the only time Doña Beatriz had emerged from her room since her son's return. Eduvige still took her meals up to her as though nothing had changed.

I had seen her in her room once, the day Laura Lamarca arrived, and I had hoped to be able to do so again by taking advantage of Eduvige's comings and goings. I made several attempts, but it was useless. Someone— either Doña Beatriz or Eduvige—had placed a folding screen embellished with golden dragons just inside the door.

I don't know whether Doña Beatriz ever thought of coming down to the dining room, as she had when her husband was alive. I doubt that Federico would have hinted that it might be better if she stayed in her room. In any case, she never once sat down at the table with the people who had invaded her house. I was still puzzled by Federico's resignation during these three hours of each day. There were really quite a few loose ends in my jumbled thoughts. One thing I couldn't forget, for example, was Doña Beatriz's accusation under the mango tree: "I'm surrounded by people who hate me. They come in and search my room." I couldn't believe that Federico knew this, behaving as he did; perhaps his mother hadn't told him about it, for some reason. Besides, I kept wondering about Eduvige's role in these intrigues. Did Federico know the answer? Did Doña Beatriz include this strange woman among the people who "hated" her?

One morning about two months after Federico's return, Herr Gunter ordered the buggy brought out and drove off alone toward Puerto Cabello. He returned that afternoon with a tall, strapping, blond girl whom he introduced as his daughter. An explanation was called for, and he proceeded to give it. He had never mentioned her, he said, because it had never crossed his mind that she might come to South America. But his life had changed so completely here, and he liked America so much, that he had decided never to leave. His daughter would love it, too. He introduced her to Federico in German; but the young man responded in Spanish, with a terseness that would have discouraged the most optimistic of men.

"How do you do?" he said to the new arrival as he took her fat, pink hand.

The girl stood there, perplexed by these words in a language she did not understand.

There were more explanations offered by Herr Gunter to the servants—and indirectly to Laura and Teresa Lamarca.

"My daughter's name is Lotha. Understand?"

Little Lotha boasted not only a robust set of limbs, but golden tresses that could have been used to tie up a ship. She wore them twisted about her head somewhat in the shape of a helmet. In spite of all this she was not without a certain grace, owing more to her innocence than to her beauty. She had the healthy, patient look of a nursemaid.

I had thought that one more unexpected guest would be the drop that overflowed the cup. But it wasn't—at least, not right away. Federico hid his displeasure—if he was displeased—with exemplary patience. Besides, Little Lotha did her best to be as little trouble as possible. She was dignified and considerate. She took over the room that had belonged to Frau Berza, and left the house every morning at dawn to stroll in the garden with a book in her hand. A little later Herr Gunter would join her; they would sit together under a tree, talking and reading. A few days later I found out that they were studying Spanish. Herr Gunter acted as teacher, at the same time perfecting his own command of the language. Within a week Little Lotha had the courage to say a few words and even string together a sentence or two.

If I had been less naive I would have understood at once many things that only later became clear in my mind. I stumbled on the answers, like small surprises. It took me quite a while to see, for example, that whenever Little Lotha found herself alone with Federico it was not purely by chance. She had been well rehearsed, not only in arranging these encounters, but in the topics that would interest him—such as Don Guillermo. The success of this strategy must have been a small triumph for her—and for Herr Gunter, too, of course—because Federico seemed to be pleased that they remembered his father. He always spoke of him with respect. European life and culture was another of her subjects. Right after her first success I witnessed a lively argument between Herr Gunter and his daughter in the garden, in the very spot where I had seen Frau Berza and Cruz María struggling. I couldn't understand what they were saying; but they were firing words at each other that snapped like whips and their eyes danced with fury. Little Lotha had lost the grave serenity we had found so appealing. I was astonished at the angry look that had come over her face; her eyes and lips were as hard as steel. As had happened the night of the scene between *El Matacán* and Frau Berza, I was discovered. Herr Gunter said something hurriedly—about me, apparently—and Little Lotha ended the conversation with a single syllable that came down like a hatchet: "*Ja!*"

A few hours later I was dumfounded to see her sitting at the piano. What audacity! Only one other outsider had ever dared touch that solemn, black ship anchored in the sea of the living room, as long as I could remember. That was Frau Berza; and then it was only to give Federico and his sister Gertrudis their lessons. When I found that intruder there with her huge, ham-colored hands splayed over the keyboard, I was filled with the fire of rebellion, and almost shouted at her, "Get up from there!" But I didn't. She was too formidable.

She began playing something slow and muddled, as heavy as her hands. The notes were not clean and transparent, as they were when Federico or his mother sat there. They stumbled. I must confess that I had never before thought of the piano as a mechanical device for producing music; it had always seemed like a huge window thrown open by Doña Beatriz or her son, allowing the exquisite, ineffable, inimitable harmonies of another world to pour into the house. But as it was being pounded by this intruder, it sounded like one of those hurdy-gurdies you find along the road on fiesta days.

What was Little Lotha playing? My God! How far was this human sausage going to carry her insolence? She was attempting the *Pathétique*, no less! And, of course, she executed it, as they say, in the same way she would a traitor: by murdering it. She must not go unpunished. It was Federico who finally did what I hadn't dared to do. He came running from his room like a man coming to put out a fire, struggling into his jacket and throwing himself down the stairs.

"No! No! No! Please . . ."

He said it in German, in Spanish, and I don't know what other language, mixing up the words, overcome by a frenzy that seemed to me to be more of terror than anger. No! No! Little Lotha was welcome to do anything she liked in the house, or in the garden, or in the whole plantation; but, by all the gods in Heaven, she must not touch the piano!

I don't know how Laura Lamarca heard about it, but never did a human face evince such fiendish satisfaction. At dinner that evening she philosophized at great length on the subject of tactless people who did not know how to keep their place.

"I know many girls like that. They try so hard to make themselves interesting that they never notice when they put their foot in it. And, naturally, they're always being disappointed.

"The thing about well-educated people is that they are discreet and modest," she affirmed. "These virtues, of course, are not acquired by knocking about the world like a mountebank; they are learned in the home—and not in every home: only in the Christian home, where there are healthy habits of piety."

She always came back to this theme: pious habits. She and her daughter never failed to take the carriage to Goaiguaza or the train to Puerto Cabello to hear Sunday mass. Had anyone ever seen Herr Gunter or his daughter going to mass?

While Laura Lamarca vented her antipathy, the targets of her attack were devouring their meat and vegetables with the enviable voracity of a couple of turkeys. Laura kept eating, too, as she talked, while her daughter Teresa picked at crumbs like a bird.

Herr Gunter and his daughter listened to Laura's cackling with such apparent indifference that I thought they had failed to understand her diatribe. But I soon saw that I was wrong: Little Lotha's glances were eloquent enough. Suddenly Herr Gunter took his head out of his plate and fixed Laura with his little eyes set in their massive lenses. His powerful jaws ground out one word:

"Windbag!"

Laura froze in astonishment—but only for a second. Then she cried, "Oh!" and began fidgeting in her chair. She seemed unable to find words for a counter-attack. As she desperately searched her mind she kept repeating:

"Windbag! Did you call me a windbag?"

This *was* the drop that made the cup overflow. Federico pushed back his plate and napkin with an impatient gesture and got to his feet.

"That's enough!"

He bowed and went toward the stairs as the others sat stupefied. Before reaching the bottom step he turned and came back to the table.

"I had intended to write each of you a note, telling you of my decision. But since we are all here together I see no reason not to tell you in person.

You cannot stay on here. You will all do me the kindness of leaving this house as soon as possible."

That same night, while I was sleeping peacefully in my little room, something woke me. I don't know whether it was a sound, or a light, or a touch; I sleep so lightly that some of my senses seem to remain awake while the rest are sleeping. I put my head out the window and saw Eduvige going into the living room. I followed her. She went upstairs as silently as a shadow. When she was out of sight I started up behind her. Just as I reached the landing a short, sharp scream pierced the silence. I ran. Doña Beatriz's door was open, and through it came the light from the sea. I didn't stop to think. I went in. There stood Eduvige, stiff and erect, like a shadowy statue. Doña Beatriz was sitting up in her bed, propped against a great pile of pillows. The filmy curtains were twisting like spirals of smoke in the gentle breeze that came in through the open window.

There was a crescent moon. A pearly mist blurred the outlines of the trees and the slender branches of the rose bushes. The sandy path that led from the house to the road glowed in the moonlight; on it stood two horses, one with a rider. I took all this in in one rapid glance out the window. Then I saw a man running toward the horses. He mounted, and they galloped away. "It's Herr Gunter," I thought. "Herr Gunter and Little Lotha are escaping." Doña Beatriz pointed toward the fugitives, but she was unable to utter a word.

My imagination, which sometimes functions with extraordinary speed, reconstructed the scene that must have taken place in Doña Beatriz's bedroom. I put it all together quickly. "I'm surrounded by enemies. They come and search my room." And what had they found?

Just then Federico came in, tying the belt of his robe. His mother stared at him, her eyes wide with terror. I took advantage of that moment to examine the objects in the room. On either side of the double bed stood a small table with an oil lamp surmounted by a large, red glass shade. Over the bed was a canopy with mosquito netting, which was now pulled to one side. Two tall wardrobes with beveled mirrors flanked the window. On the wall facing the bed was a dressing table provided with a huge mirror, and before it an armchair upholstered in blue satin. A large bureau with many drawers stood near the door. Every piece of this furniture was blue, and shone dully in the lamplight.

I expected Federico to run to his mother and take her in his arms; but he merely stood by the bed and asked, "What's happened?"

For me it was an interminable moment of anxiety and disappointment. The anxiety was caused by the look of naked fear on Doña Beatriz's face, and her inability to speak or even weep; the disappointment was because of Federico.

"What's happened?" he repeated, still standing in the same position.

Then Eduvige spoke, her toneless voice still filled with shadows and moonlight.

"Herr Gunter was here. He left through the window."

"He tried to strangle me!" Doña Beatriz was able to say at last.

"Strangle you! Why?"

"I don't know. It wasn't the first time he's come in and searched through my things."

"Did he go through anything tonight?"

"Yes, the wardr..."

The blade of unadulterated terror cut off her answer, but her pointing finger completed it. Federico walked around the bed and went up to one of the wardrobes; but a broken, desperate cry from his mother stopped him.

"No!"

He stood there without moving, while Eduvige's hovering shadow approached; her hand, invisible in the dim light, turned the key in the door of the wardrobe. She started toward the door, but Federico stopped her.

"Give me that key!"

She handed it over without a word.

"No!" his mother cried again. "Don't open it!"

He paid no attention. As the door swung open, something round and ivory-colored glowed in the darkness inside. The skull! I recognized it at once. Once more my amazing memory functioned with the speed of lightning. I saw myself as a child, in the library with Federico, erecting upon Frau Berza's suffering and humiliation a small monument to our cruelty. He had picked up the silver spade and was looking at his reflection in its mirror-like surface. I was inspecting the wheelbarrow and eagerly asking where the skull was—the Negro skull that Don Guillermo had told us about in the dining room. Was this it, perhaps, that Doña Beatriz's son was holding in his hand at this very moment?

She had gotten out of bed and was standing behind Federico, looking terribly angry. Somewhere, some time, I had seen a figure that was exactly like Doña Beatriz at that moment: the same folds in the robe, like something carved in marble; the same creamy cascade that fell about her feet like a pedestal; the same graceful white hand raised to point the way to eternity. Where had I seen it? Oh, yes—in the cemetery at the port, over some mother's grave, the day we buried Don Guillermo. As her son replaced the skull, Doña Beatriz spoke in a voice that was like an icy knife.

"If you touch one more thing in that wardrobe, I'll kill myself right here in front of you."

Completely alone now, Federico was drowning in his solitude as though in a pond. The swamp! There is a swamp for white people, too. In mine, which was a shapeless, sticky mass of superstitious fears, the only hope of salvation lay in a tiny, pale figure that recalled a childhood friend. I didn't know whether a similar figure inhabited Federico's swamp, but I did sense that he was approaching a crisis. He often sat at the piano and played the music his mother loved; it was intense and passionate, filled with dissonances that at first hurt my ears. His fingers ran over the keys like two white spiders, bringing forth great surges of sound. I could not appreciate the beauty of that music then; it was unintelligible and painful to me. Its harmonies had nothing in common with our savage, elemental rhythms, sprung from the womb of the earth. Those melodies that trickled away like water under the leaves, those nuances as slight as the breeze that does not stir the grass, bored into me as though they were trying to wrench me from a subterranean world where I had lain for thousands of years. I found myself most tormented by the abrupt transpositions, the violent changes of mood, and the crashing chords that suddenly burst from the black box to shake the house and echo among the palm trees.

Several times I was tempted to cry out, "Stop!" But I controlled myself. It would have been absurd. Who was I to ask him to destroy the atmosphere with which he had surrounded himself in his despair? This was his world; and if I wanted to draw him into mine I must be familiar with it. I must conquer it no matter how I suffered, with the same heroic cowardice my ancestors had shown when they conquered the soil and the blood of an alien world by coming as fugitives to Cumboto. And in the end I succeeded. I succeeded! I can say it now, proudly. Little by little I began to feel more at ease, and to understand. The next time Federico and I talked together, I was already convalescing from a grievous wound whose existence he had never suspected.

One night when he was at the piano and I happened to pass by as I was lighting the lamps, he reached out and took my hand. He led me to the window that opened onto the garden. The wind was galloping through the palms, making them dance. In the distance we could see, between the trunks of the trees, the red tongues of bonfires that burned to drive away the evil spirits and wild beasts of the forest. Suddenly, from somewhere far away, a man's voice cried out as though in pain.

"Natividad," Federico said, "I'm lonely and confused. I don't know whether I should stay here or go away. You're more than a friend to me; we were born and raised together here in Cumboto. If I could imagine a single human being with two separate personalities, I would say that you and I are that being. You represent the innocence of the earth, and I must represent its intelligence. But is that what I really am? Do I really belong to this earth? You'll never know how this question has tormented me lately. I don't want people to hate me—but I don't know how to make them love me. Tell me: what should I do?"

I stared at him, amazed. It was the swamp again. He himself had shown it to me, suddenly pulling aside the impenetrable curtains of his heart. His swamp was white, and in the middle a minute black figure was struggling to keep his head above the slimy waters. In my uncertainty and confusion I could think of only one thing to say. I myself didn't know what I meant by it.

"Walk."

The Shadow

I repeat that I didn't know what I was trying to tell Federico that night; but the fact is that from then on he spent all his time walking. He explored the plantation in all directions; he went deep into the woods, like Herr Gunter; and when there was nothing more to see there he began tramping the dusty roads of the neighborhood. You might say I was his shadow. I felt that I was responsible for this frenzy of perambulation that had suddenly come over Federico, and consequently believed that it was my duty to share its vicissitudes. He walked, walked, never stopping, from morning to evening, like a somnambulist. All the geographical history of Cumboto and its environs unrolled beneath our feet like a great, magic ball of yarn.

Although I had first thought it absurd, I ended by taking quite seriously a

notion that had occurred to me on our first excursion: I was his second conscience. As I watched him striding along with his jacket over his arm, almost
hidden in the cloud of dust raised by his feet, I was more and more convinced
that this was what Don Guillermo's son needed if he was to comprehend the
living essence of this world: a second conscience, a black conscience. This was
my role. As he walked through villages and settlements without stopping, as
he trudged past roadside shrines without removing his hat, I was surer than
ever that as long as he was this insensitive he would never be able to understand anything he saw, much less make the people he met love him. During
those sweaty, weary hours I believe unsuspected spiritual powers awakened
in me. There was some mysterious force that I was using, unconsciously, to
direct his steps. I employed these powers several times in apparently trivial
circumstances, with disconcerting efficacy. "Turn off to the right," I would
suggest mentally, and he would go in that direction as meekly as a sleepwalker.
"Stop at that little store and ask for a glass of water," and he would stop and
drink. "Go into the church," and in he went.

And yet these proofs of my small powers, far from delighting me, filled my
mind with doubts that hovered and twisted like a bit of smoke in a bottle. I
was trying to implant in Federico a feeling for the earth; but I asked myself
if in doing so I was not destroying it in myself. I was not sure that I could live
in the same world with him, no matter how much I learned. It was not a question of racial prejudice, but of sensitivity. Would I, in a word, ever be able
to think and feel as Federico did?

On these walks I always carried in my hand the old *zamuro* seed Prudencio
had given me in the days when we used to gather to listen to Venancio's
stories. It would protect me from the malevolence of the living and the dead.

This was not the only superstitious practice I still engaged in, in spite of my progress in analysis and reasoning. I couldn't give it up. I still can't.

Goaiguaza had a strange fascination for Federico right from the start. I remember this as clearly as though it had been yesterday; the picture of the village with its little mud houses and tall *bucare* trees afire with blossoms is one of my fondest memories. Goaiguaza is a town of strong men and gentle women. When we visited the little church, as we often did, I saw qualities in Federico that he himself never suspected. He seemed to prefer to be alone at these times; I felt this, and kept out of sight. As in all villages built by the Spaniards, the rustic church stood facing a modest park, where it was cool under the trees. It was very peaceful there, with no one but an occasional trio of dark lads lazily playing marbles. Within this low, square building, with its thick walls of earth and lime and its massive masonry buttresses, the pious early settlers gathered everything essential to the preservation of the Catholic tradition. The font near the front door was of crudely-carved greenish granite, and was covered with inscriptions that looked as though they had been scratched with a nail. Only a few were legible. *December 15, 1734, the day of San Marcos de los Reyes,* said one; another was merely a name: *Gaspar de los Reyes.* Who was Gaspar de los Reyes? I was sure, although no one said so, that his hands had carved this stone. He must have been a huge Negro, a tree of a man with long, powerful arms, glistening rolls of fat around his neck, and breasts like a woman's. With his own two hands he must have dragged the heavy block from the river bed and chiseled it out with one of those enormous iron spikes that once were used to secure massive doors. Then he installed it in the church so that all the village children—black, white, and mulatto— might be baptized.

Beneath the rotting reed ceiling, the main altar displayed an ancient color print of St. Michael driving a lance into a dragon. On the side walls hung four small platforms made of rough, painted planks, each bearing an image. One represented Jesus on the cross, dripping black, dusty blood; another depicted the Mater Dolorosa in a mantle of black velvet studded with stars and silver flowers and a crescent-shaped diadem, also of silver; the third was the statue of a saint I didn't recognize; the last was St. John, the Negroes' St. John, the reveler and warlock, in a cape of coarse red cloth and a little straw hat.

Federico never tired of looking at these things, of running his fingers over the rude, decaying benches, the rickety pulpit that leaned against one of the posts supporting the roof, and the rough stone of the baptistery. He loved to examine the series of old lithographs that served as stations of the cross, with their legends in three languages: English, French, and Spanish.

One Sunday morning a priest who had come from Puerto Cabello was saying mass. He was a tall, ruddy Aragonese who looked like a butcher; his tonsured pate was barely visible through his tousled black hair. The little church was filled with villagers, mostly women. The men remained outside, milling about in the yard, firing off rockets, and making frequent trips to the corner store for little glasses of rum. While the symbolic ceremony proceeded inside, they chatted about their small problems—the crops, their fighting cocks, and women. God's business was for women, and men's business was for men. I stood at the door near Gaspar de los Reyes' font and watched everybody. There were the mother and her two daughters from Tres Cruces, sitting on their private bench before their own prie-dieux, having come in their little buggy behind a sorrel mare. The mother was almost a cripple, for an old necrosis of her right leg forced her to walk with a heavy cane. But this infirmity, instead of sapping her strength, seemed to double it. I knew her story.

After the death of her husband years before—a poor devil who was too fond of rum—she took over the estate and proved to be an excellent manager. She had thick eyebrows and a graying mustache, which gave her the fierce expression of a hawk. With her stiff leg she rode on horseback all day around her property, giving orders. Her daughters, on the contrary, were as soft and delicate as two lilies.

I was moved and lulled by this scene. It was like an anesthetic. Against the whitewashed walls and the vivid red robes of the statues, the priest's green cope stood in a lively but agreeable contrast; the colors recalled the loveliness of growing things. From where I was standing I could see the moth holes in that ancient mantle. When he leaned to kiss the consecrated stone his white alb lifted up behind to reveal large, black boots and part of a plump, pink leg. The flame of one of the altar candles rose sharply above his head, like a small lance. The tapers were dots of gold that leaped and opened up like flowers when caught by the draft.

When the acolyte rang his little bell all the parishoners got to their knees—even the few men who were standing inside. I was about to kneel, too, when I saw that Federico had remained on his feet; I waited, uncertain. It struck me as a sign of superiority to stand erect in the midst of so much humility, and yet, aware of my own hypocrisy, I felt more humble than any of them. I tried to fix my troubled eyes on the little things that were going on about me. A poor deformed woman, a kind of human centipede, was dragging herself along the floor looking for a place in the crowd. There were lips moving feverishly, and eyes half-closed in ecstasy. The elder of the two girls from Tres Cruces, kneeling on her stool, stood out above the crowd. She had pale skin, black hair, and a long, slender neck. There was a serene solemnity about her that was rather forbidding. She was no longer a child. Although her figure was delicate, her hips were full and firm.

When the acolyte came to take up the collection I tried to calm myself by thinking, "Here is a lad who is an honor to his race. He's black, but handsome. He has a delicate profile and clear eyes. You can tell he's intelligent, because he struts around so solemnly. How much will he take out for himself before he gives the plate back to the priest?" But it didn't really make me feel any better. I was still feeling uncomfortable, even after everyone had gotten up again. I took a *locha* from my pocket and held it in my hand as I waited for the boy to come by. As the coin warmed up, my hand began to sweat. Would my *locha* end up in that crafty little Negro's pocket? The money was a symbolic tribute rendered by the material to the spiritual. But it might turn out to be just the reverse. I wondered what Federico thought about all this. Just then the acolyte held out the plate to him; Federico seemed not to notice. They held the pose for several seconds, and then the boy moved on, disappointed. I still held my slippery coin in my hand. The little Negro cast a quick glance in my direction and decided I was not worth approaching.

After mass was over, the priest turned to speak to his parishoners. He announced various events that were to take place in the parish. He said that he was saddened by the lukewarm attitude of his flock. Where before they had sent him constant proofs of their piety—chickens, vegetables, fruit—now they seldom even came to mass. The children did not attend catechism, and the men and women were living in sin like beasts, at the risk of eternal damnation. Nobody took communion. And what were the well-to-do Christians doing? More than ten years ago the church had begun collecting money for an organ, and there was still not enough in the treasury.

These were my impressions that Sunday in the House of God: confused, chaotic, contradictory, sprinkled with question marks. As I was leaving, I saw an elegant-looking man of about fifty walking past the church. He was an unusual type, and seemed totally out of place in these surroundings. He was a mulatto. What intrigued me most was his great dignity. He was dressed in gray, and carried a felt hat in his hand. For a long time after that I kept thinking about him; he represented in my mind a possible model of proper behavior. This person, whom I had never seen before and perhaps would never see again, must have been from the city. Only there could he have learned such manners, such ease, such a way of walking alone in the middle of the crowd with as much indifference to other people's curiosity as to the sun or the wind. His image gradually faded from my mind, blotted out by the mists of new emotional experiences.

One of these experiences was an unexpected meeting. I was coming along one of the lanes that run between the roads to Paso Real and Goaiguaza, when I saw coming toward me a woman dressed in rags, walking slowly and unsteadily. As we approached each other, to my astonishment I recognized her. It was Pastora, the woman who years before had passively endured the sexual assaults of the boys from Cumboto. Nothing about her had changed—neither her face, nor her body, nor her filthy dressing gown, which was still the color of dried blood. She passed me indifferently, with no change of expression, not even turning her head to look at me. Her lovely black eyes, under their long lashes, stared into space. The look in those eyes made me shudder. The life in them had not disappeared; it was simply paralyzed. She made me think of a mummy—a living, young, immortal mummy.

The roads around Cumboto are filled with revelations like this—strange, incompleted creatures, provisional first drafts of human beings in whom the hand of God suspended its labor in indecision. We came across them at all hours and watched them go by in silence. Some traveled on foot and others on burros, carrying their primitive tools and supplies in ponderous ox carts or creaking wagons drawn by skittish mules.

As Federico strode along ahead of me, I found that I could *feel* his reactions. I don't know if anyone else has ever had the same experience. It was as if that tormented, tireless young man's senses had been transferred, in part, to my own mind and nerves and pores. I *felt*—that is the best word I can find to express it—I felt his mind and heart opening up, slowly and almost painfully and yet with pleasure (as I imagine a virgin must feel when love comes) to the virile thrust of the world around us. The landscape and the people were drawing nearer, growing larger, opening their arms in a great nuptial gesture, inviting Federico's world to join with them in an incomparable copulation.

And I followed behind him like a shadow.

June

June had come again, hot and luminous. Along the jungle paths the drums were announcing the return of St. John. Once again bonfires leaped in the clearings, flinging out their long arms in a frenzied red dance. Now Federico and I went walking by night, too, eager to investigate this mystery.

These nights filled with moonlight and jungle chants brought a new uneasiness, for they took me back to that evening when Cervelión's hut had been turned into a chapel for the dark uses of witchcraft. I was not at all convinced of my own innocence in that conspiracy with the hidden powers. Perhaps I should have told Federico about it, thus revealing Cervelión's secret; but I was not sure what I thought about the whole affair, and with every passing day such a confession seemed more difficult to make.

The church at Goaiguaza was kept open at night during this time, like a heavenly antenna raised to control and direct the savage fervor in the villages. Those who do not understand these things think that this jungle madness, this barbaric rapture that at times takes on some of the aspects of epilepsy, is an expression of great joy. Actually, it is the spilling over of a racial agony, an unconscious search for redemption. The cries of these men and women are the cries of the earth. The dancing recalls the swaying of trees whipped by the storm. The little figures of St. John, roughly carved and dressed in ridiculous city clothes, are nothing but stylized fetishes which the Negroes accept by a kind of tacit agreement. In June these images escape from the village chapels and return to the jungle, where for a month they reassume their diabolical primitivism.

The statue from the church at Goaiguaza had been moved to the exact center of the adjacent park. It stood on a platform surrounded by bonfires. In its blood-red cape and its straw hat hung with ribbons of every color, it was a glittering spectacle. A crowd of Negroes of all ages, in every conceivable attire, was milling wildly about the platform, like a liquid that was kept at the boil by the heat of the fires. Three drums of different sizes and shapes, made from large tree trunks, rested on the ground; some of the men carried smaller drums at their sides. Federico looked on, open-mouthed. All at once three powerful Negroes straddled the large drums and began beating the taut leather heads with their hands. A woman screamed, and others answered her. What were they crying? I couldn't understand a word. I stood there as if in a dream, and reflected that the word is servitude's most degrading tool, for it weighs down the spirit. The sound of freedom is the howl. These Negroes were almost free, for they were screaming.

Men and women joined in the wild uproar for some time. Then, as though cut down by an invisible knife, the flower of the voices fell lifeless at the saint's feet. The only sounds were the deep throbbing of the big drums and the rattling of sticks against the wood of the drum shells. One of these drums is called the *pujao*; it has a deep, muffled voice that beats like a stone deep in the earth. I liked this one best, and tried to separate its sound from the others. The *pujao* kept repeating: *Cumboto . . . Cumboto . . . Cumboto . . .*

The hoarse concert came to an end, and the small portable drums began to speak. Their beat was high, rapid, and insolent. Voices leaped up to join them in a satyric duet. Now it was time for bodies to speak, too. As soon as this new phase of the frenzied ceremony had begun, we saw a woman advance to the center of the group; she was as dark and sinuous as a serpent. In her long, kinky hair she wore a bunch of wild flowers.

Her eyes were two coals in the handsome face that glistened like tarnished silver; her full, moist, half-open lips trembled with all the passion of the earth. She stood defiantly with her hands on her hips, then flung back her shoulders to reveal the smooth outline of her belly and the flat slope of her pubes between the quivering columns of her thighs. Her whole being vibrated like a guitar string. At that moment a young mulatto leaped out from the crowd, bringing to the drama of the dance all his savage and primal force. The newcomer played the role of conqueror deftly and gracefully, like a cock strutting around a hen. But in this case the female proved to be more agile, more graceful, and more dominating than the male. He retired in defeat before her superiority. She was then free to choose another partner, a mate worthy of her beauty. Confidently, she described a wide arc with the grace of a bird in flight, and another mulatto came to face her. In his right hand he held his beribboned straw hat, and in his left a *vera* wood cane. Not until that moment did I recognize the girl. It was Pascua!

That's who it was, all right: Anita's granddaughter, our childhood companion. I knew her in spite of the changes wrought by the years. When I turned to look at Federico, he was standing there entranced. His face seemed to be running blood where the knives of the flames slashed his face.

I don't recall what happened immediately after that. I only know that seeing that dance, that had been conceived in the mists of the jungle, brought about a change in our lives. Our walks now had a destination; we no longer set out at random. I followed Federico more closely than ever, although I was troubled by certain strange misgivings I had never felt before.

It is surprising how a man's face can change from one day to the next, even from one minute to the next. All of a sudden Federico dropped the distant, cool attitude he had brought back from Europe; now everything he did was accompanied by a kind of astonished excitement. His eyes lit up, his lips learned to speak, and—what was even more extraordinary—he began to smile. He took pleasure in discussing the things that had happened to him with the person closest at hand: me. He did this, I should say, only when we were at home.

Sometimes when I was serving him at the table or when he was at the piano playing something light and cheerful, he would talk about the plantation, or coconut oil, or cattle, or the people we had met on our walks. It was true that the property had deteriorated a great deal through lack of attention—Don Serafín was getting old—but Federico spoke enthusiastically of restoring it to its former splendor. There had been a time when he was tempted to sell it and return to Europe; but that had been merely a passing whim. He would not think of it now.

"You can't imagine," he said in a sudden fit of confidence, "what it's like living in Europe. There's beauty and culture and fun, and you can do whatever you like. For someone like myself who grew up there, it's very hard to get used to living here. My sister will never come back. But I did . . ."

Something in those recollections must have been painful, for he cut the conversation short. Luckily, the wound was superficial, and he soon recovered. At times he seemed like a child again, back in the days of our escapades and wanderings. He never mentioned his real reason for going to Goaiguaza every afternoon—and sometimes in the morning—but I knew perfectly well what it was. It's a long way. Sometimes he ordered the gig brought out, and I followed on a mule.

The first time I saw him talking to Pascua was one Sunday after the fiestas. It must have been a difficult decision for him to make. Whether it was shyness or racial prejudice, something had been holding him back; but he was being consumed by a fire that burned higher every moment. We often found her in the square in front of the church, strolling about with the other village girls who filled the air with their chatter and laughter. It was Pascua who laughed the loudest. She must have known that she had attracted Federico's attention—women have a sixth sense that might be called sexual intuition—judging from the way she behaved when he was around. I could see that at once. I believe, too, that she had recognized us the moment she saw us. As soon as we came in sight her laughter took on provocative, sinuous overtones; her words came gushing out like the melodious song of a thrush. When she talked or laughed she was like a dark, fluttering bird; when she danced she was like a serpent. She confused me, making me think of the old riddles of early evolutionary stages. I saw in her something of the bird and something of the reptile; the Coronela who came flying to perch on Venancio's shoulder, and the rattlesnake Herr Gunther had strangled with his noose.

Meanwhile, Federico stood in front of the church, went inside, came out again, and then pretended to examine the water in a nearby stream. When he thought no one was looking he raised his eyes to stare at her greedily. I did the same, and felt a wave of desire running through my veins. There were disturbing swellings on her slender body. Her hips were firm and lean like those of a splendid mare; her legs were long and muscular. Her small breasts lifted the thin material of her blouse, showing dark through the cloth. She must have smelled of pepper and limes.

That Sunday morning she and her friends started down the road to the river, and Federico followed them at a distance. As they descended the river bank to the beach, which lay in the shade of a large stand of bamboo like a similar spot in Cumboto, he stood in the road and pretended to inspect, with all the interest of a botanist, some tall breadfruit trees. Keeping at a prudent distance, I went through the fence and spied on them through the bushes. They were chattering and teasing Pascua about the little *Musiú* who was afraid to speak to her. The poor thing! Imagine coming all this way to make eyes at a girl like her! And when she's engaged, too, to a mulatto as jealous as José del Carmen!

I don't know if Federico could hear what they were saying from where he stood on the road. I didn't miss a word. My heart sank when I heard the name of that terrible José. There are advantages to being a spy. I was able to watch the bathers at my ease as they took off their clothes under the dense bamboo. Actually, they didn't take everything off; they kept on that inner garment, fragrant with intimate odors, which the village people call a

"tunic." It is so thin, however, that through it you can see the most tempting outlines. This tunic is the Venezuelan peasant's bathing suit. In the water it fills with air and balloons out over the surface for a moment like a huge lily pad; then it clings to the body, revealing every detail.

As I crouched there in my hiding place, eyes staring and nostrils trembling, I saw once more Pascua's sinuous body. Her dark skin showed through the clinging cloth like tarnished silver. Her small breasts stood up defiantly, and under the folds of the material little streams of water from her navel traced arabesques in her black pubic hair. Here was the serpent transformed, with arms and legs and gossip and giggles.

It was a long, noisy, exhausting bath. The dark bacchantes splashed about in the swimming hole; then, weary at last, they came out and began to put on their clothes languidly. As they pulled their dresses over their heads the dripping tunics fell about their ankles like the skin shed by snakes. Slowly and lazily they climbed back up to the road, filled with a sweet melancholy. Some of them picked flowers to put in their damp hair.

Federico was still bravely waiting there. I couldn't help smiling as I saw him go up to the girls and take off his hat. They seemed embarrassed. Then, with unsuspected daring, he fell in beside Pascua. I don't know what he said to her, nor what she answered. As they talked he poked the ground with a slender piece of bamboo he had cut with his pocketknife.

The next morning he was all smiles.

"I want you to come with me this afternoon and meet an old friend."

Afraid of betraying my feelings, I simply nodded. I would be near Pascua again; I would speak to her. I was excited all day, and when it was time to leave my heart began to pound brutally. This time he and I rode together in the little buggy. When we reached the village we crossed the plaza and went down a road I had never seen before. Soon we stopped in front of a small house that stood in the shade of several gigantic *bucare* trees. The setting reminded me of Cumboto. Federico knocked at the door and Pascua herself came running to open it. She was barefoot.

"This is Natividad," he said, smiling. "Do you remember him?"

But she didn't remember, or pretended that she didn't.

"I don't believe you," he said in a mocking tone. "Stop teasing and shake hands with him."

"*Hombre*! Don't be silly! Of course I remember him!"

But she didn't offer her hand.

All my happiness came tumbling down in that silent catastrophe. She had always been unfriendly toward me. Why? There was some hidden reason, but I had never wanted to know what it was. I would have been overjoyed if someone had told me, for example, "She doesn't like you because the day you first met you called her grandmother 'old Ana.'" But no one was ever going to tell me that, for the simple reason that that was not why Pascua despised me.

I followed them silently into the little living room. Federico turned to me and said, with such kindness that I was amazed, "Get ready for another surprise. Come along."

How delighted he was! His happiness showed in his face as Pascua accompanied us, her naked feet as slender and agile as two reptiles.

We went through a narrow hallway with a dirt floor and entered the kitchen. There sat Grandmother Anita, huddled in her old rocking chair, wearing her brightly-colored shawl and her enormous hat with its shiny brim. It was amazing. More than a hundred years weighed on that bent figure with its withered, black flesh and yet they had been powerless to destroy her iron will to live. All the bitterness that had shriveled my heart a moment before disappeared like a little dust, blown away by the loving breath of her presence.

"You're Natividad. Yes, I knew I'd see you again some day."

"You knew, Granny?"

"I was sure of it. We old people know a lot of things that you youngsters don't understand. I knew you hadn't forgotten me."

I pulled up a chair and sat down beside her. Just as she had done that afternoon when she was leaving Cumboto, she put out a wavering hand that was like a small, blind animal, and felt for me. Slowly, painfully, clumsily, she reached my chest; but that was the limit of her strength. I had to lift her hand to my face. Her fingers were stiff, like a charred root in my hand. Her whole being was a geological outcrop, an affirmation of the strength of the earth.

I overwhelmed her with questions. What about the trunk? Did she still make *calás*? Did she still tell her ghost stories? She shook her head. It had been a long time since she had cooked anything or told a story. Who was there to tell them to? Ernesto had been killed in a fight. Prudencio had left, just as her son Fernando had done, to seek his fortune. As if you had to go out and look for it! Pascua had other things to think about. She was in love, and was going to marry a boy named José del Carmen. The old lady lived in her solitude, in the deep river of her memories; she was tied to her rocking chair, visited by friends who spoke only in silence.

Pascua looked in from the hall, where she had been talking with Federico.

"She doesn't sleep. She just sits like that all the time. We try all kinds of medicine."

"Why should I sleep?" Anita retorted. "You young people can sleep. You haven't started counting the hours yet."

Pascua was still walking about in her bare feet in the most casual way. Federico looked down at them, frowning. All at once she burst out laughing.

"What you staring at me for? You want some coffee?"

June was still throbbing in the depths of the jungle.

Let There Be Light

That was definitely to be a time of surprises. No sooner had I recovered from one than another came along; my life was jerked about at the whim of an impish destiny. A few days after I had found Grandmother Anita again, the mulatto I had seen two months earlier in the park at Goaiguaza appeared at the White House. He said he wanted to speak to "Señor Zeus." Federico was in his bath at the time, and called out to me, "See what the gentleman wants, Natividad. I'll be down in a minute."

The visitor was wearing a straw-colored suit. I showed him to a seat in the living room and stood there looking him over. He was a strongly-built man, with a marked tendency toward obesity. His curly, unruly hair was quite gray, and the white at his temples gave his face the flat tone of a badly-developed photograph, a colorless look that he had surely not had in younger days, when his black hair must have lent him an air of virility. I reflected that Federico, without even seeing him, had referred to him as "the gentleman," and I agreed that he had used the right word. I adapted myself automatically to the circumstances.

"Señor Zeus has asked me to make you comfortable until he comes down. Do you mind waiting a moment?"

He smiled.

"Thank you. I have plenty of time."

His eyes wandered over the living room, inspecting the furniture, the pictures, and the carved wood of the ceiling. I took his hat and hung it up. It was made of gray felt, creased down the middle, with a narrow, curved brim of a lighter gray. "He must be a politician," I said to myself, without quite knowing why. His hand resting on the arm of the chair was dark but very clean and well cared-for; his nails gleamed, and on his third finger he wore a beautiful gold ring adorned with blue enamel. He began talking in a calm voice, not looking at me.

"The object of my visit is a very personal one, and it may seem—what shall I say?—a little odd, rather singular. Perhaps you can tell me . . . To be brief, I would like to know where I can find an old colored woman called Ana."

"Ana?"

The visitor must have noticed my reaction, for he looked at me with raised eyebrows.

"Do you know her?"

A wave of mingled emotions, of suspicion, and of memories suddenly washed over me. I answered with another question.

"Are you a relative of hers?"

He leaned back in his chair and began playing with the delicate gold chain that hung across his vest, gazing intently into my face.

"Why do you ask? Do you see a resemblance?"

He saw my confusion, and a sardonic smile came to his thick lips. He raised his hand and let it fall again with a weary gesture. Then he said in a different tone: "It wouldn't be surprising. I'm her grandson."

I was dumfounded. I didn't know what to say or do. With every word he spoke I was more upset by his confident, slightly mocking air; but at the same time I felt drawn to him.

"'Don't be embarrassed," he said, still smiling. "I realize that conversations like this between people like ourselves are awkward—especially when they take place in a house such as this, which is called, if I'm not mistaken, the White House."

In my now intolerable confusion, the worst impertinence of all occurred to me. I apologized. He merely laughed quietly.

"Why are you apologizing? Do you think I'm affected by such things? No, my boy. You're still very young. I have lived through things you couldn't even imagine. But to return to our subject. We've established the fact that you know my grandmother. Can you tell me where I can find her?"

All at once I began to relax. The embarrassment I had felt earlier was succeeded by a feeling of gentle seduction, a kind of rapture, in the presence of this man who brought to life the world of legend and fantasy evoked by the name of Grandmother Anita's son Fernando. Here before me was the offspring of that fabulous being who had abandoned his mother, his family, and his village to go to a different world and attempt the most ambitious and hopeless of all human experiments: to turn black into white, to transform night into day. This gentleman, drumming softly on the arm of his chair with dusky, immaculate fingers, was even more interesting than his father, the runaway Fernando. Fernando had been the experimenter; this man was the result of that experiment.

"You people never cared a thing about her," I said, so harshly that I surprised myself. I don't know what had happened to me to make me speak that way. I expected him to show some sign of resentment; instead he just sat there, regarding me with his rather prominent, bloodshot eyes.

"Apparently you're not aware that we've been living elsewhere. My father left this country when he was very young, and we children were brought up far from here."

He paused, as though searching for words, and then went on: "Whatever my father may have done when he was young, or how he treated his mother, are matters on which I have always refused to pass judgment. You'll understand this . . . some day. He's dead now, resting far away from the country he loved. You may not believe this, but as he was dying his most urgent request was that we find his mother and kiss her in his name. As I was the oldest, he took me by the hand and said, 'Fernando, find her and ask her to forgive me.'"

I was thrown into confusion again, but in a different way this time. I was on the point of being touched. In order to escape—in those days I was beginning to react intellectually against sentimentality—I asked myself: "Why is he telling me all this? Would he do the same with Federico? Is he so carried away with emotion that he's forgotten he's talking to a servant, or is this just a pose?" I decided to find out by reminding him of my position.

"The master will be down soon."

He looked down for a moment, and then raised his eyes to my face.

"I don't think I really need to see him now. You said you knew where my grandmother lived. Or perhaps you have to ask your master's permission before you can tell me?"

The arrow plunged into my chest and stuck there, quivering. At that moment Federico came downstairs. I explained the situation briefly, expecting to hear some objection; but he heard me out politely, with no change of expression. When I had finished, he said, "You know where to find her. You may go with the gentleman, if you like."

We went in the carriage that had brought Anita's grandson from the city. When I took my place beside him my face was burning as though it had been cooking over a slow fire. Federico's final words, spoken with such indifference, had not been exactly an order, nor even a request. He had given his permission, in a vague, elastic, and humiliating way. "You may go with the gentleman, if you like." And only a moment before the visitor had asked, with cutting sarcasm, "Or perhaps you have to ask your master's permission before you can tell me?" He had come closer to the mark than he had expected. And now what? I cast a furtive glance at his face, expecting to be greeted by his sardonic smile; but instead he was grave and thoughtful. There was a melancholy look in his eyes.

An odd thought came to me: this man must bear the same name as Federico and myself—Lamarca. For a while, as the horses trotted along in a cloud of golden dust, I thought about names. The very idea intrigued me. Zeus-Lamarca, Zeus y Lamarca, Zeus de Lamarca—Federico could sign a letter in any one of these three ways. He inherited the first element from his father and the second from his mother. I, as a servant born of unknown parents on the plantation, should use (although I never had) Doña Beatriz's family name—

or, rather, old Don Lorenzo's. The "gentleman" who rode beside me, this melancholy, polite mulatto with his straw-colored suit, his gold watch chain, and his enameled ring, would *have* to use the same name, since he was the descendant of slaves who had belonged to the family. This was the tradition—which is to say, the law. The words I heard on Grandmother Anita's lips when I was a child came back to me now with astonishing clarity. As she was showing us the fascinating daguerreotypes she kept in her trunk, she had told me: "These were my grandfather Mamerto's masters. If they ever came back they'd be my masters—and yours, too."

"I know this landscape," said my companion, coming out of his reverie. "My father used to describe it to me. These were the scenes of his childhood. He lived here until he was fifteen."

He put his hand—the one with the ring—on my knee in a friendly way, and smiled in his sardonic fashion. I put myself on my guard.

"Excuse me for talking about these things. You're probably thinking, 'What do I care what happened to this man's father?' But perhaps you're wrong. You might find it interesting. I'm sure you would have loved him. He was the best and most generous of men. He had his own ideas about life, about education, and about this thing called 'race.' He was not a pure-blooded Negro, like his mother. These people here have a mistaken idea of what he was like. Even his own mother didn't understand him. I tell you quite frankly that even today I don't know how to judge him. Did he do the right thing, or was he wrong? His father was white—a well-educated man named Fernando Burgos, a lawyer and politician who visited Cumboto several times with General Páez. His father promised to take him to the capital and see to his education. Unfortunately he died before he could carry out his plan. My father was convinced that the Negro must emancipate himself, not only from the protection of the white man but from this horrible pigment that is more degrading than any sin."

He stopped and looked at me. Then he asked:

"Did you notice how your . . . employer received me?" (His desire to be tactful was obvious.) "All he knows about me is that I'm a mulatto, a descendant of slaves who once belonged to his family. When he saw me he must have thought, 'What's this fellow doing running around loose?' He doesn't know that I have a university degree, that I speak several languages, or that I've published a book on tropical diseases. None of these things matter. As far as he's concerned, I'm no more than a thief. I've stolen something from him: my life, my own destiny."

The carriage was flying along the road. People stared at us as we went by. When they saw me sitting beside that elegantly-dressed figure they must have said to themselves, "Look at that black boy trying to mingle with the quality!" I didn't care what they thought. I was enchanted by my companion's conversation. He was a doctor, he told me. From a leather wallet with gold corners he took a pretty little card and handed it to me.

DR. FERNANDO ARGUÍNDEGUI, M.D.

TROPICAL DISEASES

Universities of Paris,
Berlin, and Rome

As I held the card in my hand he launched into confidences of a different kind. His father—it was true, and he was not going to deny it—had wanted to marry a white woman in order to improve the race. "To emancipate his children," as he had put it. And he had done so. After the unspeakable joy of seeing himself reproduced in two white children with flaxen curls, his last child, a boy, was born black. This was one of the things he wanted to tell Anita to console her for the loss of the son she had never forgotten. His father's great tragedy had its comic aspects: the white children changed color as they grew older. They took on a coarse, dirty shade of gray; their skin turned opaque, like that of fruit plucked from the tree too soon; their hair changed to a mottled yellow, like dishwater, and became stiff and kinky; and their variegated eyes glistened with a feline sensuality.

He explained these depressing phenomena by telling me about certain theories of inherited characteristics, about pigment, and about cross sections of human hair. I remember vaguely such words as 'homozygotes' and 'heterozygotes.' He also spoke of spiritual and pathological heredity. He had some striking ideas about the Spaniards. Their classification as members of the white race was very questionable; and yet they were the most insolent in their prejudice. They had made no contribution toward a true civilization, beyond sowing the world with their filthy, narrow-minded priests. He seemed to grow more furious with every word.

"These things make me feel sorry for other people, not for myself. Whenever I return to any of the cities where I have lived—Paris, Berlin, or Rome —I have to erect a solid wall of indifference between myself and the barbaric malice of my compatriots. They'll never be able to escape from themselves. They're frivolous, inept, and idiotic. In a poverty-stricken, servile society, whose members are prouder of what they have inherited than of what they have won for themselves, everyone boasts of being a descendant, but no one wants to be an ancestor. I've been subjected to the most amusing humiliations. I've been called black in every possible tone of voice. Those who are more educated refer to it discreetly, with everything from little smiles of polite delicacy to affable venom; the braver ones say it to my face. Some of them have had to get drunk first—or pretend they were—to work up the courage. Few of us are very brave without being drunk. I've been snubbed by tarts from noble families, who were not above sneaking up to the garret with the butler but who felt disgraced if they had to speak to a 'black' on the street. Worthless lads, thieves, adulterers, swindlers, and boys with pretty faces and wavy hair have looked down their noses at me. But funniest of all, those with some Negro blood who bear the racial stigma are quick to snub me, so that they won't be involved in some monstrous, indefinable complicity. Go to the capital, and you'll see thousands of white people walking down the street with features that betray Negro blood. They all have it. During the colonial period the white ladies had nobody to amuse them at siesta time except their Negro slaves. But they all try to hide it."

His smile hovered like a wasp. After a pause, he went on: "Have you ever looked carefully at the man you work for? I suggest that you do so. You're black, but at least you're healthy. I'm not saying that you should leave him. He's a poor, unhappy soul who needs somebody to watch over him. His mother was crazy. Is she still alive? Somewhere among her ancestors there must have been syphilis—the Neapolitan disease, they used to call it. Or perhaps alcoholism, or maybe some indiscretion with a 'black.' "

When we reached the outskirts of Goaiguaza I was relieved; I felt as if I were awakening from a monstrous nightmare. The slow, sinuous metamorphosis that had taken place before my eyes during the journey had filled me with dread, and yet at the same time had made me feel almost affectionate toward the man. Dr. Arguíndegui had never raised his voice. His face had never lost its serene expression. He had never once made a gesture that was not in good taste, as though every one had been rehearsed. But his final words dripped venom; the subtleties of his mind only made their rancor seem more terrible.

We returned almost at once, for his visit with Anita was a short one. I had decided to wait in the carriage. Pascua was home at the time; when she came out to see the visitor off her initial curiosity had changed to active dislike. Dr. Arguíndegui seemed depressed and disappointed.

"She's terribly old," he murmured as he got into the carriage. "It's amazing how long she's lived."

We rode for a while in silence. Then he said in a low voice: "How black she is! Much blacker than I expected."

And then, suddenly, I remembered something that had been fluttering around in my mind like a bird in a cage.

"Your name is Arguíndegui? I thought it would be Lamarca."

He looked at me in surprise.

"Lamarca? Why?"

"Wasn't that your great-grandfather's masters' name?"

"Who ever told you that? His masters were the Arguíndeguis, descendants of the Basques who founded Puerto Cabello."

Again he smiled his sardonic smile.

"Someone's been lying to you. Don Lorenzo Lamarca, your . . . employer's grandfather, acquired Cumboto by foreclosing a mortgage about forty years ago. He got the property for ten thousand pesos. Grandmother Anita can tell you the story. My father got the facts from some letters she had. Ask her about it."

We made the rest of the trip in silence. As I thought about it, I recalled that Anita had, in fact, mentioned the Arguíndeguis—Don Carlos and María Belén—and had said that they had been her masters when she was a girl. When we arrived at the gate to Cumboto and I was about to get out of the carriage, the doctor put his hand on my arm.

"Do you know what 'Arguíndegui' means in the Basque language? 'Let there be light.' Don't look like that," he said with gentle fury. "I'm not lying to you. If you don't believe me, ask someone. It means 'Let there be light.' I'm trying to spread some light in the world. Why don't you do the same?"

PART FOUR: *Fury*

The Tempest

The flame that had been set burning in Goaiguaza at the time of the June bonfires soon grew into a conflagration. At first it smoldered, like the beginnings of combustion in rotting straw. Then telltale wisps of smoke appeared, and finally it became a roaring tempest. In its midst there dangled a twisting skeleton—a young, white skeleton.

I know how Federico fought against the passion that was overwhelming him. I saw him pacing up and down all night long in the living room, taking down book after book from the library shelves, dashing out into the garden to stare up at the stars, his features distorted by the contempt he felt for his flesh. On the two or three occasions when he resisted the impulse to go to Goaiguaza, he took walks in the opposite direction, through the palm grove on "the other side" to the beach. He was in the clutches of a cold fury that drove him to throw himself against the thorns of bramble bushes and into ponds filled with toads and creeping things.

I pursued him there, too, like a shadow. The scene reminded me of certain unsolved riddles. It was here that Eduvige had made me chop down the *totumos*—the gourd trees that Herr Gunter had identified as *crescentia cujete* —and farther on was the spot where I had watched Federico's uncle pacing off mysterious distances with a map in his hand. What had he been trying to find? No one knew but Eduvige. Or perhaps Doña Beatriz. Nothing more had been heard of Herr Gunter or his daughter, Little Lotha. They seemed to have been forgotten; since that scene with the skull, Federico and his mother had been careful never to mention their names. And what about Eduvige? She was still at the house, as stiff and silent and ghostly as ever. She knew everything and knew nothing. But I didn't think about her mysterious behavior much any more; I was too busy worrying about my young master.

I must say once more that I did not love the sea. It brought back painful memories. It reminded me of Don Guillermo's death. Not that I had loved him—but Federico was his son, and I still owed that debt of loyalty. No one who lived in Cumboto—except possibly its owners—felt drawn to the sea. The nearest hut stood more than a league from the beach. Many of the Negroes who lived among the coconut trees on "the other side" had never been down to the rocks and had never seen a wave. Negroes are not fond of the ocean, and least of all those from Cumboto; the racial memory of crossing it as fugitives still lives in their minds. Sometimes the waves, too, seem to be saying, "Cumboto . . . Cumboto . . ." I noticed that now, as I found myself there in this new phase of our lives.

But this blind wandering was only a momentary reaction, a kind of unsuc-

cessful experiment. Convinced at last that no change of scene could liberate him from his passion, Federico decided to give himself up to it; he was like a castaway who closes his eyes and puts himself in the hands of God. When he resumed his visits to Goaiguaza there was a gleam in his eye that made me think of a desperate drug addict who has found out where the morphine is kept and is on his way to steal it. He went joyously, at peace with his conscience. "You see?" he seemed to be saying to himself, "You've fought and you've lost. There's nothing more you can do. Give up."

From then on it was pure madness. They met in the woods like two happy animals. It would be useless for me to pretend that I was not draining the cup of humiliation. I spied on them with the same insane, fierce determination that they displayed in their sin. I followed them through the brambles, lacerating my flesh, dragging myself along like a lizard, filled with a servile envy, burning with a deep, secret lust, finding a kind of delight and ambiguous satisfaction in the proof of my impotence.

Pascua's silvery body held no secrets from my eyes. Lying in the grass far from the village, they would caress each other to the fainting point and moan and roll about. When her clothing was stripped off she was all flame and serpent. She clamped his body between her soft, powerful thighs as though she were trying to squeeze him dry. I searched my memory in vain for anything comparable. I thought about taking Pastora in the dead leaves, and angrily spit out the memory at once. Pastora was as cold and damp as a rotten tree trunk; Pascua burned like the June bonfires. Serpent and flame. I watched her drowning in a sea of sensuality, wound around Federico's body, her mouth crushed against his, her trembling legs twisting and writhing, and I found myself moaning with them, transfixed and pinned to the earth with the same dagger.

This orgy took place every afternoon, day after day. Federico was exhausted. More than once, as I was following him back to the house, I was tempted to kill him—not out of envy or jealousy, but in disgust, simply to end the nightmare. It was like a cry that came from deep in my heart and threatened to burst my brain: "Kill him! Kill him!" But then came a terrible fear that blew out the voice like a candle: "No! No! You can't! What would become of you? What would become of all of us?"

At home he was impatient as he awaited the hour of their rendezvous. To pass the time he began to paint, at a little table near the large window that looked out on the sea. As I passed by one day I stood on tiptoe and looked over his shoulder; it was the figure of a naked woman: Pascua. There she stood, graceful and wanton, with her skin like tarnished silver. The background was a splendid tangle of vegetation. Behind her a bonfire was burning, and its lascivious tongues of flame seemed to lick her body. Tiny scales glistened on her skin, blood-red in the reflected firelight.

The same fire burst from the black box of the piano. One afternoon while Federico was playing, a handful of small wild figs fell at his feet. We both turned toward the window and saw Pascua looking in. Federico's consternation was indescribable. He ran toward her, then toward me, waving his arms. He raised his eyes apprehensively in the direction of Doña Beatriz's bedroom and turned pale. Then he came to me and muttered through clenched teeth:

"Please! Get her out of here! Hitch up the buggy . . ."

But Pascua was already in the room, caressing the polished floor with her feet. She strolled about and examined everything without a word, smiling, her fingers clasped under her chin in a mocking gesture. When she reached the piano she stopped and ran her thumbnail over the keys. Federico, paralyzed with fear, stood staring at the floor. I started toward the dining room door, but I stopped before I reached it. There towered the gray figure of Eduvige, regarding the scene with expressionless eyes.

"Did he bring her here?" she hissed.

"No, she came by herself."

"What's he going to do?"

I shrugged.

"He's scared."

But Eduvige corrected me: "Not scared. Ashamed. He's afraid his mother will see her and despise him." Then she added with icy contempt: "He doesn't know she hasn't been able to move from her bed since the night Herr Gunter tried to murder her."

"The night of the skull?"

I got no answer. Eduvige had disappeared. Pascua, meanwhile, had sat down at the piano and was pecking at the keys with fingers sharp as knives. Federico threw an anguished look in my direction; I reassured him by glancing up toward the second floor and shaking my head. He understood. Taking a deep breath, he said to the girl, "Are you satisfied?"

"No," she answered. "Play for me."

He hesitated. His anxiety returned, but only for a moment. He sat down meekly and began to play in a timid and stumbling way. He must have thought that his mother was listening. But gradually, as he entered into the marvelous world of music, all thoughts of living beings and mundane matters, all immediate concerns, vanished from his mind. His hands, with their reddish down, were pale, winged spiders weaving a crystalline net to ensnare us all. There were moments when they were not spiders but dragonflies; we watched as they skimmed skillfully over the surface of a deep pond, tracing delicate wounds in the water with their pointed glass tails. They were male and female in a tireless game of love. The left hand, flying over the basses with great power and spirit, was the male; the right, leaping lightly and frivolously over the treble like a bacchante, was the female. At times the two came together: the male sprang splendidly over the female and fell asleep, twitching gently. Federico was totally absorbed, every part of him dominated by those two restless, sensual hands: his head, his body, his eyes, his stern mouth, his trembling legs. Sometimes he sat tall and erect, with both arms stretched out nearly straight before him; sometimes he swayed and twisted as though in sudden agony.

He was playing Beethoven's *"Moonlight" Sonata*. Both hands stiffened on the keys, and then out of the silence surged the *adagio sostenuto* with its funereal cadence, like smoke from a censer. "They're weeping for Cruz María," I thought, leaping back to my childhood. "That, too, took place in the moonlight, and was filled with terrible pain." Swept along by my memories, I saw strange things. I saw Cervelión carrying the broken, bloody body in his black arms. He was laying it down on the ground; he was kneeling before a smoking pyre; his outstretched arms were turning into a huge, heavy serpent that took the shape of a wreath. Walking in the shadows—through this music of shadows—Cervelión was bringing his son's death to the White House, to leave it on the doorstep like an offering of hatred.

When Federico stopped playing, Pascua was kneeling ecstatically at his feet. She took his white hands in her dark, aggressive ones and caressed them. She gazed at them devotedly. She seemed blinded by their whiteness; their outlines awoke strange, superstitious feelings in her heart. She had seen them fly, flutter, and dance as though they were independent beings; they never made a false move. She kissed them passionately. She pressed them to her face. Pride in having been caressed by those fingers glowed in her eyes. Her body, too, was a piano, with its bass and treble. Although the only outward sign was a ripple that ran over her dark skin, the music was playing inside; when she was no longer able to contain it within her, it emerged as a trembling sigh, a moan, or a broken, incoherent cry.

Federico put his hand under her chin and raised her face to him.

"Once you said to me, 'You're not very strong, are you?' Do you remember?"

"I said that? I don't remember."

"It was that day we first went down to the river. There were my sister Gertrudis, Natividad, and I, and you joined us. Just before we got there, I had to stop and rest. I was a weak child, and so I never forgot what you said. I never mentioned it to anybody, but I kept thinking about your remark, turning it over in my mind. I used to dream about it. I never wanted to remind you of it until I was sure I could make you take it back."

"So you used to think about me?"

"No, not about you; only about what you had said. I had forgotten who had said it, or where, or what the circumstances had been. I kept thinking about it."

"And now, are you satisfied?"

"Yes."

"Thank God."

They sat there in silence, caressing each other, while I watched them from the dining room door. I was thinking about Doña Beatriz. She had not been able to rise from her bed for at least a year, and I had known nothing about it. Neither had her son. Only Eduvige knew. How horrible! When Pascua had appeared at the house, Federico had panicked at the thought that Doña

Beatriz might see her; but the moment he found out that his mother was help-less he was not only relieved but overjoyed. Now he felt he was in charge. Pascua had been won. There she was at his feet, like a dog, meek and loving.

On a sudden impulse he stood up and led her to the center of the room.

"Dance for me."

He spoke in exactly the same tone she had used when she commanded, "Play for me."

"I want you to dance. Take off your shoes."

At first she was taken aback; then she laughed delightedly and her mocking smile returned to her lips. She took off her shoes. As I looked at her bare feet I thought of the day we had visited her in Goaiguaza.

"Natividad," Federico commanded impatiently, "bring the rug from the library. Hurry!"

But she stopped me with a gesture.

"No. I like it better this way."

She moved her feet slowly, enjoying the contact of the cool floor. They were two sensual reptiles; every toenail glistened like an eye.

"What do you want me to dance?"

"Anything. Wait, I'll play for you."

There was a tense moment. As she looked at him, expectantly, her mocking smile gradually disappeared; an apprehensive look came over her face. Her eyes widened and her lips twitched. When Federico struck the keys she trembled from head to foot.

"Dance!"

"But what are you playing?" she demanded, terrified.

"The *Appassionata*. The *allegro* movement. Dance!"

"But how do you dance to that? I don't know it. I never heard it before."

"That doesn't matter," he cried, carried away by a sudden fury. "Dance any way you like, however you feel."

Then Pascua began to move; she stretched out her long, muscular legs, and put one foot forward as though she were about to enter a pool of icy water. Her hips began to sway with the serpentine rhythm I had seen on Saint John's Eve in the little square at Goaiguaza.

"That's it . . . that's it . . . keep dancing!"

The *allegro* is a swift whirlwind; then comes the *andante,* slow and solemn; and immediately the *allegro* again, this time interrupted by measures of silence and startling outbursts where the fingers skip about in the treble. Pascua had caught the rhythm and was surrendering joyfully to it, with wide-spread arms and gleaming, naked legs. Federico urged her on, nodding his head. The pace increased in a dizzying spiral, then suddenly dropped in a gentle, pensive *pianissimo,* only to rise again. It was marvelous to watch Pascua's tall, slender figure whirling about the room, running, halting, swaying, wonderfully anticipating the subtleties of music she had never heard before. The final furious convulsion left her exhausted. When the music stopped she fell limply to the floor and lay there fluttering like a wounded bird.

After that she came to the White House often, and her dancing became a ritual. They came to indulge in the wildest excesses. Federico painted her toenails red—the ten eyes of those two serpents. He made her dance naked. Beethoven was his favorite, but he also played works by other composers whom he admired: Bach's *Choral Preludes* and *Partita in C Minor*; Haydn's *Sonata in F Major*; Schumann's *Arabesques*; Mozart's *Sonata in B Flat Major*; Chopin's *Mazurkas*; Mendelssohn's *Songs Without Words.* She danced to them all, intuitively, improvising to the mad torrent of notes, the reflection of her dazzling nakedness gleaming in the motionless pond of the floor. Their theme was the *Appassionata,* which they preferred to call "The Tempest." They no longer had to hide in order to make love. She took her meals with him at the large dining room table, and spent hours poking about in the library, looking through the books, examining the contents of every drawer and shelf. She made fun of it all; nothing in the world mattered but love and music. Only three things in that room interested her: the silver wheelbarrow—and, of course, the spade that went with it; Herr Gunter's collection of insects and reptiles, which he had abandoned; and the album with the morocco binding and gold corners. She would turn over its stiff pages again and again. She, too, seemed to be fascinated by Doña Beatriz's youthful beauty; but she never referred to it. Whenever she talked with Federico she snuggled up to him, and in her voice there was so much warmth and passion that it was almost like an orgasm.

"Why don't you try writing some music of your own?" she said one afternoon. "You could put some of our life into it—our songs, our drums, our fields and rivers."

Another time she mentioned the organ that the little church in Goaiguaza needed. They had been trying to collect enough money to buy one for at least ten years. It would be a lovely gift, and God would be pleased. He would bless the man who gave it.

"Why don't you buy it for them?"

"Don't be silly."

Federico smiled, but he was annoyed.

"Why am I silly? Don't you believe in God?"

"I believe in truth, in art, in life. I hate sham."

"You think religion is sham?" she asked angrily.

He was flustered.

"No, I didn't say that. But why do we have to talk about things like this?"

But she was not to be appeased.

"I won't listen to you talk this way. We've already sinned enough without speaking against God."

She began putting on her shoes to leave. He took her by the hand.

"Don't pay any attention to what I said, silly. I just wanted to see you get angry. If you think an organ would make God happy, we'll write tomorrow and order one."

"And will you play it, too?"

"I'll play it, too."

Delighted, she threw her arms around his neck, as though a crushing weight had been lifted from her shoulders. She covered him with passionate kisses.

"You can play our 'Tempest' on it."

"In the church?" Federico said, stunned.

"Yes. Why not?"

Delirium

I don't know whether the notion came to her because of the discussion of the organ, or if she thought of the organ because she had already conceived the notion; in any case, the fact is that Pascua began going to church to pray every day, and insisted that Federico do the same. Now there was not a Sunday when we did not go to mass. When the priest addressed the congregation he never failed to shower effusive compliments on the pious owner of Cumboto for the magnificent contribution he had made to the church. "Without this proof of generosity and Christian zeal," he said one day, "we would never have had our organ. And he never misses mass, either. His is an example the other landowners would do well to follow, for the good of their souls and the encouragement of our communicants."

At these words Federico blushed down to his collar, and I turned the color of mulberries.

One Sunday when we were coming out of church I saw an obviously drunk man coming toward Federico. He was a powerfully-built young mulatto with a scarred face; I recognized him at once as one of the men who had danced with Pascua in the little square on St. John's Eve. I looked about and took in every detail of the scene. In the background, under the trees, stood a group of three villagers who were watching us and whispering; some women who had just came out of the church were standing near the door; and several youngsters who had been playing marbles a moment before were running across the square toward us. The mulatto had a club in his hand.

There are times when my mind works with prodigious speed, and this was one of them. I ran up to the men who were whispering under the trees and snatched a *vera*-wood club that one of them was holding under his arm. Then I ran to intercept the drunken mulatto. The man I had taken the club from shouted: "Look out, José del Carmen!"

I had no desire to get into a fight with the drunk—whose identity I had guessed at once—but only wanted to protect Federico. But José del Carmen, filled with the brutish exaltation of alcohol, gave me such a blow with his club on my left shoulder that I fell to my knees. Then I lost all sense of caution. The pain was blinding me, and I couldn't think. The blow might have dislocated my shoulder, but I could still use my right arm. I used it, and José del Carmen fell to the ground, covered with blood.

I remember hardly anything of what happened after that. I heard the distant voices of a group of men standing around us with angry eyes and tight mouths. Someone said, "Get some cobwebs to put on that cut." Another voice was insulting: "It's all that whore's fault!" The last one wounded me to the quick: "The black son of a bitch!" Racked with pain, I could dimly see Federico floating in a great, bloody cloud; he was leading the carriage-horse by the reins.

Unbearable days and nights went by. A Negro appeared from somewhere and put my shoulder bone back in place and bandaged me tightly, all the while saying something I didn't understand. The pain, the inability to sleep, and my lack of appetite made me lose an incredible amount of weight. Too, I was tormented by the fear that I had killed José del Carmen, and would have to spend long years in prison. All these miseries filled my convalescence with strange shadows and made it an interminable, roaring river of prayers, invocations, and incantations. With my *zamuro* seed clutched in my right hand and my mind swinging on a slender thread of terror, I recited every prayer I had ever learned. When I ran out of these, I made up my own. "O Almighty God, creator of Heaven and earth, I thank you from the bottom of my heart for all your goodness and kindness. Please don't abandon me now. I am worthless, Lord, and you will gain nothing by punishing me. Be good and generous. Cure my wounds without leaving any scar; save José del Carmen's life so they won't take me to prison; and keep me from the hatred of my enemies and from all evil and danger. Amen."

When I regained consciousness in my little room, I learned that Federico had carried me there in his arms. How could I ever thank him for his kindness! He could have left me there in Goaiguaza, at the mercy of those angry men who were thirsty for vengeance. It took courage to do what he did, to put me into the carriage and drive me home just to save my life. I had not seen him since; but I knew he was alive, and that was enough.

Gradually, I began to remember snatches of what I had seen and dreamed during those days of semiconsciousness. Some Negroes had come to see me, and I could hardly make out their faces through a thick, reddish mist. I was surrounded by a vast expanse of water, and then by an endless landscape that was illuminated by a sun I could not see. The Negroes bounced up and down as though they were made of rubber. There were some women who towered over the men like princesses. Something glittered in the distance, and there was a music that made me forget my pain. Everything had a primitive and absurd grandeur. The queen—a Negro who shone like obsidian—frowned solemnly. She seemed about to pass judgment on a criminal, and was brandishing a flashing scepter surmounted by a red flower that was open and moist like a vagina. She looked around her and announced that blood would soon be shed. Suddenly she began to foam and bubble, and turned into breakers, over which little dugout canoes were riding. Then the queen laughed and performed an obscene dance, her body naked and glistening. She summoned her courtiers and commanded, "Bring in the slaves!" And the slaves wore great chains around their necks. They were all white. Trembling with fear, they buried their faces between Her Majesty's black thighs.

Another of these visions was of Federico. He stood by my cot and showed me his marvelous hands. "Do you see? I'm a god. There are no secrets in this world I don't know. It all belongs to me. Once you told me, 'Walk!' Now nobody tells me what to do." He put his face very close to mine and went on: "Ever since you were a child you've dedicated yourself to me. You've lived only to serve me, to follow me like a shadow, haven't you?" I didn't know what to answer, because what he had said was absolutely true. I had often asked myself the same question without finding an answer. There was a time when I loved Federico because he stood for everything I would never be, everything I wanted to be. But after we had grown up the feeling that bound me to him could not have been called love. What was it, then? I had often been tempted to strangle him with both hands; but if we had been separated I would have suffered terribly. He spoke again: "You've probably longed to possess women like the ones who have offered themselves to me. I think you would gladly have leaped on Lotha or Pascua. Why didn't you? Tell me the truth."

Among the black visitors in my hallucinations were Cervelión and Grandmother Anita. The first repeated the things he had told me when I was a child: "You hang around the white people, but you're black all the way through. They're not going to teach you anything they know. You got to look alive if you want to live like a man." Had I lived like a man? No. I was no more than Federico's reflection, something less than a dog. The dog, after all, has a certain amount of free will; when he's driven by the sexual urge he breaks his chain. This was something I knew nothing of. I was a shadow. My mute passion for music, my secret desire to play like Federico one day, proved that. If I had told him of this dream, he would have been speechless with surprise, and then would have burst out laughing. He would have looked at my black hands with astonishment. No, I would never confess this. And yet I felt the fire of creation burning within me; I longed to express myself, to throw myself upon that magic instrument in which God or the devil had gathered together all the harmonies of existence. I would have learned quickly. I'm sure of that. I would have been a pianist at least as talented as he, and I would not have been hard and cruel. There must be some possibilities of expression in the instrument that Federico had never been able to bring out. It was this that Pascua had sensed: the possibility of depicting our own world, our trees and rivers, our red and furious blood.

Anita spoke of the Arguíndeguis, of Doña Beatriz, and of the general with the black beard. She brought me a present: her old mahogany trunk.

It was a long convalescence. I returned to reality very slowly, like a flower opening. Silence reigned in the White House, and I remained submerged in my thoughts even after I had regained all my mental and spiritual faculties. It was like lying in a soft, fragrant bed. But one day the mist suddenly lifted, and I became aware of the world about me. I realized that I had not seen Federico or Pascua, or heard the piano. What had happened?

I cornered the cook.

"Where is the master?" I asked.

She looked at me oddly.

"I don't know. We haven't seen him for days."

I ventured into the dining room and the garden, with my shoulder still bandaged and my arm in a sling. I strolled through the living room and the library. The house was empty. When I came across Eduvige's mummy figure I couldn't contain myself. I stopped her.

"Do you know where he went?"

"Yes. He's out looking for that . . . that woman."

"Looking for her? Why?"

"Because after that fuss in Goaiguaza she disappeared. She couldn't keep on living anywhere around here."

When I heard that I began to crumple inside. Eduvige looked at me for a moment, and then added: "There's that trunk somebody brought for him. I can imagine where it came from, and I think you'll recognize it."

They had put it in the library, under the big table. That's why I hadn't seen it. The sight of it filled me with an indefinable mixture of tenderness and dread. Why was Grandmother Anita's trunk here? Who had sent it to the White House? I tried to open it with trembling fingers, but it was locked. I ran to look for Eduvige.

"Have you got the key? Let me have it."

But she put me in my place with her serpent's glance.

"Yes, I've got it. But I'm not handing it over to anybody but him."

Grandmother Anita's Trunk

It was raining. High heaven was bilious, and winter's muddy blood was streaming over the wounds of the earth. When it rains there is a religious grandeur in the silence that transforms us. I think no one would dare play happy music at a time like this, when the fields have disappeared under their watery shroud.

I had been waiting for Federico for days, watching from the big window. At last, one night he arrived, soaked through, and went up to his room without a word. I had the cook make him some herb tea and took it up to him. He told me to bring the brandy. His face was like a stone that had been turned up with a pick and left standing in the rain until it was covered with a reddish lichen. It made me think of Gaspar de los Reyes. He was coughing. When he got into bed, shaking, I pulled the covers up to his chin and left.

I went up to see him the next morning and found him stretched out on his back like a corpse. I was afraid to speak to him. He refused lunch. I wished he would at least groan, or say something. Where had he been? I saw mud on his shoes and trousers; but he could have got that without leaving Cumboto, where there were mudholes everywhere. His eyes were open, and in them was a hopeless, faraway look.

On the fourth day, more out of apprehension than curiosity, I decided to say something to him. And an odd thing happened: I couldn't *tutear* him.

"Why don't you eat something?"

He dismissed me with an impatient gesture.

"You can't go on like this," I insisted. "You'll make yourself sick."

He answered that time.

"Do you think I'm not sick now?"

I was so overjoyed at hearing his voice that my words came tumbling out.

"You've got to pull yourself together. She'll come back."

"You don't know her. She'll never come back. I've been looking for her for a month. I've faced all those people who hate me. I've offered bribes, I've begged. Do you hear? I've begged—me! I've pleaded with that rabble. But nobody could tell me where she went. I've been in Morón, in Sanchón, even in San Felipe. Then I went to Borburata, San Esteban, and Patanemo. Nothing!"

"Did you go to see Grandmother Anita?"

"No."

"You should have. She would have told you. She sent you her trunk. Do you remember Grandmother Anita's trunk?"

He sat up in bed, his gray eyes fixed on mine.

"Grandmother Anita's trunk!"

"Yes. It's in the library. Eduvige has the key."

He got up, holding on to the head of the bed to keep from falling. I supported him with my good arm and helped him into his robe; then I took him downstairs. Eduvige handed over the key without a word. When the bell on the lock tinkled, I was so overcome with emotion that it was my turn to lean against something to keep from falling. All my past rang out in that jangling sound and came tumbling over me. My carefree, adventurous childhood, the colored crayons, the piano lessons, the blue donkeys, the path that led to the river, Frau Berza with her straw-colored hair, the black pony that galloped across the ancient newspaper, the colored portrait of Leo XIII, the names of perfumes printed on a chromolithographed almanac, the tales of demons and apparitions, the *calás*—it was all synthesized in one great essence that exploded in my heart like a charge of dynamite. Federico, sweating and shaking, had opened the trunk and was standing there contemplating the jumbled heap within. I stared, too, and my hands trembled.

Like two blind men, we reached out to touch and caress those things as though they were our very lives. There were the musical instruments—the mandolin, the violin, the little flute with its corroded keys—and the tiny Holland porcelain cups with their gilded rims, the gold and silver jewels, the brightly-colored clothing, the Madras scarves (like the one Anita wore) impregnated with ancient perfume. These were the old rags that had so fascinated Pascua. (I think she once went so far as to try some of them on.) And, most exciting of all, among these keepsakes were the four daguerreotypes that had been my favorites, and the little packet of letters, tied with a faded blue ribbon, that had so intrigued Federico.

The appearance of that trunk in the White House gave us a lot to think about, beginning with one question: Who had sent it? and ending with another: Why had they sent it? But in our fascination of the moment—as long as we were in the world of memory—we didn't think about that. We bent over the little trunk in silence. Every touch of our fingers, every caress, was an unanswered question. I took the daguerreotypes in my hand and looked at them for a long time, trying to discover the secret of the dark and light areas that reproduced the image. The two ladies and the two men looked out at me from a distant world, across the frontiers of nothingness. There was a time when I had thought they were Lamarcas; now I saw them as Arguíndeguis. Let there be light.

Meanwhile, Federico had untied the bundle of letters and was shuffling through them. There were at least a dozen, some long and some of them merely notes. The latter had been scrawled on scraps of paper, evidently in haste, perhaps furtively. Federico sat down in a chair with his back to the window and unfolded one of the large sheets of paper; its edges were brown and tattered, and it was covered with faded stains. Its creases were like cauterized wounds; the ink, which had in places eaten away the paper, had taken on the color of rust. I looked over Federico's shoulder and read along with him. I didn't stop to wonder whether I had that right; I simply did it.

The letter was almost illegible, for the most part, although I could make out a few words here and there. It was dated June, 1785, and was addressed to Andrés Arguíndegui.

My dear cousin:

As you can imagine . . . about the property you are occupying on the coast near Puerto Cabello, which is called Cumboto . . . seven leagues along the sea and . . . toward the mountain range that runs to the south. I have spoken . . . the consulate here . . . attorneys whom I trust, and they are all . . . it is as clear as day and cannot be challenged, as nearly as I can make out from . . . delivered by your slave Mamerto . . . this property since the founding of Puerto Cabello . . . the house established and staffed with faithful servants, with no interruption . . . Father Andrés was one of the founders of the city, two years after the company . . . since 1729, more than half a century . . . your brothers, and your ancestors were buried . . . you have? . . . I am eager to serve you. I have even discussed the meaning of your family name with these people: 'Let there be l . . . You Arguíndeguis have made . . . where our family has displayed great self-denial . . . I am returning it with this letter, and the assurance that . . .

. . . cousin, Rodrigo.

Whether Federico was able to read it all, or whether he was merely staring at the page blindly, he sat there with the letter in his hands for a long while. The fragments I had read made me think of the story Anita had told me that day when she had become so alarmed at my admiration for Roso. It all came back to me at the mention of the Arguíndeguis, the founders of Cumboto, the meaning of whose name had been explained to me by the mulatto doctor.

Federico had, in fact, been staring at the letter without seeing it. I had to take it gently from his hands and put another in its place before he returned to reality. He unfolded it slowly. This one had been written in 1836, and was almost entirely indecipherable. Most of it was one large, bluish stain, as though at some remote time it had been left out in the rain. Toward the end I was able to read:

. . . nine years when General Bolívar was defeated here and had to flee by ship. Then I remember that father had a party attended by many people from the port. You, who were a little older than the others, played the violin, and Francisco—may he rest in Glory—played the flute, and little Matilde the mandolin.

They made me recite a terribly long poem in homage to the kings of Spain. Then General Páez came. It seems to me that ever since then this great leader has had to bear all his country's burdens on his shoulders. He has just now defeated the rebels who deposed the President, and I have taken the old instruments out of the trunk again for my nieces and nephews and the servants to play. Little Carlos played the violin, and Ana, Mamerto's granddaughter, who is a gay, pretty Negress, played the mandolin very well. But since then things have gone from bad to worse. It looks like the work of the Evil One. Ana herself says, much to our amusement, that the men in this country have the devil in their bodies. I haven't seen your children for months, for your wife's family has moved to Quisandal, and they don't seem to care about me at all. I should tell you that Francisco's coconut plantation is coming along very slowly; the trees are hard to grow. But we have high hopes. I hope you will be able to come and help with all this. Write soon and encourage me, for I need it badly.

Your sister, María Belén.

It was the signature of that woman Grandmother Anita had told me about: General Páez's mistress. The "Ana" mentioned in the letter could only be Anita herself. In those days she played the mandolin and was pretty and gay. There were so many things the old lady hadn't told us! And why had she sent her trunk to the White House?

María Belén's name seemed to have awakened something in Federico, for he opened the third letter himself. It was from Curaçao—why Curaçao?— and was dated October 12, 1849.

Dear Matilde:

I don't know if this letter will reach you. I'm writing you because you're the only person who has escaped the horrible things that have happened to us. I don't know what has become of Simón since your father was put in prison and our property was confiscated by the tyrant. Give thanks to God that you were not here to see these terrible things. The soldiers came and pushed everybody about. When they captured our father and tied his hands behind his back, I lost my head and threw myself on them, calling them awful names. Then an officer with a huge, black mustache seized me by the arms and whispered in my ear: "Calm yourself, or they'll kill you. You don't know me, but I'm a cousin of yours. I am Jacinto Salcedo." And, Matilde, he was the son of Aurelia Arguíndegui, our grandfather's sister. So I was able to escape with my life, but not without seeing them beat Mamerto. He's such an old man, but that didn't stop them. They put the majordomo in the *cepo de campaña,* trying to make him tell where we kept our gold, and they shot two other servants like animals. I'll tell you now, so you'll know: there are ten thousand pesos (six hundred ounces) in gold buried in an earthenware pot at the foot of a gourd tree in the coconut grove they call "the other side." Mamerto has run away. Try to find him. I found out from a sailor that our poor father has been sent to a place called Bajo Seco, at Lake Maracaibo. In God's name, Matilde, try to get news of him and see if you can help him. My ears are still ringing with those angry cries: "Get the *godos*! Get the *godos*!" My dear sister, I'm not yet twenty-five and my hair has turned white. But it will give me courage to take my revenge. Tell Simón and his children that they must never forget and never forgive. Teach them to hate our executioners.

Your unhappy brother, Carlos.

Federico had forgotten his own troubles in the sweeping river of the past. Like myself, he was reliving the agony and sorrow of the dead who walked in Cumboto. Their feet had trod these very floors, they had read these very books, they had gazed out upon this landscape, now so gloomy and heavy with gray rain. The Arguíndeguis had written down the ancient history of the White House, with all its love, its gaiety, and its tears. Did Federico know the name, or was this the first time he had heard it? At that moment there was nothing to be seen in his eyes but the dying light of a dream; he was painfully pulling aside the curtains of that dream to let in the glare of reality.

The perusal of those letters was for Federico the beginning of a sudden, provocative self-examination. He had stumbled across an unexpected path that was leading him back to life. There were many who had lived, were living, and would live as he was at that moment: like floating snowflakes, unsupported by any contact with the earth of history. He had still not discovered anything, really; but now he knew there was something to be discovered. What was it?

He opened the next letter eagerly.

Puerto Cabello; January, 1853

Dear Carlos:

We have finally signed the papers turning over Cumboto. Simón did not want to sign because he is so angry with this Lorenzo Lamarca who claims to be a relative of ours and has hounded us so mercilessly. But we had to accept ten thousand pesos. What else could we have done under the circumstances? Simón hasn't a single suit of clothes; I haven't been able to go out on the street for years; the children need to be educated; and you need money, too, if you're going to get ahead in that horrible wilderness from which God knows if you'll ever return. Sometimes I despair and lose all my faith. Will this nightmare never end? No one even mentions General Páez any more; it's as though he were dead. How easily our people forget!

Our final attempts to find the ten thousand pesos you buried in Cumboto were useless. Mamerto, as you know, was killed by a mule; although he was over a hundred, he still worked and walked everywhere like a boy, accompanied by his granddaughter Anita, who is as great a walker as he. This Anita still has the trunk you left with her grandfather, but no matter how we try we can't find her. As you can understand, I've kept the most important secret—if that damned Lorenzo doesn't sniff it out and find the money. I'm enclosing a copy of the mortgage. Write me when you can.

Your sister who loves you,
Matilde Arguíndegui de Alba.

When Federico finished this letter, the storm that was brewing inside could be seen in his frown. Everything had been revealed in that tiny, careful script penned by Matilde Arguíndegui, the spreader of light. And this Lorenzo Lamarca was the dignified master who had been held in such respect by the Negroes and whites of the neighborhood! His grandfather, the feudal lord! What a contrast between the lives of those two grandfathers—Mamerto and Lorenzo Lamarca!

The little notes were tied in a separate bundle with a yellowed ribbon that Federico snapped with a flick of his finger. He was visibly upset. I don't know if he had noticed that I had been reading along with him. If he had, he paid no attention. Why should the spirit care what the shadow does?

There were seven notes, like the leagues of Cumboto. Some of them were mere scraps of paper with only two or three words.

Dear Jaime:
The poem you wrote for my birthday was lovely. But you're mistaken; it wasn't my sixteenth, but my fifteenth.

There was no signature.

I don't know why I love you . . . I'm afraid, but I'll meet you at the mango tree tonight if you wish. Eduvige is on our side, and so is Anita. You can write

to me through either of them. I'll do the same. Don't write a very long letter. Until tonight, with kisses from your

B.

Don't come tonight. Father suspects something.

No signature.

Eduvige will tell you what to do. I can't hide my suffering any longer. If father finds out he'll kill me.

Bea . . .

I can't.

No signature.

I don't know how I'm going to get this letter to you. Father has made me tell him everything. Everything. You must leave Cumboto at once. They're going to kill you.

No signature.

My beloved Jaime:
I'm writing this in great haste and running a terrible risk. But I mustn't keep it from you. Our baby son was born last night; I don't know whether he's handsome or ugly. I'm afraid they'll take him away from me and do something horrible to him. Father is furious, but Eduvige is still on our side. How good she is! She has sworn to save the little boy no matter what happens. I trust her. Why are you still in Cumboto?

B.

At the bottom of this letter there was a note written in another hand.

Federico read it, shaking. It was a biographical notation added by some meticulous hand of the type who enjoys filling in the lacunas of history.

Jaime Rojas, schoolmaster and piano teacher. Dark, with curly hair, green eyes, tall and goodlooking. He was Don L———'s daughter's teacher. Disappeared without a trace. It is said the old man had him murdered and buried on "the other side."

Federico stood up without a word, with no change of expression. He looked straight at me in a way that made my spine tingle, and then went slowly upstairs.

Madness

For a time the madness in our lives mainfested itself in strange ways. Federico went through a period of seclusion, during which he seemed to hate everything in the world but his own room. There he ate and read and looked out at the countryside and the sea from his window. I took his meals and books up to him. My refuge was the library, where I found a secret delight, not in reading, but in contemplating Grandmother Anita's trunk. I loved it as much as Federico apparently loathed it.

One day there fell into my hands a small pamphlet containing passages from the story of David; after having read it I developed a passion for Biblical themes. David spent his early life as a fugitive, fleeing to the mountains and taking shelter in caves. There he became one with the spirits of the forest, earth, and water; he learned to love nature to the point of ecstasy, lived with wild creatures, and watched the grass grow and the flowers open. And marveling at such wonderful things, he sang of them in his psalms.

I said, I will take heed to my ways, that I sin not with my tongue: I will keep my mouth with a bridle, while the wicked is before me.

My heart was hot within me; while I was musing the fire burned.

I am consumed by the blow of thine hand. When thou with rebukes dost correct man for iniquity, thou makest his beauty to consume away like a moth: surely every man is vanity.

I found a leather-bound Bible in the library, and eagerly began reading it. I got through almost all of Genesis, and then went on to Exodus, wherein is related so beautifully the life of Moses, that proud and pious soul.

And the Lord said furthermore unto him, Put now thine hand into thy bosom. And he put his hand into his bosom: and when he took it out, behold, his hand was leprous as snow.

And he said, Put thine hand into thy bosom again. And he put his hand into his bosom again; and plucked it out of his bosom, and, behold, it was turned again as his other flesh.

Then I read Deuteronomy and Leviticus and Kings. But the most astonishing revelation was the Song of Solomon. It was the story of Federico and Pascua, told with inimitable symbolic beauty. Had Federico ever read these pages? I would have been proud of a love like this, as proud as the wisest of kings.

The king hath brought me into his chambers, she sang in her unforgettable ecstasy. *We will be glad and rejoice in thee, we will remember thy love more than wine: the upright love thee.* And she proudly proclaimed: *I am black, but comely, O ye daughters of Jerusalem, as the tents of Kedar, as the cur-*

tains of Solomon. Look not upon me, because I am black, because the sun hath looked upon me: my mother's children were angry with me; they made me the keeper of the vineyards; but mine own vineyard have I not kept. Tell me, O thou whom my soul loveth, where thou feedest, where thou makest thy flock to rest at noon: for why should I be as one that turneth aside by the flocks of thy companions?

And, in fact, why should she be wandering and suffering the wrath of her people, when she was black, but comely and passionate?

During this parenthesis of relative solitude when I was devoted to books and almost mystical meditations, I came to some conclusions about the events that had come to throw our lives into such a turmoil. The trunk had been Grandmother Anita's revenge. She knew the whole story of the Arguíndeguis and the Lamarcas, and had kept it to herself for years. She had sent the trunk back to the White House without waiting for its owners to return, in the same way one would incite a mastiff to attack. The beautiful and beloved trunk could tear and rip. I reconstructed in my own fashion the story told in the letters, filling in the gaps with deductions or, lacking these, with guesses. Doña Beatriz had fallen in love with her piano teacher, as Solomon had with his Shulamite, and, caught up in the fire of Cumboto, had given him the flower of her youth. She gave birth to his son. But that son was condemned to die on the altar of Don Lorenzo Lamarca's prejudice. The enigmatic Eduvige had saved the child's life by leaving him on Cervelión's doorstep, wrapped in rich swaddling clothes. There were still some questions only Eduvige could answer. Did Doña Beatriz know that Cruz María, *El Matacán,* was her son? Whose skull was it the black-bearded general had unearthed with the silver spade when he was inaugurating the railroad, and that Federico's mother kept in her wardrobe? Perhaps it had belonged to her dark lover.

That's how it all must have happened. But suppose it hadn't been that way at all? If *El Matacán*'s tarnished skin could have been formed in Doña Beatriz's spotless womb, that mold fit for casting a superman, why not mine?

Wonderful! Marvelous! Incredible! And yet quite possible. It was such an audacious conjecture that I shuddered. This was the stuff of dreams. All the circumstances combined to make an ideal background for the daring embroidery of my heart—the time, the place, certain dim words that were beginning to germinate in the sensitive soil of my memory.

If I could talk to someone who knew the history of Cumboto, I might be able to find out the truth. But whom could I go to? Doña Beatriz was lying in her bedroom as though in a mausoleum, perhaps even dead and embalmed by Eduvige's icy hand to satisfy that gloomy sense of fidelity. And Eduvige herself—when had she ever been willing to tell anyone anything? The only person who could have revealed the truth was now the slave of her own revenge; she had deliberately sealed her lips and disappeared without a trace. That was Grandmother Anita. Her trunk, which was a wellspring of information about Federico and his family, had nothing to say about me.

I don't know whether Federico, in his solitude, was pondering these same questions. I would not have dared bring up such subjects. When one fine day he finally returned to the ordinary world again, he was transformed. He came downstairs and sat at the piano as if nothing had happened. But this was only in appearance. His conversation, the expression on his face, and especially his music soon betrayed the tremendous change that had taken place within him.

"Have you noticed," he asked me, "how my style has improved? I'm a great artist. You can be proud of the privilege of hearing me, for no one will ever be my equal."

He kept talking as he played, as though we were taking a stroll in the country.

"Be sure of one thing, Natividad: man can become a god. What are wealth, or love, or friendship worth? Nothing. They're the aspirations of timid souls, unworthy of a real man. Do you know what my name is? Have you forgotten? Zeus! Jupiter!"

One day he spoke of his favorite composers. When he had first returned from Europe he had shown a certain weakness for Chopin; but he soon saw that his style did not suit the environment.

"He's soft and frivolous; his music represents precisely the decadence of what we call love—although it should be called misery. I love only one thing: depth, the suffering that can change a man into a god. That's why I prefer Beethoven.

"Do you know what my dream is? To combine the classical spirit with the essence of this soil. We need a new musical form, and I shall create it. You Negroes have your chants and your rhythms, but there is only one music. Listen to this."

He closed his eyes and bent over the keyboard, waiting for some secret signal. His hands hovered over the keys, as limp as two withered blossoms about to fall to the ground. All at once they came down, and the chord resounded like thunder. What followed was a dark, tormented music that flew back into the past, moaning: *Cumboto . . . Cumboto . . .*

He may have forgotten Pascua, but I couldn't. The thought of her flight tormented me. Where had she gone? To the city, probably, just as Solomon's passionate beloved had done: *By night on my bed I sought him whom my soul loveth: I sought him, but I found him not. I will rise now, and go about the city in the streets, and in the broad ways I will seek him whom my soul loveth: I sought him, but I found him not. The watchmen that go about the city found me: to whom I said, Saw ye him whom my soul loveth?*

I imagined thousands of fantastic things, and my nights were filled with erotic visions. There she was, not in the city but in the deep jungle, writhing and gleaming at the center of a group of naked Negroes. She was dancing to the beat of the deep drums, whose music took on Beethoven's rich harmony and yet retained all their telluric vigor. I knew that this was a strange and absurd synthesis, and yet in my dream I heard it happen. It was like a monstrous hybrid—of a dolphin or an albatross and a panther, say. It was so powerful that I was swept up in a kind of whirlwind, and I twisted and vibrated like a bow when its string snaps. This was the goal toward which the uncontrollable, fiery cataract of my life was rushing. The dream reoccurred many times; it was the work of a clever succubus who came to my cot regularly to conduct her oneiric concert.

Federico had begun to drink a great deal; but he never got drunk. His face began to show the signs of progressive deterioration. He was composing now, writing down on music paper the notes that moaned at the touch of his fingers. I watched apprehensively. His composition was, in fact, the monstrous musical hybrid of my dreams. The succubus lived in Federico's piano. And yet in waking reality I did not hear that tremendous beauty that had so moved me in my dreams. The result was coarse and stiff. Federico's jungle drums lacked the deep throbbing, the diabolical rapidity, the desperate struggling of a captured bird or a wounded wild animal that the black man's soul has put into his hollowed-out tree trunks. The two harmonies could blend only in dreams. The panther was the wrong sex ever to mate with the albatross.

One night I found him asleep on the big, black leather sofa. He was clutching his pillow and moaning. There was a strange, wild odor in the room—the odor of a dark, naked woman. A perfume of pepper and lime. The window was open, and a soft breeze was stirring the linen curtains. Federico groaned softly and turned over in his sleep. Suddenly his body tensed, like a bow whose string has snapped. I wondered if he was having the same experience I had had, if the same succubus was paying a call on the young god. I went to the window to close it, and stood there looking out at the trees glazed with moonlight. The memory of Cruz María and Frau Berza came back and struck me like a blow.

It was in this very garden, under this very moon. All at once I noticed something. A long shape that had been lying motionless near the house began to move; it wound off into the bushes. It was a serpent. The rod of Moses. Now all I had to do was put my hand in my bosom and take it out again, leprous as snow. As white as snow, the versicle said.

The Messenger

The miser counts his money every day, but he never counts his days. We were exactly the opposite: every morning we brought out the coins of our thoughts and arranged them in little piles, with the resigned impatience of those who know they are helpless to change their destiny. Just as David had watched the grass growing and the flowers blooming, we watched the ashes sprinkling down upon our heads. Each new gray hair and wrinkle took us one step farther from our misery. How good it was to look at each other and say to ourselves, "We're getting old!" And we were only approaching fifty.

A quarter of a century has been enough to bring peace to our hearts. The landscape, too, seems calmer—not as green, perhaps, but not as savage.

Federico—Don Federico, rather, as I call him since he has grown his beautiful white beard—Don Federico now takes his walks in other parts of Cumboto, and doesn't cover as much ground as he used to. As soon as the sun begins to drop in the west he puts on his straw hat, takes his cherry-wood cane, and leaves the house. Sometimes he goes west, toward El Palito, and sometimes east in the direction of Paso Real. I follow at a distance, doing my best—an old man's futile mania—not to let him see me. He knows I'm there, of course; he knows I'm his shadow. But he enjoys the game, and pretends not to notice me.

Cumboto's Negroes and mulattoes have learned to love their employer. They feel that he belongs to them. Whenever they see him strolling through the shadows they seem a little surprised, and say to one another, "There goes Don Federico . . . *Ave Maria!*"

And they cross themselves.

Then one of them asks, "Why do you suppose Don Federico never got married?"

It is precisely for that reason that they cross themselves. There is no woman in the White House now to insure the continuity of the master caste. The Negroes are afraid that death will come one day to settle his accounts and dispossess them.

There was a time—at the beginning of the tempest—when I wondered whether my unhealthy devotion to my master was not a betrayal. Now I think differently: I know now that I was never more heroically faithful to my people and to myself. The meeting yesterday afternoon on the path supports this opinion. If I had not been as faithful, the young traveler whom we met would have found no one to direct his question to—"Isn't that the owner of Cumboto?"—or anyone to tell him: "Come to the White House tomorrow." Yesterday's tomorrow is today. The young man will probably be here soon, for the sun is well up and I specified no particular time. I merely said, "Tomorrow"—that is, today.

I spent a bad night, stirring up the sleeping swamp under its crust of the past twenty-five years. The sleeping swamp! The ghosts came tumbling out like demons. The last were those of Doña Beatriz and Eduvige, poor sorrowing shades. They took their secrets to the grave. The skull and the silver spade are now in my little room, under the old cot, in Grandmother Anita's trunk; the bell on its lock has never tinkled again. Everything is still there, all that motley collection: the clothing, the musical instruments, the jewelry, the letters, the daguerreotypes, the silver spade, and the skull. I'm sorry that some things are missing: Cruz María's swaddling clothes, the bullet that killed him, the rattles of the *Crotalus terrificus* I saw in Trina's hands that night in Cervelión's hut. Perhaps when all these objects have turned to dust and their particles have become indistinguishable it will be easier to see everything clearly through the shadows of our loyalty.

It is twelve noon by the old clock in its glass bell on the library table, and I see the young man coming up the sandy path. As I watch him through the window, once again I find his slender figure disturbing. As he comes closer I can make out his dark face—the color of tarnished silver—and his greenish, luminous eyes. When he reaches the front door, in the shadow of the broad tile roof, I go to let him in.

"Are you the one who told me to come back today?"

"Yes. Take a seat, and I'll tell him you're here."

I leave him standing in the living room—that calm sea—and start up the stairs. When I reach the landing I turn and watch him examining the furniture, the paintings, and the piano. In a few minutes I come down again and find him standing by the piano, running his long, tapered fingers lightly over the black, shiny lid.

"He'll be down in a moment. Do you like music?"

He flashes a smile at me.

"I love it."

"Don Federico is a great pianist."

I say it deliberately, to see how he will react. He replies, simply, "Yes, I know."

When Federico comes in I leave them alone. Everything is so clear in my mind at that moment that I have no need to see what is going to happen or to hear what they will say to each other. So I go out into the garden and walk up and down along the path. Half a century before, in this very spot, I witnessed a disturbing scene one moonlight night. "Frau Berza has a secret," Federico had informed me. It was a secret of death. I could say to him today, "This young man has a secret, too; but it is a secret of life."

When Don Guillermo was still alive the family would be having lunch at this hour. There is the dining room table, with its spotless linen cloth. Don Guillermo used to sit at one end and his wife at the other, and between them the two children, Federico and Gertrudis, and the governess with her straw-colored hair. It had been just about this time of day when Doña Beatriz had appeared in her billowing, sky-blue crinoline to announce that the bearded general was coming for lunch. After lunch we used to sit down to draw with colored crayons while Frau Berza dozed, her open book on her lap. And all the while Eduvige came and went as silently as a ghost.

I come to myself with a start. How long have Don Federico and his guest been talking in the living room? I have no idea. But if they're still there they must have had a great deal to say. Determined not to listen or watch, I stroll farther away from the house. I cross the garden and head for the *coquera*. New generations of Negroes and mulattoes have sprung up on the Zeus property. These young people seem to me more aggressive and restless, but their laughter and their chatter sound the same as always. They still play the game of "popping coconuts," and still address their *gallos* with the same incantation:

> *Coquín, coquito,*
> *coco, cocón ...*
> *Viejo virulo de verde ropón;*
> *pónmelo bueno,*
> *pónmelo pon,*
> *dame la agüita con este pelón;*
> *coquín, coquito,*
> *coco, cocón ...*

More houses have been erected, and some new buildings, including a large cow barn. Juan Segundo, *Luango,* can still be seen moving among the animals with his milk can on his shoulder.

Suddenly I am astounded to hear something I haven't heard for years. Someone is playing the piano. My whole body is like one gigantic ear. The notes come winging over the treetops in joyous, crystalline flocks, as gaily as they did so long ago. It is one of the sonatas I used to hear Doña Beatriz and Federico playing. The *Appassionata*? No, the *Aurora*. My young master told me, after his return from Europe, that its original title was the *Waldstein*— The Stone in the Forest. The execution is not very clean—poor Federico's fingers must be stiff after so many years of inactivity—but what feeling! The trills and figures for the right hand soar above the solemn basses and spiral heavenward. Heavy footsteps on the floor of the forest, a bustle and confusion, and the approaching thunderstorm. Now he's playing the *allegro*. Then comes the *adagio molto,* as thoughtful as if it were trying to convince itself that it had been so surprisingly gay a moment before. The notes drop from above, one by one, into a quiet pool, and turn to song; the cascade grows in speed and intensity, becomes more insistent; it leads the way to the *allegretto moderato,* which is like running lovers who suddenly come to halt and begin a kind of march. In the *prestissimo* those poor fingers try to skip over the keys as they once did, like dragonflies skimming the water. The basses hold back, timidly; but soon they, too, are caught up in the dizzy pace.

Astonished Negroes and mulattoes are beginning to pour out of the sheds, the huts, and the bushes; they stand and stare in the direction of the White House.

The new generation does not know this kind of music. It may be that some of them thought that black box, standing in the living room like a ship anchored in the sea, was a coffin. The *Aurora* fascinates them with its gaiety. A spontaneous pilgrimage begins to move toward the sound of this unexpected revelation.

I join them, of course. I want to see my master, my friend, my brother in his moment of triumph. I want to show him to these young Negroes and say, "Behold! Here is our god!"

But when we reach the window and look in, I am dumfounded. It is not Don Federico at the piano, but the young man. Pascua's son—his son!

The music is ringing out like a hymn. As I look about me the whole world seems to be in flames—even the blue sea that gleams in the distance over the coconut trees. My joy is tinged with a vague uneasiness, as though I were hovering on the edge of a dream, about to awake. I sense that there are three people there in the White House's polished, echoing living room; two are visible, and one is not. The invisible one is Pascua, the fugitive. Her son has brought the tidings of her love, her sacrifice, her immortal flesh and spirit. I wonder what this messenger has come to tell us—the past or the future? I tremble when I consider the magnitude of the task destiny has cut out for him.

Meanwhile, the young man is sitting up very straight and smiling. He looks toward the window, filled with black heads that are like a cluster of some monstrous fruit, and smiles again. He is an adolescent god of tarnished silver.

The sonata ends, and there is a short silence. Has he finished playing? No. His audience has not yet had enough. He understands; his dark fingers—ten reptiles with alabaster eyes—take their places on the keyboard again. The chord resounds like distant thunder. But this time it is not the transparent, stylized voice of traditional music that bursts from the piano; it is the roaring beat of the *pujao* and the insolent exultation of the little drums.

The men and women around me, sweating and enraptured, are swaying and groaning like trees in the midst of a storm:

Cumboto ... Cumboto ...

GLOSSARY

adivino: prophet.

arepas: fried corn meal cakes.

bachaco: a fierce red ant.

banana-stobat: a dish made of plantains, fish, ham, and other ingredients.

bucare: a large South American shade tree.

buñuelos: fritters made from the flour of a tuber called *apio*; they are served with molasses and cinnamon.

caimán: cayman.

camaza: a bowl made from the fruit of the bottle gourd tree.

campate: a fierce black wasp; also, the nest of this wasp.

cariaquito: a plant credited with magical properties against bad luck.

cepo de campaña: a form of punishment or torture in which the subject is tied in a sitting position with his arms hooked around a rifle placed behind his knees.

chaparro: a quirt made of braided leather.

chupa-huesos: a kind of owl, believed to announce the approaching death of the ill.

coquera: the processing area on a coconut plantation.

Coquín, coquito, etc.: a nonsense verse addressed to the "fighting coconuts."

Cruz de Mayo: the Feast of the Holy Cross, May 3.

culebrita: little snake.

custodia: a medallion of gold or silver representing the Lord's Supper.

gallo: a fighter; literally, "rooster."

gente de paz: literally, "people of peace"; an expression from revolutionary days.

godos: literally, "Goths"; a conteptuous term for the royalists.

guacharaca: the chachalaca, a ground-nesting bird that cries continually while in flight.

jabillo: a stout tropical tree.

león: lion.

locha: a Venezuelan coin worth about half a penny.

Luango: one of the kinds of Negroes brought from Africa as slaves.

mapanare: a black and yellow serpent native to Venezuela; it is venemous and aggressive.

María la O: a fantastic personage in Venezuelan folklore.

matacán: a small deer.

mato: a South American lizard.

medio del estreno: the forfeit—in this case, a *medio real*—that must be paid to anyone who demands it when one is wearing anything for the first time.

medio real: a Venezuelan coin worth about a penny.

merengue: a popular Afro-Antillean dance.

Musiú (feminine, *Musiúa*): a Gallicism, from *Monsieur*.

paraulata ajicera: a South American thrush with white breast and black wings.

Pascua: Easter or Christmas; as a nickname, it suggests a gay, cheerful nature.

petateo: something that takes place on a *petate*, a palm mat commonly used as a floor covering.

piqui-juyes: literally, "stings and runs away"; a small insect.

pitirrí: the gray kingbird.

quimbombó: gumbo, a thick soup made with okra and other ingredients.

resadá: a small, sweet-smelling plant of the mignonette family.

samán: a tropical tree similar to the cedar.

sopita: a kind of soup.

tigre: jaguar.

tocayito: the diminutive, affectionate form of *tocayo*, namesake.

tutear: to address someone using the *tú*, or familiar form; its use suggests intimacy or social equality.

ventas: things offered for sale.

vera: a tropical shrub whose branches are extremely hard and heavy.

zambo: the child of a Negro and an Indian.

DATE DUE

New Books 9-14-70			
GAYLORD			PRINTED IN U.S.A.